K.C. SMITH

A THIRST FOR POWER

To those who wish for fun and adventure in a world that often feels bleak.

N
W
E
S
SVAKLAND
STORM
FROSBURG
WHITE GIANTS
SARDORF
SHIPWRECK
COVE
PHANTOM WOODS
FROST SEA
RANDIER
DAYLIGHT ROAD
ELSCAR
VARIAN
BAY OF SORROWS
KING'S ROAD
SANGALIA
MINES OF DURIAL
SPARKLING SEA
CIRUS
ISLE OF THRAY
BOILING SEA

ESDAR SEA
ESDAR SEA
THE EMERALD PEAKS
GNOMEIC
SYLPHIN
MITSTAD
UNDINAAM
SALAMAAND
SCORCHED LANDS
AWNDAR SEA
SEA
EMMORIA
FELLHAVEN

A THIRST FOR POWER

PROLOGUE

As the dark cloak of night fell upon the land, the purple moon glimmered, looking down at Verhaven, the world of the Zydells, casting a gentle glow over the lush landscape. The trees swayed, leaves rustling in the pleasant breeze as Orrick crept his way through the shadows of the evening.

In the distance, a circular building could be seen in the center of an intricate garden maze, bathed in the moon's violet glory and completely unguarded.

The archives.

He wasn't surprised to see it unguarded. The Zydell have lived in peace, far away from the Gods, meaning they believed they had no reason to hide or protect anything in their world. Their one mistake was that they assumed the Gods would listen to the Cosmic law to never step foot in their world. But Orrick wasn't one for rules. He found that rules were put in place to be broken rather than followed.

He breathed in the warm air that carried the ancient scent of power and secrets to his nose, a malicious smile spreading across his lips as he weaved his way through the maze of flowers, trees, and bushes, closing in on the structure. The energy of this world was extraordinary. It hummed through the air, vibrating his bones in an exciting, almost intoxicating way.

As he approached the entrance, he could see the towering stone pillars that encircled the interior vault more clearly. They were etched with intricate designs carved into their marbled surface, but it wasn't what was depicted on the columns that held his interest. It was the small domed building in their center. He strode past the towering marble pillars, pushed the heavy brass doors open, and stepped into the cavernous room.

The walls were lined with thousands upon thousands of neatly shelved books. The shelves reached from floor to ceiling, dripping with ancient knowledge, just waiting for their spines to be cracked.

Orrick shut the door behind him and made his way toward the back of the vault, trailing his fingertips along the spines of the ancient tomes as he went.

Each of them was titled in a different way, with scribbles of black ink scrawled along their spines. Some were dated, while others had the names of worlds he himself created, which made him raise a brow in curiosity of what those may contain. Several of the books were marked with what seemed to be people's names, and absolutely none of the titles held a rhyme or reason to their order.

"Glad to see their organization is so well thought out," he grumbled, the sound echoing around him in the large, quiet space.

The problem was that he wasn't entirely sure what he was looking for, how it would be labeled on these books, or if it was even here at all.

Ever since he left Svakland—left his sister and her halfling companion—he was obsessed with finding out where Ada, the Zydell queen, had hidden the other two triplets away. Garren held a power unlike any he'd seen or felt, and that kind of power three times over was enticing. He wanted to know what it could do and how it could be used—how *he* could use it.

And so the search began. One by one he read the spines, opening and flipping through any that seemed promising. He discarded them haphazardly on the floor when they provided nothing of use, leaving breadcrumbs of yellowed pages and leather bindings in his wake.

After what seemed like eons of searching, reading, and exhaustion, Orrick looked up at the domed ceiling made entirely of glass. The late hours of dusk were giving way to dawn. He had been in this place all night. The Zydells would wake soon and he couldn't be here when that happened.

Orrick looked behind him to the trailing mess of discarded tomes he'd created and waved a hand over them. Each of the leather volumes placed themselves back onto the shelf, whether in the same place or not, Orrick had no idea. Not that it mattered since there seemed to be no actual method to the madness of this archive. Nothing made sense in this place.

With a heavy, annoyed sigh, Orrick made his way toward the only way out, but just before he passed the final shelf, a name on the spine of a tome caught his eye.

Honoria.

Orrick raised a brow as he reached up to pluck the volume from its place high above him. Honoria was the reason he found the Zydell archives in the first place. He spent the last three months gaining her trust and entangling himself in a rather rewarding relationship with her. One that often had him aching for more.

It was a pleasant surprise to his ultimate goal. Not only had he discovered the location of the very information he had become obsessed with these past months, but he was sleeping daily with a stunning and rather ravenous woman. Fucking her was thoroughly enjoyable.

They kept their relationship a secret, of course. She had no idea he was a God, but believed him to be a Zydell. He held his ruse well and avoided direct contact with anyone else whenever he visited her, knowing that if anyone in the high council of Zydells were to discover him, they would know instantly he didn't belong. The consequences would no doubt be dire.

There were two other names just below Honoria's on the spine. He was curious to learn more about the woman he was sleeping with but even more intrigued about the fact that her name was included with two others.

Orrick's eyes lit up with anticipation as he opened it, studying the delicate pages.

"Well, lucky me," he said with a snort of disbelief. "To think I've been fucking one of the triplets this whole time. Little Honoria is much more than she seems."

It was strange, he hadn't felt the same kind of peculiarity with Honoria that he did with Garren the first time they met. He knew instantly that something was off about Garren, but with Honoria, there was nothing out of the ordinary. Maybe it was because Garren was in one of his mortal worlds, and Honoria was here, surrounded by her own kind. Still, if she was as powerful as he imagined each of the triplets to be, shouldn't he have felt a piece of it? Especially with how close they were.

Orrick shrugged it off and continued reading the volume. He read of their parentage, of their detriment to the Cosmos and the need to keep them separated. All things he already knew. His father wanted to use them for his own desire, to rule as the single God, but Ada stopped him, hiding them away before he had the chance to steal them. Their existence was long forgotten—until now.

He read further, flipping the page, and there just beneath Honoria's name was another—Alvar, who was taken to the mortal realm of Fellhaven. "Hmm, that must be Garren," Orrick mused. "Alvar is a way better name."

He moved on to the third and final name listed. The first and last few letters were smudged into an unreadable smear of ink, leaving only what remained in its center—ari. They were taken to the world of Zsaro.

"Interesting," Orrick narrowed his eyes on the page. That wasn't a place he would have thought the Zydell queen would leave one of her offspring. That world was a brutal one, full of magical creatures who were ruthless and territorial. A half-Zydell, half-God being wouldn't really fit in there. They would be the only one of their kind, unable to blend in as Garren did in Fellhaven.

As he stewed over it further, it was actually rather smart of Ada. Zsaro was probably one of the last worlds anyone would ever look for one of the triplets. It was often forgotten by the Gods, left as a sort of misfit world that no God wanted to deal with. They would rather leave it to its own devices than keep tabs on the beings that inhabited it.

He chuckled, a smirk spreading across his lips. He did it, he had actually found the location of all three. Orrick flipped to the next page to see what other knowledge the book might have to offer when a small scrap of paper fell out, floating down to the marbled floor. He bent and picked it up to find a messy script written on it. It looked as if someone was in a hurry when they jotted it down, almost like they wrote it with their eyes closed.

He read the words on the page aloud, "*Three bound by fate, born of both God and Zydell. They hold the power to break the Cosmos. War and death stalk them for their own means. Immortal weapons wielded hold the key to salvation. But discovery by the hungry Gods and all will be lost, the Cosmos unmade until only silence remains.*" He frowned, rereading the words in his head. What was this? Some kind of sad attempt at poetry? Or was it something more?

"Put down the book, God." A voice echoed behind him. Orrick jumped, slamming the tome shut, dust billowing around him as he turned to face Ada, Queen of the Zydells.

"Fuck."

PART ONE

Fuck

I

ORRICK

"Fuck, fuck, fuck!" Orrick cursed as he sprinted naked through the city streets. He knew this city well—in fact, it was one of his favorites.

The buildings passed by in a blur, his appearance gaining more than a few curious glances, some lingering far too long, and he fought the urge to stop to allow them a more intimate view.

He knew these streets inside out, navigating through them with ease. This was a place he visited frequently, more than any other of the worlds he created. Yet, as he weaved his way down the familiar roads, he couldn't help but notice much had changed. It suddenly dawned on him that he hadn't been to this particular continent of Emmoria in a very long time, possibly centuries or longer. These days, time seemed to pass him by without him even knowing.

The streets were now cobbled with large stones, the buildings taller, and the streets once full of vendors selling their wares were now empty of carts. Instead, people quickly darted in and out of alleyways and doorways.

It made him miss the sights and sounds of this place, creating a sense of nostalgia that tugged at his center, reminding him of simpler times long ago. What happened to this once vibrant city?

A sharp pebble dug into the bottom of his foot, and Orrick growled but didn't slow his pace. He only sprinted faster, bare feet slapping against the cobbled streets. Finally, a shadowed alcove came into view, and he practically dove into it, taking a moment to catch his breath as he leaned his back against the cool stone wall, bringing his hands up over his head as he took in big gulps of air.

It was the first chance he had to actually stop and process what just happened. His mind raced as the creeping feeling of catastrophe crawled along his spine, caressing that vital piece of himself deep inside. A vital piece that didn't feel quite right any longer. Something was wrong. Something horrific.

Orrick took one final lungful of air and reached down to that spot deep down, desperately searching for his power source, pulling on his godly gifts, but there was nothing there. He was completely empty.

"Fuck!" he yelled, slamming his fist against the wall behind him. He turned to face the arching stone wall, lashing out, punching, kicking, hitting as pain lanced through his hands and feet, dust and pebbles raining down on him.

When he finally stopped, knuckles dripping blood beneath him, he leaned his head against the wall, closing his eyes with a sigh of defeat. What the fuck happened to him? He thought back to the day before, the week before, and nothing came to mind. He couldn't remember anything after his last visit with Honoria—the Zydell woman he used for information.

As a God, it was forbidden for him to go to Verhaven—the world of the Zydells—but that hadn't stopped him from sneaking his way into their world and forming a rather fun relationship with one of them.

Honoria was all too willing to allow Orrick in. She was as feisty and rebellious as she was stunning, commanding the male attention like a siren's call. She was the perfect Zydell to unknowingly help him in his goal. The last thing he could recall was her finally telling him where the archives of her world were located.

Something must have gone terribly wrong while he was there, so wrong that he lost the only thing about himself that he truly cared about. But how? Orrick growled, his rumbling annoyance echoing through the tight alcove he was in. He ran a hand through his hair, slamming his fist into the wall with one final swing, the stone cracking, spreading out like a spider's web around the impact. At least he still seemed to have some of his godly strength.

Only moments ago, he'd woken in such a good mood, not realizing anything was amiss. He was pleasantly surprised to wake entangled in a rather delicious position with a lovely pink-skinned beauty. He hadn't thought twice before pressing his naked body against hers, feeling the smooth warmth of her skin against his hardening length, nibbling lightly at her pointed ear.

What he didn't expect was for the girl to scream and for her rather large father to barge in, practically pulling the bedroom door off its hinges. His anger permeated the room, his skin turning a fiery red as he stormed toward them.

Orrick closed a fist, pulling forth the well of energy that was always present inside of him to crush the man where he stood, but nothing happened. He frowned, looking down at his hand as he shook it out, opening and closing his fist before reaching deep down once more, but he was greeted with only emptiness—a void where limitless power had always been present. The air around him suddenly felt thick, sucking the air from his lungs as panic clawed at his chest.

"You want a fight, do you?" the man spat.

"Shit," Orrick mumbled, not even taking a second to think before he pushed himself from the bed and jumped out the open window. A blast of flame followed him, just barely singing the bottoms of his feet as it erupted through the window behind him. He landed with a diving roll and sprinted as fast as his legs would take him down the uneven, rocky streets.

Orrick shook his head with a snort; now here he was, naked and practically a useless bag of bones, left to run through the streets of this city in a world he had created. He barked out a humorless laugh.

"A Salamander," he said through clenched teeth, looking down at his slightly burnt feet as if the girl's fuchsia-pink skin hadn't instantly given that away. Salamanders were the most brutal of the Elementalists—the people of this continent in Fellhaven—with their fire sorcery and hot tempers. Their breathtaking shades of red hair and alluring beauty were such a stark contrast to their burning and, frankly erratic behavior. They were not ones to be trifled with, lest you want your hair burned off or worse, your dick set aflame. A sudden ache settled between his thighs at the thought, and not the good kind.

Orrick peeked his head out of the alcove to the empty street he had just come from. No one was chasing after him. Good, because he needed to figure out what the fuck was going on with him.

He peered back into the dark alcove to the far end, creeping his way further into the alley until it opened up to a courtyard filled with snaking vines and flowers of every color—so different from the city streets he had just run through. It was quite beautiful, serene even. He felt the tension in his core ease a little.

A chorus of giggles shifted his focus to the left where he found a man and two women looking at him, smirking as they let their eyes travel up and down the length of his naked body.

He raised a brow and squinted at the sign hanging above the building behind them: *The Mount and the Mare.*

"Fancy a tousle?" Orrick looked back at the three prostitutes standing before him. It was the silver-haired woman with large pale blue eyes like glass who spoke. She was a Sylph, one of the fair-skinned air Elementalists. Her gown barely held in her ample breasts. Orrick could see the delicate edge of a plump pink nipple peeking through, beckoning him forward.

"We'll give you a ride you won't forget," the man said. His voice was smooth and cool, like a babbling stream. His azure skin gleamed in the warm rays of the sun, dark green hair twisted into thick corded locks, his purple eyes glittered like amethysts. Orrick bit down on his bottom lip, trying to hold back his arousal. He had a soft spot for the Undinas—water Elementalists. Historically, they were always the best lovers, in his opinion.

"All three of us for the price of one."

Orrick finally let his gaze travel to the third Elementalist, who had just spoken. The woman had curves in all the right places, enough to make a grown man beg. He took his time studying every rounded swell of her body. She was a Gnome, an earth Elementalist and it seemed that she was currently in her natural form. The Gnomes were the most cunning of all Elementalists, able to shapeshift, replicating the look of anyone around them. However, this woman was no clone. That body and face were all hers.

Her umber skin was absolute perfection, and Orrick wished to wrap himself in her long purple tresses, cascading down her back, stopping just above her rounded ass. Orrick groaned, biting his lip harder. She was stunning in a particularly tempting sheer gown, leaving little to the imagination. The look of want in her hazel eyes was one that made him begin to throb in desperation.

Orrick looked them each over once more, imagining the delicious things he would do to each of them. He could certainly use a distraction from his current predicament.

He looked down at himself, to his swollen cock standing at attention, and shrugged his shoulders, "Why the fuck not?"

2
GARREN

"Cut off its fucking head!"

Garren smirked, arms crossed over his chest as he watched Oriana struggle to hold on to the creature they tracked here.

"You look like you've got a good handle on things."

"Garren!" she yelled, grunting as the beast freed a bright orange arm covered in bouncing threads of fur from her grasp. Oriana ducked and dodged the loose, flailing arm of the hairy creature. "Gods damn you, Garren. Kill it already!"

He laughed, finally drawing his long sword. As he unsheathed it from along his back, the sing of steel was like music to his ears. It was heavy in his grip, a weight that made his hand tingle in anticipation—anxious for the kill.

With one arching swing, the blade connected with its target, cutting clean through sinew and bone. Green blood sprayed in its wake just before the beast's head slid from its body, hitting the ground with a solid thunk.

Oriana squealed, releasing the monster, where it crumpled to the ground alongside its head. Thick, bright green liquid streaked down her face, dripping from her chin and staining her cerulean robes. She gagged, wiping the blood from her skin. "Gods, I forgot the smell that accompanied a Cherlkur. Their blood is like shit mixed with rotten cheese." She shivered, covering her nose and mouth with her hands while stepping over the twitching body of the beheaded beast. "You could have been a little quicker. You know I can't use my enchantments against a Cherlkur."

Garren chuckled, using a cloth to wipe the putrid-smelling blood from his sword. "I still don't understand why. You can do pretty much anything with your enchantments. I've seen the extent of your powers many times." He tossed the used cloth to Oriana.

She caught it and stuck her tongue out at him, trying to find a spot not covered in the green liquid to wipe off her face. "It's how Orrick made them. He wanted to unleash them on the Gods and didn't want it to be easy for them. Luckily, he never followed through with that plan. Unfortunately—for us—he decided to send them all here instead."

Garren snorted, "Asshole."

"Couldn't agree with you more," Oriana huffed, standing beside her dapple gray steed. "You know, you could try to use your abilities on one next time. You never know. You aren't fully God, so it could work and it would surely be a lot less messy." She scrunched up her nose, watching as blood continued to pour from the beast's neck, forming a steaming puddle of molten green that slowly seeped into the earth.

Garren began covering the creature in brush and twigs. The metallic clink of flint hitting steel echoed through the forest as a fire quickly engulfed the oozing demon, burning away all remaining presence of it, once and for all.

"Why don't you ever use your powers when fighting these creatures?" Oriana suddenly asked.

"Because it's not as much fun," He grinned and winked at her, and she rolled her eyes in response. "If you want to coexist with the mortals and fully immerse yourself in this world, you have to live like them, too."

"We do live like them," Oriana said, mounting her horse. "But we can still live like Gods sometimes." She winked back at him just before digging her heels into her horse's side and taking off at a galloping speed.

Garren snorted, sheathing his blade before jumping onto his own midnight black mare, taking off after her.

Oriana's white locks trailed behind her, whipping in the wind as she looked back at him, a playful gleam in her sparkling green eyes. Garren smiled, leaning forward as he urged his mare faster, catching up to her just as they broke through the forest's edge. He had never felt more alive than in the past months spent with her. She was the only person who had ever made him feel this way. She was a Goddess—his Goddess—and there was a wildness in her gaze that matched his own.

Over the last few months, she had transformed, finally embracing who she truly was, which only made her more beautiful in his eyes.

But one captivating trait that had stayed with her at both her lowest and now at her highest was her compassionate soul. She always prioritized others over herself, using her gifts selflessly to help those around her.

His own gifts remained in the back of his mind. If they could be used to help others, he would use them without thinking, but what little he'd seen of whatever power he possessed scared him.

If he used it, would it change him? He was afraid of not only what his powers were capable of, but he was terrified of becoming someone else entirely—becoming something like Orrick.

Garren pushed the thoughts away because it didn't matter. He would never find out. His power was too dangerous to ever be wielded again.

"Yah!" Garren kicked his mare faster, overtaking Oriana's steed, grinning broadly as he looked back at her, watching a scowl form on her features.

Suddenly, a piercing screech rang out like a knife to his ear and he pulled back hard on the reins, his horse digging its hooves into the pebbled earth, dirt and dust billowing around them in a cloud of brown until they came to a complete halt.

Garren gritted his teeth, covering his hands over his ears. Oriana barreled past him before circling back around and sidling her mount up beside his. "What are you doing?"

"Do you hear that?" Garren slowly brought his hands away from his ears. The high-pitched screech was dying down, now just an even-toned hum. It vibrated through the air and thrummed through his body, almost moving his limbs with its energy.

"Hear what?" Oriana looked around them before returning her gaze to him and furrowing her brows.

"It's late, Garren. Maybe you just need rest. It's been a long day of hunting." Oriana gently touched his arm. "Let's go home."

Garren frowned but nodded. It *had* been a long day and there was nothing more he wanted to do than take a nice hot bath and eat a good meal in the comfort of their home.

The city of Elscar wasn't far. The city gates could be seen off in the distance. It was late, nearing evening, and the Cherlkur was their third and final kill for the night. The demons had definitely been dwindling ever so slightly after Orrick left all those months ago. The three of them seemed to have formed a kind of nonverbal understanding between one another. They all wanted the same thing—Anthes gone. Orrick hated his father just as much as Oriana did, but that little bastard hadn't completely stopped the onslaught of beasts. Apparently, their understanding didn't go that far. He still scattered his creations across the land every now and again. Garren supposed he hadn't really expected anything less from the unhinged God. He was chaos incarnate after all. It would be uncharacteristic for him not to keep sending demons for Garren to kill.

They rode in silence all the way to the city gates before dismounting and leading their horses home. The hum was finally fading into the air around him, but he could still feel it singing in his blood, stroking his bones. He shivered in response.

"Are you alright?" Oriana raised a brow, grabbing his hand and pulling him to a stop, forcing him to look down at her. "You're worrying me."

"I'm fine. It was just a strange sound. I've never heard anything like it." His eyes glazed over as he tried to think of what it could have been.

"Do you want to go back to where you heard it and see if something is there?"

He shook himself from his daze and smiled down at her, "No, no. All I want to do right now is take a nice long bath with you."

She smirked, "That sounds absolutely delightful."

They walked hand in hand all the way back to their home on the western outskirts of the city, leading their horses beside them. It was a beautiful yet simple home, offering everything they needed. It was fairly similar to Haldis' home back in Sardorf, but with the addition of large floor to ceiling windows in their bedroom to let the evening air flow through. Ivy snaked its way up the stone walls, flowers in an array of vibrant colors sprouting from every crack and crevice. It was all Oriana, of course. The entire town was her, built from her enchantments—just a small ounce of her true gifts.

Oriana pushed open the door to their home and pulled Garren up the stone steps to their washroom. The tub was already full of water, steam rising in swirling wisps from its surface.

He chuckled, "You were ten steps ahead of me, weren't you?"

She only smiled with a sheepish look in return, untying her leather corset and riding gear before slipping off her dress and letting it fall to the floor.

He groaned as she slowly let each piece of remaining clothing fall away, revealing more and more pale, soft flesh until she was fully naked before him.

"Why am I the only one naked?" she teased as she stepped into the steaming bath, submerging herself in the milky lavender-scented water until just the tops of her breasts could be seen, her nipples peeking tantalizingly through the water's surface.

Garren dropped his sword from his back and quickly began pulling off his tunic and trousers, not even bothering to unbutton them.

"That's better," she said in a low, throaty voice that sent his cock throbbing.

She moved forward in the tub, allowing room behind her that Garren eagerly took, joining her in the soothing bath, submerging himself fully, and then pulling her toward him until her back was flush against his chest. She sighed, resting her head against his shoulder, and he wrapped his arms comfortably around her waist, placing a gentle kiss on her temple. She closed her eyes with a smile.

The tension of the day practically melted from his shoulders. He was so happy to be here, in this moment with this beautiful woman. This was peace. This was all he needed in this world. He and Oriana had found solace in one another, a connection that ran so much deeper than the physical, and Garren wanted nothing more than to hold onto the tranquility of their life together for the rest of his days.

Garren couldn't sleep. He could still feel that strange hum vibrating through him. It had him on edge. He groaned and rolled out of bed, walking over to look out the bedroom window.

It was a clear night. The moon was just a sliver in the sky, stars dancing around it like tiny sparks, giving the night a dark indigo hue. The city streets were quiet; not a soul could be seen. He sighed, looking back at Oriana sleeping soundly in their bed. He had to know what this noise was. He had felt it the most when they were just east of the city on the road that led to Varian.

He needed to go back. He needed to follow it.

Garren slipped into his black linen tunic and trousers, grabbing his riding leathers and longsword before snatching his knee-high boots and tip-toeing barefoot to the door. A floorboard creaked beneath his weight, and he held his breath, taking a quick peek at Oriana, who was still motionless, her gentle breathing heavy with sleep. He blew out a quiet sigh of relief before closing the door behind him and walking down the steps to the front door.

Pulling on his boots, Garren strapped his longsword on his back and stepped out into the quiet stillness of the night, but it wasn't truly quiet, not for him. The hum was ever present, like an incessant fly buzzing in his ear.

He made it to the stables, where he saddled his horse and led it out into the moonlit street.

"Where are you going?"

Garren jumped, hand gripping the handle of the longsword at his back.

Oriana chuckled and walked out from the shadowed edge of the stable.

"Gods, Oriana. I could have killed you."

She was fully clothed in her riding leathers, choosing to wear her favorite blue flowing pants and linen top, ready to join him, it seemed.

"I love how you actually thought you could sneak out on me in the middle of the night." She crossed her arms over her chest. Her white locks braided into a single plait that laid over her left shoulder, shimmering in the milky rays of the moon. "So, where are we going?"

"*We* aren't going anywhere. *I'm* going back to the Daylight Road."

"Why?"

"I just...I have to."

"What's going on, Garren?"

Garren pinched the bridge of his nose and took a deep breath, "The sound I heard earlier. I don't know how to describe it. It's like a million bees buzzing in my ears, traveling through me like a shock of electricity. It won't leave me."

Oriana frowned at him.

"See, I knew you wouldn't understand." He turned away from her, more frustrated than angry.

"Hey," Oriana grabbed his arm, whirling him toward her, pulling him against her, and looking up into his eyes.

"I might not understand, but I believe you. I'll always believe you."

His face softened, and he brought his lips down to hers. They lingered there in one another's arms until he broke the kiss, "It was louder on the road to Varian."

Her soft, ruby lips curved into a playful smile, "Sovereign City, here we come."

3
ORRICK

O rrick groaned, forcing himself to roll from the large bed full of pillows and furs and several naked bodies. He let his hand graze across a soft nipple, squeezing a butt cheek or two as his feet found the solid wood of the floor.

He felt awful. The events of the previous evening were a blur of passion, sweat, and far too much wine. He didn't remember feeling this bad since—well, ever.

Orrick snapped his fingers, fully expecting the glass of water he had wanted to be within his grasp. When nothing appeared, the reality of his current predicament came crashing down upon him like a sack of rocks. His powers were gone. Was that why he felt so bad? Was this what not having his godly gifts felt like? *Fuck.*

Orrick lost track of the time he spent in *The Mount and the Mare.* Had it been a day? Two or maybe three days? A muffled snore came from the bed, and he turned to see all three of the exquisite creatures he had spent however many hours or days with, contently spent into exhaustion. He had a way of doing that when fucking. They would probably all sleep away the entire day.

He glanced down at the floor, where the Undina's clothing lay carelessly scattered. A pair of black linen pants, which he knew would barely reach his ankles, lay crumpled next to a vibrant blue vest adorned with intricate gold threading that shimmered under the dim light. Beside them was a pale blue tunic, its fabric delicate and unfortunately marred by several tears. Orrick had a vague memory of ripping that now tattered shirt off of the beautiful blue-skinned man breathing softly on the bed beside him. He smirked, putting on the blue vest, his chest far too broad to button it closed. Orrick shrugged; it was better than nothing. Luckily, the man's feet were nearly the same size as Orricks, so he grabbed the pair of sandals and strapped them on. Slipping a hand into the pocket of the borrowed vest, Orrick raised a brow and smirked, pulling free two coins and tossing them on the bed where the three prostitutes were still deep in sleep.

He stumbled down the spiral staircase, pushing open the front door of the establishment, sucking in a sharp breath as the blinding rays of the sun assaulted him. He raised an arm to shield his eyes, squinting until his vision adjusted to the stark brightness of the morning light.

On instinct, he reached out in an attempt to pull the white, fluffy clouds together and hide the sun from view, but of course, nothing happened.

"Fuck!" he yelled, nostrils flaring as his anger boiled in him like a raging river of fire. He clasped his hand into a fist, squeezing tight, fingernails digging into flesh until blood dripped from his palms onto the cobbled streets below.

It was time to find answers. What in the Cosmos had happened to him? He was sure if he could remember, he would be able to fix it. But there was nothing, just a gaping hole in the center of his mind as if someone had ripped the memory of the last few days out of him.

He lashed out with a growl, grabbing a potted plant beside the brothel's entrance and hurling it into the sky. The pot shattered in front of him, his breathing heavy as he tried to reign in his temper. He closed his eyes, letting out one final huff of annoyance before he walked through the alcove and onto the main street of the city.

He was in Mitstad. It was the only city in this world—more specifically, the continent of Emmoria—where all the Elementalists resided, not in peace exactly, but in a sort of strange harmony. Emmoria was a continent at war, having been so for nearly four centuries.

This land was divided into four regions, and the city of Mitstad was at the very center of them all. Northeast of the city was Sylphiin, the region of the air Elementalists.

A place covered in thick forests and verdant hills. It was the smallest of the four regions, bordered on the west by Gnomeic, which was home to the Earth Elementalists. Theirs was the largest, most mountainous of the regions. To the south of Gnomeic was Undinaam, home to the water Elementalists, and east of that was the powerful fire region of Salamaand. They had burned their once-thickly forested and richly lush region down to ash and sand long ago; all that remained was a desert wasteland full of their large and menacing cities. Their armies were brutal, and their ruler merciless.

Orrick sighed. The heat of the sun beat down upon him, fueling his irritation at being unable to use his powers, which had been his constant companion since birth. Being without them was an ache without relief. Where the fuck should he even start to find answers? He gritted his teeth, trying desperately to hold in his ire.

He raked through his mind, searching for any piece of memory, but it was as dry and barren as the fire Elementalists lair. Orrick growled, and a sudden burning sensation scorched through him with a vengeance. He could no longer hold in his fury. Out of habit, he whipped his arm out to the side, something he always did when his anger rose, trying to send out his power to destroy anything in his path. He knew full well nothing would come of it, but it made him feel just a smidge better, releasing the fiery tension that had corded through his muscles.

A screeching yell stopped him in his tracks as he turned toward the sound with a brow raised. That sound was like music to his ears, causing a smirk to curve the left side of his mouth.

He was surprised to find a cart full of what looked like fruits or possibly confections. He could honestly no longer tell what the cart was selling because the entire thing had been engulfed by dancing green flames.

"Well, that's interesting," he mused, taking a step closer out of curiosity.

Suddenly, a woman ran out from behind the cart of emerald fire, wielding the air around her like a whirlwind. The breeze encircled the flaming cart, creating a tornado of flickering green that was pulled up high above them. The fire extinguished into nothing more than black smoke—a smear across the pale blue of the sky.

Orrick looked back at the cart, now a barely recognizable, charred hunk of wood with spirals of smoke curling above it.

"Might I suggest a less flammable cart for your next business venture," Orrick said to the woman who was staring at what remained of her wares.

She spun on him, silver hair gleaming in the sunlight as it whipped around her. She glared, pointing a pale finger at him as she yelled, "You!"

Orrick frowned, looking to either side of him, but there was no one in the vicinity. This Sylph woman was talking to him. He looked back at her to find her now prowling toward him.

"Me?" he snorted, placing a hand on his chest.

"Yes, you!" She barked, "What do you think you're doing? You could have killed me. You aren't allowed to use your gifts here. It's forbidden. Mitstad is a free city. You are going to pay for this!"

Orrick chuckled, "You're mistaken. I didn't do that. I'm no fire wielder."

The woman's silver eyes turned eerily dark, and Orrick found himself strangely taking a step back from her. She had no idea who she was dealing with; if only he had his gifts, he would turn her into dust where she stood.

"Are you daft? I just saw you do it!" She screamed, throwing her hands up in the air.

A gust of wind came toward him, and he stumbled backward, almost falling onto the cobbled streets below. Orrick dug his feet into the ground and narrowed his eyes on the woman. "If you knew who I am, you would not have done that." His voice was low, lethal.

"I know exactly who you are, Salamander."

That same burning rage that he had felt since he found out his powers were useless burst through him. A slight twitch of the Sylph woman's hand was all he needed to see before he struck. Not even allowing another moment of thought, he threw out his ire, lashing everything within him at the woman.

The Sylph burst into a cone of green flames.

Orrick froze, watching in stunned fascination as the woman fell to the ground, shrieking as her skin bubbled, melting away to reveal the corded muscle beneath. He observed until her body no longer writhed, until she was simply a smoking corpse of charred bone and ash.

"Huh," he huffed, looking down at his hands, the final lick of emerald extinguishing from his fingertips. "Intriguing."

"Hey, you!" someone yelled from behind him. Orrick turned sharply from the smoldering embers to find a man running toward him, the cobbled street beneath his feet moving, a distant rumble pricking in Orrick's ears. A Gnome. It was time to go.

"Fucking Elementalists," he groaned, rolling his eyes before sprinting away from the man and the evidence of his newly discovered ability.

Orrick wound his way through the streets until he finally came upon one of his favorite establishments in this small city. It was a tavern named after him. Not that anyone would know. The place had been around for at least nine centuries now.

A bronze plaque nailed beside the wooden door read, *Tavern of Chaos.*

Orrick smiled before entering. As soon as he pushed open the door, the warmth of the place wrapped around him, the scent of the most delicious drink this world had to offer hitting him like a comforting hug—mead.

"Oh, thank the Cosmos," Orrick almost sang the words as he took a seat at the gilded bar. He finally had a moment to think, to sip mead, and try to understand what exactly was happening here.

A tankard of the honeyed drink was placed before him, and he gulped it down, reveling in the taste and feel of it gliding down his throat.

"Another," he said as he let the events of what just happened run through his mind.

He no longer had his godly gifts, but he had elemental ones—fire, specifically, but not like the Salamander's sorcery, something more. Whereas the Salamanders could use fire, only manipulating it to their whims, Orrick had created it. There was no fire source near that cart. The flames had come directly from him. The Elementalists of this world could never create; that was an ability only meant for Gods—for him. It was possible that his gifts hadn't truly left him, instead changing somehow to fit this world. But why? And more importantly, how?

This wasn't an act of the Gods. Changing one's abilities was not a punishment they could inflict upon him. So, what was causing this strange change in the most significant part of himself?

Orrick slammed a fist onto the bar counter, causing the tankards of several patrons beside him to jump, their contents sloshing and spilling free. A chorus of disgruntled Elementalists cursed on either side of him as a chair screeched against the floorboards to his left, and footsteps strolled towards him.

Orrick prepared himself for another fight or execution, he supposed. He would kill everyone in this bar if he needed to. He had made them, after all; he had no qualms about annihilating them.

He pushed his own chair back, standing and closing his eyes, feeling that now more familiar burning irritation rising inside of him. He bit the insides of his cheeks to try and keep it just there before the strike. Letting out a long, steadying breath through his flared nostrils, Orrick opened his eyes and turned toward the Elementalist.

Stunned surprise rocked into him as he was greeted by a well-curved woman instead of a gruff, drunken male. She had her tanned hands placed on her ample hips in what Orrick could only interpret as annoyance. He let his eyes travel languidly up her length, drinking in every one of her swells like a fine glass of wine.

She was wearing a tight, light orange top across her chest, which pushed her heaving breasts up nicely. It was sleeveless, with a deep plunging neckline that barely covered anything. She might as well have been topless. Her midriff was completely exposed down to her wide hips, where a pair of flowy trousers hung, rimmed in gold and cinched at her ankles. Sandals were strapped to her feet, one of which was thumping impatiently in his direction. When his gaze finally settled on her face, gorgeous gray eyes ringed in a subtle violet stared back at him. They were framed by a stunning and familiar high cheek-boned face. His smirk suddenly turned upside down as recognition dawned, and he raised his brows, "Honoria?"

"I'm going to kill you."

4
GARREN

The Daylight Road always offered stunning views of the surrounding landscape. They rode at an unhurried pace past the rolling hills and bustling forests, enjoying being in one another's company without the impending threat of a new demon tearing through a town and pushing them onward.

But the beautiful landscape was wasted on Garren, who was on edge and irritable. The imminent battle was now a mysterious noise that only he could hear, and that was almost worse than the anticipation of fighting a brand-new creature.

Discovering the unknown. That was truly terrifying.

The sound pulsed behind his eyes and pounded in his head, only growing harsher and more insistent as he followed its path. He gritted his teeth against it, wondering how bad it would be by the time he found its source.

Golden rays of sunlight danced upon the trees, casting cooling shadows across the road. Honeysuckle and lavender lined either side of the dirt path, filling the air with their vibrant fragrance. Usually, the sound of leaves rustling in the breeze, bird songs echoing across the lane, and his horse's hooves beating along the packed earth provided tranquility that he languished in. Still, every one of those sounds was now drowned out by the ringing that only grew louder the closer they got to Varian.

"We're almost there," Oriana's voice was like a beacon of light through the imposing noise. "You can just see the city gates on the other side of the Emerald Lake."

She pointed toward the horizon, and sure enough, the gleaming gates shimmered in the distance. As they continued their journey around the perimeter of the lake, the rest of the city gradually unfolded before them. Majestic spires and intricately designed buildings emerged, glimmering beneath the early rays of the morning sun.

Garren winced as another screeching wail ricocheted through his head like bells. He gripped his head in pain.

Oriana grabbed the reins of his horse, pulling them both to a stop before letting go. "Garren, are you alright?"

"We're close. It's getting louder." He gritted through the stabbing in his head and kicked his horse into a gallop once again, yelling back. "Come on. I want to find out what it is before my head explodes."

He rode hard, Oriana keeping pace behind him until, finally, the magnificent pearl gates of Varian stood before them like sentinels. The gates were always open during the day but locked and guarded at night—a habit Garren understood, especially with Orrick's demons still roaming throughout Svakland.

Varian was named the *Sovereign City* for its cunning ruler, substantial wealth, and towering citadel. But Garren had always thought a more apt name would have been the *Emerald City*, for its viridescent glittering rooftops and green sparkling sea. The sunlight reflected from them, casting the entire city in a strange emerald glow. Even the air swirled with the scent of pine and cypress, immersing the city and its surroundings in a sense of comfort that lightened the tension tightening along Garren's shoulders.

It was captivating, enchanting in its decadence, even from a distance.

As they came up upon the magnificent city, Garren pulled his mare to a stop just outside the gates. The ringing in his ears had suddenly changed. No longer a high-pitched screeching wail, but a low pulsing drum beating against his eardrums in a rhythmic pattern.

"What is it?" Oriana pulled her steed to a stop beside his.

"It changed. The sound."

"Well, let's go inside and figure out where it's coming from. Maybe we are so close now that the frequency has changed." She looked so hopeful that Garren tried to gather strength from her.

"Maybe." Garren sighed. He appreciated how accepting she was of this.

He couldn't help but think, what if it was some strange trap? They had no idea what they were walking into. He had no idea who might want to trap him or lead him somewhere, but seeing how much he had learned about the Gods and Zydells over the past months, he wouldn't put it past them. No matter if some were good or bad, they all had their agendas and their own schemes, and he wanted no part of it.

"Come on," Oriana nodded toward the open city gates. "Only one way to figure it out. Lead the way."

He stared at her unblinking for a moment, Oriana, the Goddess of enchantments and bloodlust. The thought often sprang to the forefront of his mind unbidden. It was hard to believe that she was one of them. A God, like Orrick or Anthes. She was so much more accepting of those weaker than herself, embracing them with an unwavering warmth of genuine love and kindness. He may have only faced two other Gods besides her, but neither of them put a good taste in his mouth. Even just thinking of them made him want to spit upon the earth and curse their names.

Garren took a deep, shuddering breath, shaking the unwanted thoughts from his mind, and walked onward, leading the way through the winding, cobbled streets.

They soon realized that riding their horses any further was impossible as the streets only grew more and more crowded the further they rode. Dismounting, they found a small stable to board their horses for the day.

Garren took a deep breath, closed his eyes, and listened closely to the drumming in his ears. He turned his head slowly from right to left. The beat picked up speed to the left, "This way."

He grasped Oriana's hand and pulled her along behind him, steering them through the streets, never loosening his grip on her. With each step, the sound picked up speed until they came to the docks on the outskirts of the city. Varian was a major seaport. All of the best seafood came from these waters, and it was a massive hub for passenger ships making their way north or south. Every ship, whether transporting people or cargo, stopped in Varian.

Garren stopped, closing his eyes again, listening for a change, anything to put him in the correct direction, but there was no difference.

"I–I think we need to go out to sea. We need to find a ship."

Oriana frowned, "Are you sure? There is nothing out there. Only the Storm Sea."

Garren nodded, "I know, but it ends here. It's so steady, and it's no longer directing me through the city. The only way to go is that way." He pointed out to the calm green sea, sparkling under the sunlight. The waters were crystal clear, and schools of fish could be seen swimming beneath the calm lapping of the waves. But the further you looked out to the horizon, the darker it became. No longer were there steady, beautiful seas and cloudless skies. Menacing dark gray clouds replaced them, along with waves large enough to capsize most vessels.

Garren thought back to a story he had read in Haldis' family book. It spoke specifically of the Storm Sea—although it was once known by a different name. It told the tale of a people who were trapped there endlessly, stuck beneath the churning sea, cursed to live there forever.

Garren shuddered at the thought of being trapped in such a place. A chill ran down his spine as he recalled the cruelty and havoc one of Anthes' curses could wreak. The ominous noise persisted, seeming to beckon from that very direction. He grumbled to himself, fully aware of the futility of the venture. The Storm Sea was notorious, a treacherous expanse that devoured and spit out anyone daring enough to sail into its depths. Despite the danger, he knew they needed to cross it, if for nothing more than to find the source of the relentless sound nagging at him to follow. He feared he would go mad if it filled his head much longer. "We need to find a ship. A ship that will sail into that."

Oriana barked out a laugh, "No one will sail into that. It's a death sentence." She smirked up at him, "Well, for anyone in this world except us."

"I know, but that's where it's coming from. Maybe we will be able to help a ship make it through?"

Oriana raised both brows, crossing her arms across her chest, "That is no natural storm, Garren. You know that, right? That storm has been raging for centuries. It's a curse. We won't be able to save anyone in it."

"I saved you, didn't I?"

Her features softened, "That was different, you know that."

"I know, but you almost trapped yourself within the storm, couldn't you use your gifts to help a ship cross through it safely?"

"I honestly don't know." She frowned, eyes growing distant as she looked out at the imposing black swirling clouds. "I guess it wouldn't hurt to try. You go that way, and I'll go this way. Let's find a ship."

Garren's lips curved into a half smile. He fucking loved this woman. No matter what happened, she was always accepting and ready to help.

She took a step to turn away from him, but he reached out and grabbed her wrist, wrapping his other arm around her waist. He pulled her flush against him, and her breath hitched in surprise as he pressed his lips against hers. She melted into him, bringing a hand up to the back of his head, gripping his hair as she pushed to her toes, pulling him closer against her.

"Get a room!" someone yelled through the crowd, a few laughs rising around them.

Garren broke the kiss, placing his forehead against hers, smiling at the heat that had built in her cheeks, giving them that delightful sun-kissed pink glow. "I love you." He whispered.

She smirked back at him, "I love you, too, you big brute. Now, let's go find a ship and sail away into that storm."

5

ORRICK

"Argh!" Orrick groused as Honoria grabbed him by the tip of his ear, pinching tightly as she yanked him past the bar full of amused patrons and up the wooden steps that led to the inn's rooms. She pulled him all the way to the far end of the fairly cramped hallway, where she opened a door and practically threw him inside.

"What the fuck, Honoria," He rubbed at his sore ear, turning to face her as she slammed the door shut behind her.

"You're dead, Orrick. Dead!" She screamed and ran for him with a flying fist, her nearly sheer terracotta pants flowing around her. He dodged it just before she could connect with his left eye and grabbed her wrist before she could prepare another punch.

She growled, "Let go."

"And let you take another swing at me? I think not."

Her face was screwed up into an unpleasant scowl. She was normally so beautiful, but that look made her ugly.

"Fine," she sneered, ramming her shoulder into him as he lost his balance, and she tackled him to the floor.

"Whereas, normally, I would be quite pleased with this kind of foreplay," Orrick grunted beneath her weight as she threw her free hand at him spastically like a kitten trying to attack a much older and larger cat. He finally grabbed ahold of her other wrist and gripping both tightly, he yanked her arms above his head, pinning them to the floorboards. Her face now pulled down to his, their noses touching, breath hot and ragged, mingling in the small space between their mouths. "Something tells me you're mad at me and not interested in pleasure right now. Am I right?" He asked, brow arching with uncertainty. If there was even a small chance that she might be up for some *fun*, he didn't want to risk letting the opportunity slip away.

She huffed, blowing hot air into his face, "Whatever gave you that impression? Let go of me."

"Only if you promise not to swing those fists at me again."

"Fine."

He released her, and she sat up, pushing herself off him. Orrick sat up and glared at her, fully expecting what came next. She brought a hand back, slapping him so hard across the face that his head snapped to the side. He could have sworn black dots blurred his vision.

"Feel better?" He ground out, resisting the urge to rub his cheek or show her that it actually kind of hurt. That would give her far too much satisfaction.

"A little," she said, standing and walking over to the small bed opposite him, where she perched on its edge, crossing her arms over her ample chest.

"What is going on, Honoria? Why are you here? Why are we here?"

"You don't remember?"

"The last thing I remember is being tangled in bed with you, and then I woke up here, in bed with a different woman, and nearly had my head melted off for it."

She snorted, "Nothing more than you deserve."

Orrick's nostrils flared, and he gritted his teeth against the rage he felt bubbling. "My godly gifts are gone. I am stuck in this world, and it seems you are too, so tell me why and maybe we can both get out of this fucking place."

She sent an icy stare in his direction, chin raised in defiance.

Orrick sighed, pulling a hand down his face. He was exhausted and pissed off, and she knew it.

"Are you going to tell me what happened, or just sit there with murder in your gaze?"

She narrowed her eyes at him, "You really don't remember?"

"Why do you think I'm asking you?" he growled. "Listen, Nor, I'm not in the mood for games. I've had a rough few days. Can you please just tell me what the fuck is going on?"

"*You've* had a rough few days?" She barked, "You fucking bastard, this is all your fault! And don't call me that...that pet name. You lost the right to call me that after what you did."

"I beg your pardon, but how is this *my* fault? I haven't done a wrong thing in my godly life."

Her eyes blazed with a fury so intense her face flushed crimson. She looked like a boiling kettle ready to explode, steam and sparks shooting from her ears. Orrick knew she was going to dive for him before she pounced, nails poised to dig into flesh.

"Honoria, wait!" He yelled, but she crashed into him once again, pinning him to the hard wooden ground. Her breasts hung heavy, grazing his chest as his dick rose to attention. He smirked at her, and she snarled, feeling the evidence of his arousal.

Shrieking in disgust, Honoria scrambled off of him, pushing herself against the opposite wall, shoulders rising and falling with deep breaths.

"Oh, come on, you used to love roughhousing with me." Orrick sat back up, only then noticing that tears welled in her eyes, threatening to spill free. "I can't help what turns me on, Nor."

"This isn't a joke, Orrick. This is serious. We are stuck here. There's no way for us to change what happened."

"What happened!? If you don't tell me, then we will be well and truly stuck. I have no idea how my gifts were taken, and without knowing, I won't be able to get them back and get us out of here." He would be damned if he allowed himself to get stuck in a world of his own making. How fucking embarrassing would that be? The Gods didn't take him seriously now, but after hearing about this... Well they wouldn't hear about this because he was going to find a way to reverse whatever shit had been done.

"Wait, what about you? Can't you use your gifts to get us out of here? Maybe if we make it out..."

"I—I don't have gifts either," she cut him off with a whisper, tears fully streaming down her cheeks. "It's a disaster. Why did you have to use me like that, Orrick? What did you even want from the Archives so bad that you used me to access them?"

It was as if the floodgates of his mind had burst open, filling the void that had been there since he woke up in this world. "Fuck, I remember. I—I remember it all."

He rose to his feet and began pacing the room, running a hand through his hair over and over again. His footfalls were heavy as he navigated through the tangled web of his memories. "Your mother did this. She stripped me of my gifts after finding me in the archives and sent me here as punishment." He looked over at Honoria, who was still sitting opposite him, and frowned. "But why would she send you here too?"

It didn't make any sense. Why in the Cosmos had Ada sent Honoria here with him? Why would she trap her own daughter in a world with a God? A God who was having intimate relations with said daughter. Honoria was much safer in Verhaven, where she had always been.

"Because you didn't tell me you were a God!" Honoria yelled, standing and stomping toward him, tears long dried in streaks down her cheeks, replaced by her ire. "It's forbidden! I can't believe I didn't realize you are something else. She punished me because she thinks I invited you in. What God are you anyway? You can't be one of the Six Eternal because they would have been able to put up some sort of a fight against my mother at least. But you were too weak for that."

Orrick bit the inside of his cheek to keep from allowing her to see how much that jab stung, "I am the God of creation and chaos."

"Wait," she frowned and then raised a brow. "So you created this world? You are the one who has created all of the strange new worlds in the Cosmos?"

"The one and only," Orrick bowed, stiffening as Honoria barked out a laugh.

"So, let me get this right, you made this world, and now you are stuck in it? How does that feel? Do you feel weak, useless?" Honoria smirked maliciously.

Orrick clenched his jaw, feeling the steam rising in him, boiling with rage, but he kept his mouth shut, not giving her the satisfaction of a response.

"Honestly, that does give me a small amount of joy. My mother sure knows how to dole out a punishment."

"Still doesn't take away the fact that she punished you right along with me," Orrick spat back.

"Cosmos," she breathed, shoulders sagging in defeat. "I'm so stupid. I can't believe I fell for your lies. Let you seduce me so that you could steal whatever information you were seeking in the archives. You're such a fucking bastard. You deserve this fate."

"I would argue that you do as well, for your naivety."

She stared at him for a long moment, her expression unreadable, before finally saying, "You know nothing about me, God."

"I beg to differ. I know you pretty intimately in fact."

"You're such a fucking bastard. What would it take to wipe that smug look off your face?"

"Not sure, I'll let you know if the day ever comes."

She sighed heavily, crossing her arms over her chest, and glared at him, "I can't believe I used to think that look on your face was endearing. Now it just makes me sick to my stomach, knowing its truth."

"And what is that?" He asked, walking to the window and looking down at the cobbled lane.

She ignored him and instead said, "How did you even get into our world? It's impossible for a God to enter Verhaven."

He looked back at her, making eye contact as he said, "There are always ways, Honoria. Nothing is impossible."

Orrick turned his gaze back to the window, looking up at the clear sky, and rubbed a hand along the back of his neck, where he suddenly felt a soreness tightening along his shoulders. The memories of what happened in Verhaven swam in his vision.

He had been searching for information on Garren's two siblings—the God and Zydell halflings who were hidden away in the Cosmos.

Zanos, God of life and death and the King of the Six Eternal ruling Gods, had been lying to them all for thousands of years. It was forbidden for a God to step foot on the Zydell's home world of Verhaven, let alone to mate with one.

Zanos himself forbade the Gods from mating with any being in existence other than a God. It was now Cosmic law, punishable by death. Upon enacting his law, Zanos had ordered any and all halflings in existence to be executed—though apparently, that didn't include his own offspring.

So while Orrick's father, Anthes, was off doing Zanos' bidding by traveling the Cosmos and killing off every single halfling that still dared to draw breath, the fucking

King of the Gods was having an affair with Ada, the Queen of the Zydells. An affair that resulted in the birth of the three most dangerous halflings ever to exist, ones that Zanos should be the most scared of because they were the ones that posed a legitimate threat to the Cosmos. Instead of coming clean and executing them himself, he and his Zydell lover had hidden them away, hoping no one would find out.

Well, someone did find out—Orrick. And he was more than mad. He wanted Zanos dead.

He wanted the Six Eternal dead. How dare they make rules and dictate Cosmic law but not follow it themselves? Orrick wouldn't allow it. He didn't want the triplets dead—no, he had a much better use for them. He wanted to find Zanos and Ada's forbidden offspring and use them to kill off the Six Eternal once and for all.

He had seen what Garren was capable of—had quite literally felt it. Ada had separated the three of them for a reason. What could all three do together? The three most powerful beings in the Cosmos fighting as one against the six ruling Gods. It would be epic. It would be beautiful. It would be catastrophic—in Orrick's favor. His lips spread into a wide grin.

A flash of the small scrap of paper he had found in the book about the triplets suddenly came into view behind his eyes. It spoke of the destruction of the Cosmos, its undoing, but also of its possible salvation. "A prophecy,"

Orrick mused, but had it already been set into motion? He would think that the triplets would need to be together for that to happen. That was the reason they had been separated, Orrick pieced together. The Zydells and the Gods were trying to avoid the prophecy that the triplets posed on the Cosmos. *They are scared.*

"So—" Honoria's voice pulled him from his scheming thoughts. "You never answered my question. What were you looking for, Orrick? What was so important that you got us banished to this world for it? I have a right to know."

Orrick ignored her, his mind pulsing as he tried to figure out what to do next. Yes, he had used her, pretended to be a Zydell, gained her trust, and she had led him right to the Archives, to the answer he was looking for, but he had discovered even more than he intended. The triplets' prophecy was far more intriguing, teetering on the cusp of terrifying. Orrick wasn't dumb. He knew that if something was enough to scare the Zydell Queen that it was something much larger than himself.

He glanced at Honoria. The hurt shown in her features, lining her face, and it pushed against the beating organ in his chest. *Fuck.* She didn't even know what or who she was, did she?

"I have to go," Orrick suddenly blurted out, walking out the door and slamming it closed behind him. He listened for the sound of movement on the other side of the door to see if she would follow, but she didn't. Orrick released a sigh of relief. He needed his powers back and he would stop at nothing until he had them. He needed to talk face-to-face with the Zydell Queen. There were too many questions that needed to be answered. He only hoped she would heed his call.

6

GARREN

It was useless. No frigate, no vessel in this city would go anywhere near the Storm Sea. He knew it was a pointless endeavor. No one in their right mind would sail headlong to their death. And it wasn't like he could point out that two powerful beings would be onboard to save them. No one would take them.

Garren sighed and pushed his way through the crowded docks back toward where Oriana had gone when the thrumming sound that was loud and ever present in his ears, directing him into the storms, suddenly went silent. He looked out over the sea, peering into the gray, searching for something, an explanation, anything to tell him what the sound had been or where it was coming from.

A nagging at his nape urged him to turn around, a prickling that made the hairs along his arms stand on end. He turned slowly.

Garren's eyes locked instantly with a man standing on the end of a gangplank coming off a rather large ship. Everything went still and quiet as the stranger's eyes found his. There was something so familiar about the man. An unspoken connection lingered in the air, one that seemed to extend beyond this moment, beyond this world even. The man's eyes were dark, piercing, and black. They bore into him, studying, shifting into a strange brightness as if his eyes were the night sky and stars had suddenly come to life within them. It sent a tingling down his spine, setting the hairs at his nape on end. Time seemed to slow, everything around them falling away until it was just the two of them.

The man raised a single gray brow in intrigue and then narrowed his eyes. The rest of his face was covered by a black cloth that wrapped around his head, hiding all of his features except for those eerily expressive eyes. The man cocked his head and took a step closer. Garren tensed, holding his breath at whatever was about to transpire between them. His hand twitched, ready to go for his blade. The sea breeze wrapped around Garren, pushing him toward the man. He held his feet firm, not wanting to get any closer to the stranger.

Oriana's face popped up in front of him, blocking his view as she stood on her tippy toes with an excited smile, severing his enraptured gaze with the man.

"Garren! I found us a ship!"

Garren shook his head, the bustling chaos of the docks coming back into focus around him. The high-pitched squeal pierced his eardrums once again with a vengeance. He winced at its sudden reappearance. Not the low drum that had begun since arriving in Varian, but the one from before. The one that rang out with an urgency, like a beacon directing him. The low drum had brought him to the docks where he assumed he was meant to go out to sea, but this high-pitched wail was practically pulling him into the storms, urging him forward.

"What?" he blinked, "W—Where?"

"This way," she grabbed his hand and pulled him in the opposite direction of the man.

Garren looked back to the spot where the stranger had been, but he was gone. Nowhere to be seen.

Who was that? What had that strange pull toward the man been? Garren couldn't shake the feeling that something was off. Something in Svakland had shifted suddenly. First, the strange buzzing in his ears, then a persistent ringing that was pulling him towards an unknown destination. And now a stranger who felt so familiar to him, but he was certain he had never seen or met them before. Those eyes were distinct, not ones to forget, yet their presence seemed to tug at him almost in the same way the ringing was. He didn't like it. He didn't like any of it. Nothing made sense anymore, and it only left Garren feeling unsettled as he followed Oriana down the docks.

"There she is," Oriana stopped abruptly, Garren practically running into her as she pointed toward the smallest ship in the port. He had to look down off the dock even to see it.

It was the most unusual ship he had ever laid eyes on. It was long and narrow with two triangle-shaped sails. Its hull—if it could even be called that—was so shallow he was sure the minute too many passengers got in, it would sink below the sea's surface and capsize.

"Absolutely not." He said, shaking his head and backing away.

"Garren, it's the only option."

He glanced back out to the darkness beyond, to the thick imposing clouds, to the seas that he knew swirled with deathly currents.

"Tell me, how do you expect that ship to make it through there?"

"Because it's made it before," said a voice from behind them, carrying an unfamiliar accent.

They both spun in unison and were greeted by a man the same height as Garren, his skin a dark glowing umber, his eyes a strange mixture of light brown and blue. But the most unusual thing about him was his hair. At first, Garren thought it was a dark brown, corded into thick, tangled locks, but upon closer inspection, he could have sworn it was a very dark purple.

"Who are you?" Garren asked, narrowing his eyes on the man. He definitely wasn't from around here. Even his clothes were strange.

"Atlas, Captain of that vessel," he nodded toward the longship. "Happy to meet you. Your friend here tells me you are looking to sail through the Storm Sea."

"That's right." Garren couldn't remove the distrust from his voice. The man's words were rolled together almost in a melodic way. Where was he from? Garren had traveled the entirety of Svakland and never heard that dialect.

"Well, it just so happens to be where we're headed." A wide grin spread across his lips, revealing a set of perfectly white teeth.

"You're joking, right?" Garren scoffed, "Come on, Oriana, he's just looking for coin."

"Suit yourself," the man said with a chuckle, " We'll be leaving with or without you in just under an hour."

Atlas turned, leaving them alone to talk as he headed onto his vessel.

Garren grabbed Oriana's hand, pulling her through the crowded docks to a small alcove shrouded in shadow, hidden from any wandering eyes. "Listen, that thing doesn't look like it would survive a rain cloud, let alone a fucking massive storm curse that has been churning for centuries. What if you just took us there, you know, jumped us through time and space, whatever it is Gods do to get into a new world?"

Oriana's brows raised in surprise, "Honestly, I'm not entirely sure why I hadn't thought of that to begin with. Cosmos, that would have saved us so much time today. Although I can't follow whatever sound you're hearing, I can at least get us on the other side of the storms, and then you can direct us from there."

Garren nodded, a smirk on his lips. "Let's do it. I would do just about anything to not get on that boat."

Oriana rolled her eyes, "Alright, hold my hands; this won't feel like much of anything since it's really not far and in the same world. Just a slight jerk and a blink of your eyes. Are you ready?"

"Yes, the sooner I can get rid of this fucking noise, the better."

Oriana let out a long, steadying breath, closing her eyes, and Garren followed suit. It was just as she said, a sudden yank of his torso and darkness, but then a hard smack.

"Uff, what the fu..." Oriana grunted, and they both opened their eyes, looking at one another just before they fell, tumbling at the edge of the massive grey whirlwinds that were the Storm Sea. The wind rushed past them as the choppy waves of the sea rose closer to greet them just before they both plunged beneath its icy surface.

The shock of the water pushed all the air from Garren's lungs. His senses reeled as bubbles swirled around him, the murky depths blurring his vision. Disoriented, he swam, not entirely sure if he was headed for the surface or farther into the dark abyss. Finally, his head broke through the surface, and all thoughts went to Oriana. He yelled out her name, spinning, blinking through the torrential rain, trying to find her bobbing within the white peaked waves.

"Oriana!" he said again.

"I'm here!" He finally heard her call out, spotting her white-locked head floating in the dark blue several lengths away from him. He swam to her, grabbing onto her waist and pulling her against him as he kept them both afloat.

"What happened? Did we make it across?"

"No," she gasped, pushing the wet hair from her face. "It stopped me. The Storms won't let me through. We have to go back!"

Just then, a massive wave crashed over them. Garren's fingers slipped against her slick skin as the icy tendrils of the cursed sea threatened to pry his grip from Oriana. For a split second, it felt like the ocean might swallow them whole, but then he felt a sharp, deep tug in his stomach. Darkness engulfed him, and in the next heartbeat, his feet were on solid, dry ground again.

They both doubled over, gasping for air in the narrow alleyway from which they had disappeared only moments before.

"I've never had that happen," Oriana coughed, wiping the salty water from her face. "I couldn't jump us through.

It felt like I ran headfirst into an invisible wall. It must be the curse. It's the only explanation."

"So what does that mean?" He asked, ringing out his tunic and trousers.

"We have to take that ship." She pointed to the small, oddly shaped vessel bobbing in the calm waters at the dock.

Garren only grunted. He really didn't want to get on that thing.

Oriana turned to Garren with pleading eyes, "This is more than likely our only chance unless you want to try and purchase a ship and sail through on your own."

"That's not a ship, it's a damn dingy. Sailing on that ship will force us to swim through those storms regardless."

"We'll be okay. We can keep it safe through the storms—hopefully."

Garren scowled at her, grunting again, because that phrase rested entirely on that one word—hopefully. If the storms hadn't let her through, would they let her use her powers inside to fight it? They were both powerful in different ways, and he believed they could help the ship navigate the sea one way or another. That curse was designed to trap an entire civilization—a civilization that might no longer exist. Its purpose was to keep anyone from reaching those people, not to trap those who ventured within its depths. So maybe all they needed to do was guide the ship through the storms, away from the heart of the curse. He hoped so, but uncertainty lingered in the back of his mind.

Many ships had tried to cross it over the years, but none had made it. Every single one was cast back out, their ships in pieces, their passengers never to be seen again.

Except for this man. Garren narrowed his eyes at the strange Captain who claimed he had not only made it through but was already planning to go back.

Garren grunted his annoyance, which only made Oriana smirk. She knew she'd convinced him. "I have a few questions for this Captain first."

She gestured an arm out toward the gangway, "After you."

7

ORRICK

Orrick wound his way through the city with graceful ease. The one good thing about being trapped in a world of his own making was that he knew everything there was to know. He knew every path, every tree, every blade of grass. He had created it from nothing, after all, built it into what it was, allowing his creations to continue on in his direction. They created new life on their own, life that he didn't know, but would sometimes spend time learning, choosing few out of the many to observe from time to time.

Most of his creations were simply experiments. Random ideas pieced together like patchwork linen out of boredom or just for his own amusement. This particular world was one of his favorites. It featured several continents separated by vast oceans, each teeming with life. He had named it Fellhaven, because it was the mortal version of Verhaven, home of the Zydells. Although he hadn't set foot in Verhaven when he crafted this world, it had been his inspiration. He let his mind run wild with the possibility of what their unknown home was like.

Verhaven had always been a place shrouded in mystery, an unknown within the Cosmos that he had meticulously crafted. It would be empty without him. Once, it had been nothing more than a streak of black, desolate, a void. Now, the Cosmos was a picture he painted with life, no longer empty but brimming with worlds. Yet, Verhaven lingered out of his reach, taunting him with its secrets. That was until he learned of Zanos' treachery. If the almighty God of life and death was going to break his own rules, then why did Orrick have to abide by them?

So he had finally figured out how to sneak his way into the world undetected simply by pretending to be a Zydell himself. The Gods and the Zydells had such subtle differences that all he had to do was cover those differences and they were none the wiser. Once there and positive that his ruse had worked, he lured in a naive, foolish girl with pretty words and promises of love, adventure, and a better life. That was all it took. Honoria fell quickly for his deceit, questioning nothing, too smitten with him to notice or care that he might not be who he said he was.

That did him a lot of good. He assumed seducing a girl who lived in the Zydell palace would give him the best chance of getting what he needed. It had, but it seemed he had dangled himself a little too close to the tip of the

Queen's blade. He hadn't known Honoria was actually her daughter, not until he read from that book in the archives.

Honoria was a pretty plaything, but ultimately just a necessary means to his own ends. Although now that he knew who she was, he was inwardly cursing himself for being so careless, because now the truth was he needed her. She was one of the only three people in the Cosmos who could help him destroy the Six Eternal once and for all. And she hated him.

Which begged the question of why Ada banished her here with him? It made no sense, so she had to have a good reason. Honoria was the only child she raised herself, her most precious possession. Yet, it seemed as though she cast Honoria aside, discarding her as if she were nothing more than a worthless trinket. And if the scribbled message tucked within the ancient tome were to be believed, keeping Honoria close and under her protection would limit any threat to the destruction of the Cosmos. It was an oddity that Orrick planned to understand by asking the Queen herself.

Orrick continued his trek south through the city. The closer he traveled to the desert sands of Salamaand, the more he saw the evidence of the war that riddled these lands.

Mitstab had always been a bustling city for those seeking pleasure and an escape from the constant fighting and war that plagued this world. The last time he had visited, the air was laden with the scent of roasted meats, the roads lined with vendors, the bakers always tempting passersby with their delectable treats. He remembered how the sound of laughter and the soft melody of music echoed off the tall buildings. It always remained a small oasis, offering a respite from the chaos and destruction that ravaged the world around it. Now, the streets were littered with debris as buildings lay in crumbled ruins around him. Their stone facades were marred and scorched with blackened scars from relentless battles as the acrid scent of smoke lingered heavily in the air. It was just a constant reminder of the perpetual struggle in this world.

As he navigated his way through the scattered rubble and remnants of collapsed buildings, a sensation crept over him, a strange mix of nostalgia and sadness—something he hadn't felt in a very long time. He looked up to the sky choked with ash and heavy with the scent of decay. This world was his masterpiece. Once full of vibrant beauty, it had been a sanctuary. He created it for himself as an escape, a place where he could be free of the burdens that plagued him as the son of the Six Eternal and relish in what he had breathed into existence.

At some point, it had transformed into a bleak, desolate wasteland. How long had it been since he last set foot here? Centuries maybe, he couldn't remember, but this much decay and change seemed unfathomable. Was this devastation a consequence of his neglect?

He hadn't kept tabs on the Elementalists of Emmoria in so long. Guilt gnawed at him. He should have done more to shield this place from the raging inferno of war. It was never his intention to abandon them, but he had been caught in a web of punishment by the Six Eternal for nothing more than doing what he was destined to do—create.

They banished him to the far reaches of the Cosmos, where he only continued to forge new worlds, each more intricate than the last. Angered by this, the Six Eternal imprisoned him, locking him away in the dark world. He wasn't proud of it, but it took him much longer to escape that fate than it should have. Once free, he became a bit sidetracked by the news of Oriana's curse, sparking a mischievous intrigue that led him astray.

And so, centuries slipped away as one thing led to the next, and this place faded from his mind. If only he had remembered them and taken the time to visit them once or twice over the years, maybe this city wouldn't now be a smoldering shell of what it once was.

He gripped at the foreign feeling in his chest, rubbing at it until it dissipated. Orrick sighed, finally making it to the edge of the disaster that Mitstad had become. He wondered what the rest of Emmoria looked like, as well as each of the Elemental regions. What had this endless war done to the surrounding lands? His lands.

Orrick shook the thoughts away. He could think about those things and explore Emmoria another time. He had much more pressing issues to figure out at present.

He stared out at the desert landscape before him, surveying the vast expanse of golden dunes that stretched farther than he could see. In the dunes, he would call out to Ada and make her heed him. The woman sent him here, along with Honoria, with no apparent way out, so she better come when he called.

The sun blazed mercilessly overhead, its intense heat beating down, scorching his skin. With a frustrated growl, he threw up a hand toward the sky, wishing to pull the clouds together and block the fiery rays. The gesture was futile and he cursed when nothing happened. This whole not having powers thing was getting old fast.

With each step, his feet sunk deep into the golden grains of sand. The grains shifted beneath him, making every movement a struggle as if the dunes were trying to pull him under. How did anyone walk through this?

The desert was home to the three large fire cities. The Salamanders were the most destructive of the Elementalists and had the largest army. If Orrick bet on one of the four kingdoms winning the war, it was them. Long ago, they practically annihilated the Undinas from existence. It was the only time Orrick interfered with the Elementalists' fight. If he hadn't the Salamanders would have continued their slaughter through Gnomeic and then into Sylphi-in, annihilating everything in their path. He enjoyed this world and these people he created too much to see them all burned to ash. He wasn't done playing with them, although when he got his gifts back, he might change this fucking desert into a frozen landscape of snow and ice instead.

Orrick felt like his throat was on fire, so dry that he wished he could conjure a large glass of water to gulp down and then another one to pour over his head. Not only that, but his legs were so heavy he was sure if he took one more step, he would fall face-first into the sand. Was this what it felt like to be mortal? Fuck. He didn't like it at all. He was so exhausted just from walking through the damn sand.

Orrick fell to his hands and knees. "Ada!" he yelled out, "What have you done?"

He kneeled there in the sand, waiting for several excruciating minutes, but his pleas went unanswered. Orrick grunted and stood, brushing the pesky sand from his hands and knees. He tried another tactic, "I know of your folly. I know everything, Ada. Come and face me, you coward."

A sudden breeze swept across the desert, whipping around him and sending sand spraying. He shielded his eyes against it until, just as quickly as it came, the wind ceased, and the sand settled back onto the sprawling land-scape of gold. When he finally dared to look up, he was greeted by the sight of Ada standing before him. Her white gown billowed around her on a non-existent breeze as her long blue hair flowed behind her, giving her the appear-ance of swimming through water. The silver of her eyes glowed with an otherworldly light that was stark against her dark skin.

"How dare you," He punched the air, fire bursting from him. Ada stepped aside, letting the fire pass behind her as it smothered itself out in the sand. "Change me back, now."

"You knew the risk in coming to our world, God. My punishment does not come lightly."

Orrick's laugh was full of hatred. "Fucking hypocrite. You and Zanos haven't been playing by the rules for quite some time. You have no right to enact punishment when you have done far worse than I, oh mighty Zydell queen," he spat, a sneer spreading across his face. "Imagine what your people will think when they hear of your indiscre-tions. That you, in your selfishness, have created the very thing that can destroy the Cosmos itself. " She flinched ever so slightly, and he took great joy in that small chink he had chipped from her statued exterior.

She stood her ground, not offering a response to his claims. She wasn't going to deny it. At least she wasn't a liar as well as a whore.

"Why did you banish her too?" He needed to know, to understand. It didn't make any sense.

Ada looked away from him, breathing in sharply before saying, "She belongs here. She has been asleep for far too long, but here she will awaken. Her destiny was written long ago and not even I can stop it from coming to pass. I am just a small tool in the Cosmos' plan. Just as you are."

A glimmer danced in her eye, and Orrick thought he saw a tear forming, ready to fall, but then she sharpened her gaze, glaring at him with an unnerving intensity. It made his skin crawl; her stare felt as if she were peeling back all of his layers, revealing his deepest self.

Orrick shifted uncomfortably and said, "Me? How am I a part of her plan?"

"All of our fates were written in the stars long ago. To attempt to change the inevitable is fruitless."

Orrick furrowed his brows, scowling at her. What did she mean? What future had she seen? He did not like uncertainties. They gnawed at him like an itch that couldn't be reached. He clenched his jaw in frustration.

"You saw the prophecy, did you not?"

"You mean that messy writing on the random parchment shoved carelessly into that tome?"

Ada's lips tightened, nostrils flaring slightly. "That is only a piece of their fate."

Orrick sighed, closing his eyes and bringing a hand down over his face, "So what is the rest? What was missing from that prophecy, as you call it?"

"A fate known is a powerful thing, God. You are not ready for that kind of power."

Orrick pursed his lips, holding his tongue and forcing down the intense desire to lash out.

"You can break free, you know." She suddenly said, "All you need to do is understand, chaos God. Your gifts aren't gone, just out of reach."

Orrick brought the palms of his hands up to his eyes, pressing against the pressure building behind them. "Can't you just tell me how to get them back? Why do all of you ruling beings have to be so secretive? Doesn't that get exhausting? Always skirting around the point."

She came closer to him, her movements so ethereal it looked like she was floating. Her dark skin glimmered in the harshness of the sun like gemstone, creating a glow around her. The Gods really weren't all that different from the Zydells. Each of them possessed powerful abilities, but Ada was on another level entirely. She seemed to transcend the rest, the full extent of her powers a mystery that Orrick yearned to discover. Was she more powerful than the triplets? That thought shifted his mind back to Honoria.

"Wouldn't she be far safer with you in Verhaven? Surely, you aren't daft enough not to realize what I truly desire." She wasn't daft at all. That was the problem. There was something more to this. Something he was missing. If one of the triplets was happily tucked away in the one place the Gods couldn't go, wouldn't that be the best way to keep the prophecy from being fulfilled?

"In time, you will know what to do."

He rolled his eyes, crossing his arms over his chest, "It would be a lot easier and quicker if you just told me."

"You aren't ready."

"Cosmos above! Ready for what?" Green flames licked along his fingers again. Something that he noticed happened anytime someone pissed him off. "Also, why the fuck do I have fire magic? You took away my gifts and replaced them with elemental magic? For what purpose?"

She turned and began walking away from him, cobalt locks still floating around her as if alive, moving on their own accord. "The flames are merely a placeholder for when you find yourself once again."

Orrick groaned. This conversation was growing tedious, and his anger was wobbling precariously just on the edge of an explosion. He didn't want to play games with her any longer.

"Tell me, can the triplets kill the Gods? Kill you, even?" He fished, trying to reel in the answer to his suspicions about them. He watched, amused, as unease seemed to ripple through her, and she went rigid, shoulders tensing and hands balled into tight fists.

"Are you so frightened of them because of the threat their existence poses on you?" He prodded, "I have seen what only one of them is capable of—all three together would be catastrophic, wouldn't it?"

A flash of trepidation shone in her gaze, barely perceptible, but Orrick saw it, and it was all he needed to know that he was right. She was afraid of her own children, fearful of what their existence posed to the Cosmos, and it gave him nothing but pure joy.

"Do not pretend to know me, God," she spat. "Your fate is not exact. You play a dangerous game, one that could alter the course of your destiny forever. Make all of your choices wisely lest you want to be stuck here for eternity." And with that final cryptic statement, she was gone like a spirit in the wind.

"Well, that was entirely unhelpful," Orrick groaned.

He turned back toward the crumbling city of Mitstad far off in the distance and began stomping his way through the sand like a child whose favorite toy had been ripped from his grasp.

He stopped abruptly as a thought hit him. Ada said his gifts weren't gone, just out of reach. But out of reach, how? He closed his eyes, reaching deep within himself, feeling for that well of power that had always been a constant within him, but it was as empty as it had been since he arrived in this God's forsaken place.

Out of reach, my ass. Orrick opened his eyes and continued the long trek back to Mitstab and Honoria. He was desperate to escape this world. As long as she was here, away from her mother's protection, she was vulnerable and exposed. If Anthes came for him only to discover her in this world, he would stop at nothing to manipulate her into his confidence. At least he knew Garren was safe with Oriana and wouldn't fall for Anthes' tricks, but he wasn't fully convinced about Honoria or the third sibling. One thing that Orrick could agree with his father on was how to use the triplets. Orrick craved the chance to witness the immense power of all three together, but that desire warred with his fear of Anthes using them for his own gain. Orrick wanted them to annihilate the Gods, but Anthes, he was positive, wanted them for much more. So he needed to get Honoria out of this world and safely back home to Verhaven.

After what felt like an eternity, Orrick finally made it back to the center of the city, where he left Honoria in the *Tavern of Chaos.*

He barely remembered how he managed to reach Honoria's room, but when he looked up, he was outside her door. Without knocking, he strode inside, slamming the door behind him.

"I take it you didn't find a way for us to get home then." Honoria's voice was laced with sarcasm and just the slightest hint of poison. She sat on the bed, leaning against the wall behind it with a book lying open on her lap.

Orrick only growled in response. He was in no mood for her derision, and where the hell had she gotten a book? Visions of her in Verhaven, lounging in her room with a book in hand, sprang to his mind, and his mood only soured further. He was out there trying to figure out something, and she was sitting in bed, reading a book.

Honoria shook her head with a snort, "You know if you weren't so conniving, so damn manipulative and stupid, we would both be rightfully where we belong, not stuck in this shit hole of a world you created."

That was it, Orrick sprung. His rage filled him to the brim, and he was on top of her in two seconds flat, pinning her to the bed. He wrapped a hand around her throat, flaming fist pulled back, and ready to swing. His breathing was heavy, chest rising and falling as anger bubbled to the surface.

Honoria's eyes were wide with surprise and fear as she lay beneath him, unmoving. She swallowed heavily, and he watched as a single tear rolled down her rosy cheek. It made something foreign wriggle deep inside him, something uncomfortable and equally terrifying.

"Fuck!" he yelled, slamming his fist into the wall above her head, smoke billowing and sparks scattering as the green fire engulfing his hand extinguished. He had become weak. Since when did someone's fear cause him to back away?

He growled again, releasing her and pushing himself off the bed, sagging wearily into a wooden chair against the wall. Orrick buried his head in his hands, elbows resting on his knees. He didn't know what to do. He felt so powerless. He had been bested and felt as if he was little more than the creatures he created—meaningless, worthless.

Honoria coughed, gasping for breath, and scuttled away from him, refusing to look him in the eye. He was an idiot. She was just as desperate to get out of here as he was. They were in this together, even if she hated him for it. If they didn't work together, they would never get out of this world.

He looked over at her to see her glowering at him, that spark she always had in the bedroom coming out to play. Good, she wasn't completely broken then.

"You know this place better than anyone. What do we do?" She finally said, voice quiet but firm.

"I don't know yet. Let me think." He grumbled, because she was right. He should know what to do, but he had never been in a situation like this before. He was in new territory, and the one person who could help—the very reason they were both stuck here—hadn't helped at all.

His mind reeled. He knit this entire world together thread by thread. There had to be something here that he could use to return home and regain his power.

Closing his eyes, he pictured the full map of this realm in his mind. They were in Emmoria, the land of the Elementalists, but this world of Fellhaven also contained the land of Griovian and the continent beyond the stormy seas—Orrick gasped, his eyes shot open again, and whispered, "Svakland."

How had he not thought of it before? Oriana and Garren were in Svakland, which meant they were all currently in the same world together. The thought suddenly made Orrick frown because that also meant that two of the triplet siblings were together. *Fuck.* This was bad. If Anthes discovered two of them in this world, well, then they were all doomed.

A plan began to form in his mind. They would find Oriana so that she could get them out of this world and send Honoria back to her rightful place, tucked beside Ada in Verhaven. He would figure out how to regain his power afterward.

"What's Svakland?" Honoria questioned, still glaring at him from her spot huddled on the bed, arms wrapped around her legs.

He sighed, feeling a slight twinge of regret over what he just did to her. He needed to get a grip on himself. He was the God of this world. He should be better. He was allowing his anger to cloud his judgment. "My sister is in Svakland. She can help us."

"Where is that?"

"Far away," he groaned. "Across the sea. We need to go west."

Honoria nodded, still hugging her knees to her chest on the bed, quickly wiping away the tears that pooled in her eyes.

Orrick sighed, "Listen, Honoria, I—I didn't mean to—" he stopped inwardly, cringing at what was just about to come out of his mouth. What was this fucking place doing to him? What was this powerless life doing to him? He had almost apologized to her. *Fuck.* He wasn't himself right now. His mind was more fragile than usual.

"We leave first thing in the morning," he finally said. "Better get your beauty sleep."

8

GARREN

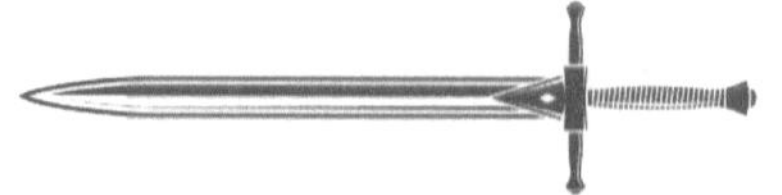

"Decided to join us on our dingy after all, aye?" The Captain smirked, making Garren's nostrils flare in annoyance. There was something about the man's body language and the air of superiority he held, slithering over him like a snake. Garren didn't like him.

"I've never seen a ship like this before, that's all. It doesn't look like it could handle sailing through a light breeze, let alone that." He said, cocking his head toward the dark horizon, raising a brow.

The vessel sat low in the water. The head of a great beast was carved into the bow, jutting up toward the sky, making it look like a vicious sea monster waiting to attack its prey. Its wood was rough and calloused with age, and Garren frowned at its appearance. The scent of salt and brine emanated from its surface, mingling with the musty perfume of decaying wood. It almost made him gag with the rankness of it, making him question the age of the ship.

It looked as if it had endured a decades-long journey merely to make it to this dock. Garren groaned at the thought of sailing through a cursed storm in this sad excuse for a ship. Maybe Oriana could hold it together with her gifts long enough to get them through.

Other than Oriana, himself, and Atlas, there were three other crew members aboard. Two of the men were working with the sail while the other was fixing ores into place.

Garren narrowed his gaze at the number of oars ready for rowers.

"She might not look like a lot, but she's treated us well. Gotten us through many rough seas safely."

Garren took his time, thoroughly scrutinizing the Captain standing before him. There was an unsettling energy that hung around him, sending a sense of unease through Garren. Beside him, Oriana had gone very still, and he knew she felt it too. It wasn't just his striking purple hair, something that made him instinctively think of a demon, because only demons tended to have eccentric colored hair. No, there was more to it than that. The man's voice was an odd mix of foreign inflections with the Svaklandian tongue, yet none of them fit with any region he had been to before—and he had been to every single piece of this continent. Even the man's clothing set him apart, full of rich fabrics adorned with intricate patterns, making him stand out in the crowd of traditional, modest Svaklandian styles throughout the city.

"Where did you say you were from, again?" Oriana asked beside him, cocking her head at the man with narrowed eyes.

"I didn't," he said with a wide smile. "Now, it's my turn to ask a question. Why do you wish to sail through the storms? Where are you looking to go?"

Garren exchanged a quick look with Oriana, "Honestly, we aren't entirely sure. It's the adventure we are seeking."

"We want to find out what is on the other side." Oriana added with a sweet smile, "We are explorers."

For a split second, Atlas' eye twitched in a way that told Garren he didn't fully trust them, but it was gone just as soon as it had come, the skepticism replaced by the wide-toothed grin he had shown multiple times in their short interactions together. "Well, you are in for quite the adventure then. Those storms left us stranded here for quite some time. This is our first sailing since. We've spent the past two months repairing our vessel and we are anxious to get back." He looked up toward the city, squinting against the harsh sun, pressing his lips into a firm line as he shook his head with a sharp exhale that sounded like a frustrated snort. "This place doesn't suit us. It is very—powerless."

What did he mean? Where were these people from? In all his years, Garren hadn't known there to be anywhere outside of Svakland. Yet these men had him second guessing what he knew about this world. Was there more land, entire groups of people he'd never encountered?

"Powerless?" Oriana raised a brow at the Captain. "What are you trying to say, exactly?"

Atlas cocked his head, his light amber eyes assessing her in a way that made Garren growl beside her, but Oriana placed a hand on his arm, stopping the rumbling in his chest.

"Your hair is very unique." He said, altogether avoiding her question.

"I could say the same about yours," came her quick reply.

But he only ignored her again, an amused smirk spreading across his lips. "A true white. Where exactly are you from, madam?"

Oriana held her ground and Garren was impressed she didn't bristle at the questions, but he wasn't so inclined to ignore the man's comments. Taking a step forward, Garren closed his hand into a fist, ready to strike, but one of the men at the sails interrupted his assault.

"All ready, Cap."

Oriana grabbed Garren's clenched fist, her soft, delicate skin soothing the anger roaring inside him. It didn't help that the damned ringing in his ears had picked up speed. It grated on him, incessant and throbbing, keeping him on edge.

"It's alright," she whispered into his ear. "He's harmless, believe me. I sense no ill will, only curiosity in his gaze."

"Mmhmm," Garren grumbled, not entirely in agreement with her.

He hadn't taken time to actually look at the three other men aboard until just then. The man who had spoken was so pale it almost seemed as if his skin had no pigment at all. His hair was just as light, similar to Oriana's white tresses, but sprinkled with darker threads. He looked at Garren with blue eyes so light they were like shards of ice.

The second man, who was tying off a knot at the mast, was covered in clothing from head to toe, leaving not one piece of him exposed. Leather gloves protected his hands, a long-sleeved linen tunic shrouded the rest of him, and he wore a hooded vest that buttoned all the way up to his neck, his face hidden behind a black cloth. The only piece of him that could be seen were his eyes, though they were still heavily shadowed and just as dark as the black hood pulled over his head.

Atlas spotted Garren staring at the man and said, "Jespin there doesn't do well with sunlight." As if that was plenty of information to explain why the man looked like an assassin ready for a nightly murder spree.

Garren nodded as he let his gaze travel to the last man, who had positioned himself at the back set of oars. This man had umber skin almost as dark as Atlas', but he lacked the long dreaded locks. His head was completely shaved.

He wore the same intricate flowing clothing that Atlas did. The only one of the crew that wasn't dressed in strange garb was the man who was hidden beneath layers and layers of black linens, which was strange in its own way.

Observing all of this, traveling with these men suddenly felt like a very bad idea and Garren turned back to Oriana, "Are you sure about this? This feels like we are enlisting ourselves in some kind of extreme cult. Something is very off about them."

A sharp squeal pierced through Garren's head as if the very mention of turning around angered whatever was creating the sound.

Oriana didn't miss his wince and rubbed a hand along his back. "I'm not completely sure about these men and this ship, but I am sure that we need to figure out what you are hearing, and the only way to do that is to go with them across the sea. We can only hope that since they made it through once, they can do it again. With our help, of course," she added in a whisper.

Garren looked back at Atlas with a sigh and nodded. "Alright then, what's your price?"

"Grab a set of oars. That's payment enough."

Garren's brow arched at the man's words, and he glanced to Oriana beside him only to find her already sitting on a bench, grabbing a set of oars. "Oh, come on, you big bad Zydell. We gotta earn our keep."

He huffed, rolling his eyes as he sat on the bench behind her, gripping onto the splintered handles of the oars.

Atlas pushed them off from the docks, and Garren watched as they drifted away from the sparkling city, grumbling under his breath, "I guess there's no turning back now."

Another screech assaulted his eardrums as if to agree, and he bit back a curse.

"Rowers ready?" Atlas called out, the other men grunting in approval, Oriana shouting her excitement as Garren only groaned. "And we're off! Row!"

Garren and Oriana rowed in rhythm with the men, and he couldn't help but think they were only helping them row to their doom.

Garren looked out at the storms they were about to sail into as the ocean's color changed from the beautiful crystal clear green along the coast into a dark, muddy brown that couldn't be seen through. His mind wandered, remembering the tale he read about in Haldis' book of Gods and curses.

He leaned forward to whisper in Oriana's ear, "You know these storms must have been one of your father's first curses in this world, right?"

Oriana looked back at him with a solemn expression and nodded. "It was here many centuries before I came. If it's true, and there is a city under there..."

"What if they are still alive?" Garren interrupted. "What if they are just trapped like you were in Sardorf?"

Oriana looked out at the storms and furrowed her brow, "I'm not sure any mortal could survive that."

"I could use a rest from fighting demons. We should try to break it."

Oriana dropped her oars and spun around completely, putting up an enchantment around them, one that made it look like both of them were still rowing yet hid their conversation from prying ears, "Are you crazy? We barely broke my curse with our lives intact. How in the Cosmos do you think we could tackle whatever curse created those storms? I don't even know what it is or why it was cast."

"It was because of Balthar," Garren said. "Do you not know the story?"

Oriana shook her head. "What does it have to do with my father's axe?"

Garren smirked at knowing more than her about this world for once, "The story commonly told throughout Svakland is one of whimsy and wonder, but I read the true, more harrowing tale in Haldis' ancestors' book. There used to be an island called Barinsia in this sea. The Barinsian people stole your father's axe and used it to conquer Svakland quickly, amounting to considerable power and wealth." Oriana's frown grew deeper as he continued the tale. "They sought to rule the world with the most powerful weapon in the Cosmos. When Anthes found out who had stolen his axe, he cursed the island and its people, replacing it with endless storms and swirling seas." Garren pointed to the horizon, "The Storm Sea."

"How did a random group of mortals in this small world steal Balthar from my father? *We* had a hard time doing that."

Garren thought about that for a long time, and all points led to a single culprit— "That's a question I would love to ask your brother if he ever shows his vile face again."

"You know we are twins, right? Our faces are fairly close in the looks department."

Garren scrunched his nose in disgust, "You look nothing like Orrick, believe me."

She snorted, "If you say so."

"Personality changes a person's features and your two personalities couldn't be more different, thank the Gods—literally."

"So Orrick played another one of his tricks on an entire civilization. A trick that caused my father to curse them for eternity." She sighed, shaking her head and turning back around, picking up her oars and rowing once again along with Garren and the others. "What a family I have."

"I know we don't have knowledge of the words of the curse, but maybe we could find a way?"

"No one could survive in a place like that, Garren. Breaking it is all well and good, but if there is no one to save, what's even the point?"

"No one to save? Men lose their lives attempting to go into these storms and find the lost treasure of the Barinsian people every year. Just sailing through these waters is a death sentence."

"And what do you think would happen if we break the curse, the storms clear, and there is the knowledge of a massive pile of riches at the bottom of the sea?" she scoffed. "It would be a frenzy, a free-for-all to find it, and even more people would lose their lives killing each other for treasure than they do dumbly sailing straight into the storms. It's a no from me, Garren."

Garren blew out a heavy sigh. He knew she was right, but the what-ifs were nagging at him. What if the people had actually survived the storms? What if they were still there in need of saving? Wouldn't the Godly or Zydell thing to do be saving them?

"He wasn't always this way, you know." Oriana suddenly said.

He raised a brow, "Who wasn't?"

"My brother. He wasn't always an unfeeling, egotistic asshole."

"I don't know why, but I find that highly doubtful."

Her facial features took on a sad, faraway look, "When we were little, he was a carefree, loving, and fun brother. And when he came into his powers and began to create, he was just as in love with this world and all others he created as I am of them."

Garren furrowed his brow and listened. He honestly couldn't imagine the God of chaos loving anything.

"But then something happened. Something that I don't even know, and he changed," she paused, shaking her head a bit from whatever memory was still lurking there. "We both changed."

"Well, even so, the fact remains that he changed for the worse while you changed for the better."

Oriana looked down at the oar in her grip, shoulders sagging with dejection. "I haven't given up hope on him yet, Garren. He might be a conniving prick, but that goodness and love are still there somewhere. If we ever come across him again, just give him a chance. He did help us after all."

And with that, she ended the enchantment that had been around them, leaving Garren without the opportunity to retort.

Garren grunted, thinking about what she had said. He didn't care if, once upon a time, the God of chaos was the most caring, compassionate God there ever was. He didn't trust Orrick in the slightest. He would keep his guard up constantly if they were to meet again. He might have helped them, but it was for his own reasons, not for the good of Oriana. The God was still a bastard. He could only hope that Orrick would stay far away from them and leave them both to their lives here in this world.

9
ORRICK

If there was one thing Orrick could do without right now, it was Honoria. She was not a morning person, so he allowed her several hours of sleep before pulling her from the bed. She should be grateful he allowed her to rest at all.

The town was practically empty this early, the sun not even cresting the buildings yet. It was the perfect chance to see more of it, unbothered and hopefully without setting anyone else on fire.

Behind him, Honoria dragged her feet. The scraping of the rough soles of her shoes across the loosely cobbled street grated at his ears until he finally had enough and spun on her, "Is it too exhausting to pick your feet up and walk properly?"

She came to a stop and glared at him, "You're the one who woke me up no more than three hours after I fell asleep and wanted to leave before the sun even came out."

"Yes," he rolled his eyes. "So that we aren't bothered by these..." He stopped, wiggling his fingers toward the buildings full of sleeping Elementalists around them. "Beings."

She snorted, "You created these *beings* and you don't even like them, do you?"

It seemed that the restless night of sleep had turned her into a raging bitch. Orrick's nostrils flared as he said, "That's not true. I like them immensely."

A door creaked open to their left and Orrick grabbed her hand, pulling her behind him through the back alleys of the city.

"You show that so well."

"Shut up," Orrick bit back, finally letting go of her hand when they made it to a quieter part of Mitstab.

He cursed inwardly, looking at their surroundings. The signs of war and unrest were evident here, too. They were headed west toward the water Elementalist region called Undinaam, where he was hoping they could steal a ship and head to Svakland. How he would make it that far and through their territory, he hadn't quite figured out yet.

The Undinas were a hostile people; they traveled in large swarms, much like the fish in the seas, and they wouldn't hesitate to kill you the instant they found you trespassing on their lands. Neither Honoria nor himself would be welcomed. If only Ada had given them both blue skin to blend in. He snorted at the thought, shaking it off. They would just have to be careful and stay in the woods along the Gnomeic border until they made it to the coast. The Gnomeic people were slightly more lax on their patrols. Their cities were sheltered in the far northern mountains with vast forests lying between them and the neighboring kingdoms, so they didn't watch their borders as closely as the other regions.

The further they headed toward Undina territory, the worse things looked. It was much like the area near the Salamander border, except instead of scorched earth and smoking buildings, the entire edge of the city was flooded. It looked as if a massive wave crashed down upon it, which he realized was probably exactly what happened.

An entire row of buildings had toppled, their structures cracking and crumbling atop one another like a precarious stack of cards. Orrick stopped just before his feet touched the still edge of the quiet waters, which formed a vast, somber lake before them.

This entire section of the city sat slightly lower than the rest. Originally, it was nestled in a quaint valley once filled with beautiful stone structures that climbed with ivy and surrounded by lush, verdant gardens. The city had expanded beyond the valley over the centuries, sprawling outward like a growing web, but this spot had always been the start. The beginning. It was once a breathtaking picturesque scene, framed by the tall, majestic trees in the background. But now, it had been reduced to nothing but ruins sunken into a lake of dark water, a shadow of its former beauty.

"Cosmos," Honoria whispered beside him. "What happened here?"

"War."

"How long have they been at war?"

"A long time."

Honoria huffed, "This is quite some place you've created. I've been here barely three days, and I've seen almost forty murder attempts by these strange, colorful Elementalists. Everyone is so angry." She bent down and touched the water, her fingers sending ripples across the still sea. "One man almost severed another's head with a shard of stone over some spilled wine. Why is there so much unrest here? What was it like when you first created it?"

"Like this."

"What do you mean?"

"It's always been at war. I was kind of in a bit of a mood when I created it."

"So you're telling me you created this entire realm to be in perpetual war?" Her tone dripped with disdain, her hands placed firmly on her hips, eyes narrowed with skepticism.

"Not exactly," he said with a shrug. "It's more like a world of passions. Well, the two best passions, hatred and desire."

Honoria's eyes widened, her face contorting with shock as she stood back up and struggled to respond.

"You are absolutely insane. You are creating life, actual living things in the Cosmos. Things that have wants, needs, feelings, and desires, just like you and I, and you think of them as no different than the dirt beneath your feet. You trample over them, smearing them through the mud with not even a thought. Practically using them as your play things," Honoria shook her head in disgust. "I think you are the one true evil in the Cosmos, the one thing that we could all do without."

Orrick kept his features frozen in place, not allowing her to see what those words were truly doing to him beneath the surface. They pierced through him, stirring something locked deep within his chest. The dull ache he felt there was unpleasant, and he wished desperately for it to go away. Emotions were foreign to him, and he only vaguely remembered why he chose to avoid them altogether. Now, they hurt, and the more he tried to push the knot of feelings tangled in his center away, the stronger they grew.

He finally turned to face her, "Without me, none of this would even be here. If you asked the people of this world if they would rather be alive or not exist at all, what do you think they would say?" He stepped closer to her until their faces were no more than a hand width away from one another, "What I've given them is a gift. All of this," he gestured to the trees that surrounded the ruined town that swayed gently in the breeze, the leaves that rustled on low branches, the birds that chirped happily in them. "Is a gift."

Honoria held her ground, not even remotely afraid of him. He cursed inwardly at the lack of his power, the one thing that he could use at this moment to make her quake.

"This is not a gift. This is a cage," she said in an even tone.

Orrick's breathing quickened as rage built inside of him, and fire licked along his fingers. He wanted to swing with everything he had, watch her face shatter and her hair engulf in flames. Orrick bit his tongue hard instead, reeling himself in.

"Come on," he grunted, stepping into the cold dark water. "We have a long way to go, and I'd like to get there sooner rather than later."

The sting that struck him at Honoria's words wouldn't leave. He grumbled as they trudged through the waist-deep water. This was not a cage. The beings here lived whole lives. Yes, they were at war, but they also had fun, enjoying the lives he had given them, didn't they? He looked at the toppled buildings and the drowned world around him, and suddenly, doubt filled him.

Orrick cursed inwardly; Honoria had gotten in his head, and he was second-guessing himself. These people were alive, and that was enough. How they lived, he didn't care.

He had created them for fun, and that was all that mattered in the end—his own enjoyment.

They finally made it out of the valley of water and onto dry land once again. The large forest before them towered above, its ancient trees stretching toward the sky. Orrick always loved trees and the greenery of a dense forest. Long ago, when he had first created this world and this very wooded landscape, the trees could move. They would walk their way to all corners of this world, planting themselves where they wanted, but Orrick hadn't thought much about how greatly that would affect this place and the rest of the creatures in it. The entire world had begun to crumble in front of him.

With life came a need for balance. A balance that, when disrupted, destroyed itself. So he had taken away the tree's ability to move, creating this vast expanse of forest instead. Orrick smiled up at the monstrous trees as they swayed gently in the breeze, their leaves whispering secrets of those ancient times.

Honoria was staring at him, and he turned to her with a brow raised, "What?"

"Your face looked strange just then as you were looking up. Almost...happy," she snorted. "What were you thinking about?"

He smirked at her, wiggling his brows, "Just your naked body sprawled beneath me on this forest floor, moaning my name."

Her face contorted with anger, and she crossed her arms, "I don't know why I even try with you. Which way?"

"Follow me, Nor," he whispered the intimate pet name against her ear, his hand brushing along her hip. She cursed, smacking him on the back of the head as he passed her.

The ground crunched beneath their feet from brush and fallen leaves as they walked on. Sunlight filtered through the canopy high above, casting a marbled pattern of light across the forest floor. The air was thick with the scent of pine and earth, filling his lungs with a sense of tranquility. He had forgotten how much he truly loved this world. Funny, how he had originally created it as an escape for himself, and now he was stuck here. His oasis had become a nightmare. That same anger from early crashed back down on him with a vengeance.

Orrick's throat was dry, his legs burning as they hiked their way through the forest. "Why is walking so damn insufferable?" he groaned, stopping to lean up against a tree and catch his breath.

"You're such a drama king," Honoria scoffed behind him.

He spun on her, "Oh, I'm so sorry that all of my powers have been unwillingly stripped from me, and I'm a little salty about it. It feels like a fucking piece of me has been ripped away. You should understand that. I don't know why you aren't sulking just as much as I am. You don't have yours either."

She looked away from him, pushing past him as she stomped her way across the uneven ground, stepping over rocks and fallen limbs.

He growled, pushing away from the tree, and called after her, "You can't tell me you aren't feeling the same emptiness inside. The same anger at what your mother has done to us."

"I am angry," she said. "But it's not for the same reasons you are."

"What is that supposed to mean?" He snorted, "What else could you possibly be angry about? I mean, besides me, I already know you hate me."

She turned and glared at him before rolling her eyes with a sigh, "I–I'm angry because..."

She shook her head, obviously deciding she didn't actually want to tell him what it was, and continued walking.

"Oh, come on, Honoria. Tell me, what else do we have to do but talk? We are alone in this world, and we have another few days of hiking in front of us. I'm all you have, and well, you are all I have at the moment, too." He blew out a breath of annoyance. He would get out of this world, get his powers back, and he would murder Ada, Queen of the Zydells. That was his only goal.

Honoria was quiet for a long time before she finally said, "I never had any powers to begin with."

Orrick frowned, "What do you mean?"

"I don't have any abilities. I have no Zydell gift. I never have."

"That's not possible," he snorted. "You have a gift. What is it? Why must you always play games with me?"

She stopped and spun to face him, "I'm not playing games. It's the truth. I don't have any gifts."

Orrick stared at her with narrowed eyes, crossing his arms over his chest. "I don't believe you. Your mother is the most powerful Zydell in the Cosmos."

Honoria threw up her hands with an annoyed groan, "See, I knew opening up to you was pointless. You're such an ass. Do you even care about anyone but yourself, Orrick?"

He cocked his head, glancing up to the leaves of the trees fluttering in the wind, "No."

Her face fell, and she looked down to the packed earth beneath his feet and whispered, "Why would my mother banish me here with you?"

"Beats me. I asked her that exact question, and she gave me some fucked up riddle that made no sense at all."

Her head shot back up, eyes wide, "You talked to her?"

"Yesterday."

Honoria's cheeks began to turn bright red, her nostrils flared, and her ears practically shot out steam. "You talked to my mother, and you didn't think to tell me about it, or I don't know, bring me along to talk to her too?" she ground out. "Y—y—you are the actual fucking scum of the Cosmos. The worst being I have met in my entire existence."

She balled her hands into fists at her sides and took several slow steps closer to him. He smirked at her, ready for the attack this time. Expecting and honestly encouraging it. She was sexy when she was angry like this. It was a whole new side of her he hadn't had the pleasure of seeing before, and he had to admit he liked her a little more now.

The ground began to rumble beneath them, and Orrick's brows rose in surprise. Honoria no longer looked like she was about to pummel him into the ground. She looked scared. "I knew you were lying about your gifts."

"This isn't me," she squeaked out. "I'm not doing this."

"Sure you aren't." He huffed, rolling his eyes at her.

Suddenly, several walls of rock shot up from the ground, enclosing them in a circle of stone that reached several feet taller than Orrick. He was just about to make a cheeky remark about her trying to trap him for her own raging desires when a shadow loomed overhead. Confused, he glanced up just in time to see a massive boulder plummeting from the sky directly over him. Instinctively, he punched a blazing ball of fire at the falling rock, but the flames flickered out upon impact with the giant stone.

"Shit," he cursed just before the rock fell atop him.

10
GARREN

The strange ship moved surprisingly fast through the increasingly choppy waves. These men were strong, rowing with fluid ease and powerful pulls.

Garren watched as Oriana cocked her head, surveying each of the odd men on the ship. He could tell she was trying to figure out the same thing he was. Where were they from?

She spun in her seat, leaning to look around Garren to the man at the back of the ship who was unnaturally pale. Garren was surprised the man hadn't turned completely red from the harshness of the hot sun in Varian.

Oriana finally focused her gaze on Garren, setting down her oars for a split second, whispering just loud enough for him to hear, "These people aren't like any Svaklandian I've ever known. They definitely aren't from our continent."

He couldn't have agreed more.

The ringing in his ears had picked up speed and timber, which could only mean they were going the right way. It was now a stabbing at the base of his skull, growing worse with each moment. He tried to focus on the storms ahead, on the oars rowing through water, on anything to take his mind off of it.

Lightning struck the sea just in front of the ship, sending ocean spray raining down on them.

"Weigh enough, men!" Atlas yelled out. Each of the crew pulled their oars from the sea and brought them into the boat, Garren and Oriana following their lead. The wind picked up around them, whistling through the mast and rigging like an angry swarm of bees. Atlas stood at the front of the vessel, eyes fixed on the churning seas ahead. Thunder clapped as lightning split the sky, illuminating the towering waves that they were moments away from sailing into.

Oriana turned to Garren with a brow raised. The storm loomed ahead, causing an anxious foreboding to settle in Garren's gut. There was no doubt the storm was Anthes' doing. A curse. And he understood all too well the struggle of trying to break free of one of his curses. The damage they could inflict was not lost on him. The uncertainty of what might happen sailing straight into it gnawed at him.

Garren stood to talk to Atlas, wobbling slightly as a wave crashed against the hull, when the man who was covered entirely, suddenly took off his hood, revealing his face and hair fully. The man was blue, and his hair was green, tied into a knot upon his head, shorn to his scalp on the sides. Garren watched wide-eyed as the man took off his gloves, revealing the same blue skin that was on his face. Instinctively, Garren reached for the sword along his back. Was this man a demon?

Atlas placed a hand on Garren's shoulder, squeezing tightly, "Whoa, there, warrior. Let's not be hasty. Sit, we have some things to explain."

Oriana grabbed Garren's free hand, yanking him back down onto the bench seats, and said in a hushed tone. "They aren't demons, Garren. Sit and listen. I believe these people are from the continent beyond the Storm Sea."

"What? How do you know?"

"You forget I used to watch over this world many centuries ago." She whispered, " It's been a long time and they have certainly evolved over the centuries, but let's listen to what they have to say."

Atlas smiled down at them; the storms swirled behind him, relentless as another streak of lightning shot into the sea, illuminating the thick clouds that spread out behind him like an eerie plume of poisoned darkness. It almost looked like they were framing him, and suddenly Atlas's smile felt different, baleful. Garren suddenly felt as if he shouldn't trust this man, but it was too late for that. They were just outside of the cursed storms, and this man was the only one who would take them through.

"We are from a world called Emmoria, on the other side of the storms." Atlas finally said.

Garren frowned, glancing at Oriana.

Atlas continued, "We came through the storms by accident, really, several moons ago."

"By accident?" Oriana asked, "What happened? Did you get sucked in?"

"Yes and no. We were headed south of our world, looking for new land to trade with, when we ventured a little too close to the storms, mostly out of curiosity about what was inside, but as we tried to sail out of it, it pulled us in. We barely made it out on the other side. Our ship was damaged considerably. We managed to make it to the port in Varian, where we spent the past three moons repairing in order to journey back home."

Garren narrowed his eyes, "So why is he blue?" he nodded toward the man sitting on the edge of the boat, glaring at Garren.

"Jespin there is what we call an Undina in our world. He is a water Elementalist."

"What does that mean?"

"He can manipulate and control water." He made a motion to the man, and Jespin rolled his eyes, dipping a hand into the waves. When he brought his hand back out a shimmering blade of dripping water was gripped in his palm. He released the liquid hilt and it hovered in the air in front of him, the blade angling its tip toward Garren before it stabbed toward him. Garren's reflexes were quick as he drew his own longsword and slashed through it, water spraying in a mist across both him and Oriana.

"Impressive, warrior," Atlas said with a smirk. "You're fast with that blade."

Oriana's voice drifted up beside him, "Extraordinary! What can you do?" She pointed at Atlas.

Garren stared at her like she was crazy. These people were powerful, and they had magic—abilities he had only seen from the Gods.

"Sometimes Orrick has good ideas when he creates beings, you know," she whispered, elbowing him in the ribs.

"I am a Gnome myself, able to manipulate the earth, same as Valic over there. And Steg," He nodded to the man at the back of the ship, "is a Sylph, an air Elementalist."

Garren let his gaze travel to each one of the crew and then finally landed back on Oriana, who was grinning from ear to ear.

"Beautiful," she whispered. "So you used your gifts to travel through the storms? That's how you made it out?"

Atlas arched a brow at her, "Yes. Well, we tried. These storms are something different. The water, the wind, it fights back." His eyes grew distant as he turned to look out over the gray churning clouds and the swirling seas. "It's something foreign."

A crack of thunder echoed around them as if waiting with anxious anticipation for them to enter its realm.

Garren and Oriana cast a quick glance at one another. The fair-skinned man frowned, noticing their exchange, but didn't say anything. The curse, no doubt, was trying to destroy them, kill whatever ventured within its grasp.

"Is it possible to go around the storms?" Garren asked.

"We don't know, but it could take weeks to figure that out, and we don't have the supplies to survive that long."

"Do you think we can make it through again? Since you've been inside before?"

"Well, that's what we are about to try. At least this time, we know what we are in for." Atlas said with a heavy sigh, "We'll be relying heavily on Jespin and Steg. There's not much we Gnome's can do without earth nearby. If we are lucky, the seas will have churned up enough sand to reach the ocean's surface, and we might be able to create a shield around the ship, but like I said, even using our gifts to fight against the storm takes an immense toll. These storms are alive. Using our gifts to manipulate and bend the elements in those storms is akin to attempting to tame a sand lion."

"A what?" Garren asked.

Atlas ignored him, "It takes immense focus and strength. We have to fight the sea in the same way we use our gifts to anticipate an opponent's actions."

"Well, I, for one, have complete faith. What magnificent people you are," Oriana was practically bouncing in her seat with excitement. "I can't wait to see Emmoria up close and in person."

The crew members frowned at her choice of words, and Garren quickly cut in, "Well, what are we waiting for? It's now or never."

"You both are very accepting of all this, coming from a world without abilities."

"Believe me, we've seen our fair share of oddities in Svakland. We are just exhausted and ready to get this over with."

Atlas's face fell and he glared at them both, "Before we risk our lives for you lot, how about you tell us the truth. Why are you really so keen to cross the storms?"

Garren just stared at him. He couldn't tell him the truth, and he had no good excuse to give him.

"It's my brother," Oriana suddenly blurted beside him. "He's been missing for months, and the last time we saw him, he was on the northern cliffs where the storm sea rages close to shore."

Garren raised an eyebrow at her.

"Did he fall in?"

"We don't know. He was there one minute, and then he was gone."

"I hate to be the one to say it, lady, but if he got sucked into that." Atlas nodded his head toward the storms, crossing his arms over his partially bare chest, "He's gone forever."

"No!" Oriana yelled, rising to her feet, "I won't give up hope. He's out there somewhere. I just know it." She sat down heavily, putting her head into her hands, making choking, sobbing sounds as her shoulders quivered.

Garren's mouth fell open slightly. It seemed Oriana was a little actress. This was a new side of her, an unexpected yet beneficial side.

"Stars," Atlas said, reaching a hand out and patting her on the back. "I didn't mean to upset you. I was just saying what your boyfriend here obviously isn't able to." He cast a quick glare at Garren before continuing to rub soothing circles along her back.

Garren snorted and was about to retort when the ringing stabbed at his ears, traveling almost entirely through his body with electricity. He yelled out and covered his ears. Just as soon as the sharp pitch had come, it was gone, and all that remained was the incessant ringing pulsing out toward the storms.

Jespin narrowed his eyes, "Looks like he might have troubles of his own, Cap'n."

"Can we please just get it over with and get through these storms," Garren growled.

Oriana turned to him, concern etched into her features. He shook his head discreetly to let her know he was fine.

"Alright, alright. Let's get sailing, men, and lady," Atlas said with a wink at Oriana before adding, "For your sake, I hope your brother is alive somewhere on the other side."

"I don't," Garren mumbled, and Oriana brought a hand behind her and smacked his leg. "What? I'm just being honest." He dropped his voice low, barely above a whisper, as he said, "What the hell was that?"

Oriana flicked her wrist, and Garren could feel a shimmer of her power wrap around them both. "We don't want them overhearing us, Garren." Her enchantment firmly in place once again, she said, "Now say what you want to say."

"That was a nice little sob story you created out of thin air."

She shrugged, "Well, when you're a Goddess living in a mortal world, you get good at stretching the truth. Technically, the last time we saw him was on those northern cliffs in Shipwreck Cove."

Garren snorted, lips curving in amusement, and Oriana let go of the illusion as he felt its caress leave.

"Hoist the sail, brothers," Atlas said.

Two of the men pulled along a rope, and a white sail rose with each tug before they tied it off. The sail puffed out, the wind instantly pulling them into their waiting doom.

The storms raged like a pack of angry wolves as they sailed directly into them. The instant they crossed into the cursed waters, it was as if they had sailed into a completely different world. Garren suddenly felt very small, shrunken in a place so vast it didn't seem possible.

The clouds turned from gloomy gray wisps to a swirling vortex of wind and rain reaching out toward them like the fingers of a giant. They followed them as the wind whipped the ship left and right, battering them like a cat with its toy. Thunder clapped, sending a roaring symphony around them, lightning following quickly, slicing into the sea dangerously close to the ship. Waves taller than the sails threatened to crash down upon them.

Garren grabbed a hold of Oriana, wrapping an arm around her waist, pulling her fully against him as he held on tightly to the bench.

Jespin stood at the bow, making strange motions with his arms that Garren didn't understand. It was only when a massive wave curled overhead, casting its threatening shadow over them, that Garren understood what the man was doing. The wave suddenly split in two, crashing down on either side of them as they sailed safely through.

Steg stood just beside him, fighting against the onslaught of ferocious gales that threatened to capsize them.

Garren could see what they meant about this place. The elements were actively fighting against them like an opponent on the battlefield, and not once did it let up or show a weakness.

As the two men fought as best they could against the savage force of this cursed place, they couldn't fully deflect its blows.

Every time they blocked a wave or shielded themselves from the whipping winds, the currents of the sea would shift, and the swirling air would hit them from another direction.

"I think they need help," Garren said to Oriana. She looked back at him and nodded in agreement but stopped short as the ship was suddenly no longer sailing through the sea but was hit from underneath by a great force that sent the vessel airborne until it crashed hard into a wave. Jespin was quick to react, pulling the water that had flooded the ship's hull in his palms.

"What was that?!" Valic screamed from the water he had been thrown into, grabbing the railing to haul himself back on.

"I don't know," Garren said, locking eyes with Oriana. "But it can't be anything good."

Just then, the tip of a blinding orange fin poked out above the surface of the churning seas.

Garren groaned, nostrils flaring at their luck, "As if these fucking storms weren't bad enough, looks like Orrick left one of his little gifts here." He let go of Oriana, grabbing Valic's hand to help pull him on board, but he was suddenly ripped from Garren's grasp and yanked violently beneath the water's surface.

"Valic!" One of the crew members yelled out in anguish.

"Shit," Garren growled.

Oriana was concentrating, her brows drawn together, eyes narrowed at the sea, "I've put a shield around the ship. The demon won't be able to penetrate it, but I can't fight against these storms. It's the same as when I tried to jump us through it. It blocks everything I try."

Garren swallowed hard. These storms were most assuredly Anthes' doing, and there was only one way to fight them—fulfill the curse.

"Go kill that beast and save Valic before it comes back around for a second attack." Oriana yelled, "I'll keep trying to help here and see if anything works."

Garren nodded. He had already decided he would go in after the demon. He gave her a quick kiss and dove into the waves. Just before he hit the water, he could hear one of the crewmen yell out, "What the bleeding skies is he doing?"

Garren let himself sink beneath the water's surface. The currents were strong, and they pushed and pulled at him as if they were trying to tear him apart, but he held himself firm, swimming against the force as he spun, looking for the creature and Valic. He swam beneath the ship when something touched his leg, and he jerked, pushing himself away, ready to fight, but it wasn't the creature. A severed arm floated up toward him, blood seeping from its frayed flesh, followed by Valic's severed head, the face caught in its final dying scream.

Garren closed his eyes. He hadn't known the man, but his death still struck a chord in his heart. He couldn't have saved him. He had to remember that. As soon as the creature took him under the sea, the man was gone. But that didn't quench the rage that traveled through him. He needed to find the beast and kill it before it could pick off any more of the crew.

The water was dark; he could barely see a few feet in front of him. He looked up, making sure to stay close enough to the ship so he wouldn't get lost in this cursed place.

He spun, looking for the bright orange he had seen of the creature on the surface, but there was no demon in sight through the murky haze of the ocean.

Garren cast his gaze downward, noticing a faint, ethereal glow shimmering from the depths. The light pulsed softly, flickering in the dark water like a beacon calling out to him.

They were now well into the middle of the storm sea, and it was disconcerting to see any luminescence in a place that should be shrouded in darkness.

Garren swam lower toward it, deeper and deeper he went, the light growing brighter all the way. It reminded him of his journey through the Phantom Wood all those months ago, following the light to get out of the gloom. Finally, he made it to a depth where the currents calmed, and the murkiness of the sea seemed to dissipate as if he had crossed over some invisible threshold into a different ocean altogether.

Surveying the seas around him, Garren froze, his eyes widening in disbelief. Beneath him lay an entire sprawling city encased in a mesmerizing, shimmering bubble. He surged forward, heart pounding, desperate to discover if anyone lived inside. Was it possible the Barinsian people had survived all this time, trapped in a pocket under the raging storm sea?

He swam so close he could almost feel the electric hum of the strange barrier surrounding the city. He peered inside, hoping that life thrived inside, and there they were—not one or two, but hundreds of people bustling about. The sheer number of them, oblivious to his presence, sent a shockwave of adrenaline coursing through him.

Garren wanted to study the world further, but even he couldn't hold his breath for that long. Soon he would need air, if the burning in his chest was any indication.

He took one final look, noticing a woman with beautiful cascading blonde hair standing atop one of the buildings closest to him. As if she felt his stare, she spun, exquisite light blue eyes locking on him. He watched as she squinted up at him in confusion, her eyes suddenly growing wide. Her grip slackened on whatever she had been holding, and it slipped from her fingers, crashing to the ground. Her mouth gaped, and she stood frozen in utter shock.

Garren reached out a hand toward her, toward the bubble encasing the city, but just before he touched it, something forceful knocked into him, sending him careening away from the city and into the deep emptiness of the sea.

He grunted, pulling his blade free from his back, only to see the orange creature coming straight toward him. It was a massive beast with a long neck, four powerful fins propelling it at an alarming speed through the deep blue, and a long slashing tail whipped behind it like a scythe. Along its back were several rows of white spikes, but the most imposing of them all was the spike perched prominently at the center of its snout. It was longer and sharper than the rest, menacing and calamitous.

The creature swam toward him at a harrowing pace, mouth wide, revealing several rows of jagged teeth ready to bite down to shred, cutting him in two. Garren held his ground, waiting for the inevitable attack. He noticed how its long neck and tail moved side to side in opposite directions as it propelled toward him. He waited until it was so close it could have swallowed him whole before he kicked up to the long spike jutting from its nose, grabbing it, and pulling himself over its head. It stopped abruptly, but before it could turn its head to bite him, he slashed, severing its neck in one fell swoop, repaying the beast for what it did to Valic—a head for a head.

Dark blood enveloped him as he watched the severed neck of the demon sink to the bottom of the sea along with its motionless body. But he was forced to turn away before it fell completely away from view because he was in desperate need of air.

Garren sheathed his sword and swam toward the surface, bursting through the waves and filling his lungs with air while looking for the ship. He spotted it several meters away. Had they tried to wait for him?

"Garren!" Oriana yelled, waving her arms at him.

He began swimming closer to the ship when something clasped around his ankle and yanked him back under the sea. The last thing he saw was Oriana reaching a hand out to him, brows drawn and lips parted in stunned silence. He looked down to see the same bright orange of the sea monster wrapped tight around him. What the fuck?

He gripped the beast's tail with both hands, trying to free his ankle with little progress as it dragged him deeper and deeper. Giving up, he grabbed the bit of tail beneath his foot and began to pull himself down along it until he was at the base, where it met with the creature's back. Unsheathing his blade once again, he sliced through the tail, fully severing it from its body. The monster roared, a sound that Garren could hear even through the water, a sound that shouldn't be possible for a creature without a head. Was this a second one? How many of these sea monsters were down here?

Garren balked when not one but two heads looked back at him along its back. This one had two heads. Shit.

Garren pushed off the demon's back hard, propelling himself high above it, and he watched in horror as the tail he had cut off began to grow back, split into two new tails sprouting from the wound.

"Fuck," Garren garbled into the sea.

The creature turned, swimming for him once again, two mouths chomping as he weaved and dodged them, swinging his blade at their attacks. Blood pooled, moving around him, blocking his view of the heads as he sliced gashes into their flesh.

A monstrous head suddenly shot through the gloom, and he grabbed its horn quickly, just as he had before, pulling himself along the neck and severing one neck and then the second.

His eyes widened and he choked on salt water as he watched each severed neck begin to sprout not one but two heads just as the tail had done. This was the same creature then, and it got stronger with every blow. Shit, this was bad.

Garren swam frantically toward the surface, sword still in hand as he broke through. The ship was still a few strokes in front of him, and Oriana looked relieved to see him, but her relief turned into worry and then horror as he yelled, "I made it worse! Get me out of the water!"

Oriana moved a hand in the way she always did when using her power, and suddenly Garren was on a solid surface. He pushed himself up to his feet and sprinted atop the water for the ship, diving into the hull. "Go! Quick!"

All four heads of the creature emerged, snarling.

"Holy shit," Oriana breathed, "It's huge."

Garren coughed up the water from his lungs, "What were you saying about Orrick having good ideas? It only had one head when I started."

"W–what is that thing?" Jespin stammered.

"We don't want to wait here to find out. Use your air magic to propel us faster!"

"I'm trying!" He grunted. It was only then that Garren noticed how pale the man was. They weren't Gods, they were mortals, and their gifts had limits that were far smaller than that of a God. They wouldn't make it out before the demon got to them.

Garren grabbed Oriana's arm, spinning her to face him. "It has to be you. A blade can't fell it, it only makes it stronger. You have to kill it."

Oriana swallowed hard, looking over at the Elementalists, who were practically frozen in bewildered fear as they stared at the four-headed creature. "You should use your gifts," she said suddenly.

"Oriana!" He growled, "You know I can't. There's no time. Do it!" He glanced at the three men shivering beside them, "They'll all die if you don't."

As if the monster heard his words, it growled, snapping its jowls and charging toward them with immense speed, creating a tidal wave in its wake.

"Oriana!" Garren shouted.

She exhaled sharply, brushed his hand from her arm, and closed her eyes tight. The shield she had conjured around the ship expanded outward. Garren realized she had stretched the barrier to create a safer distance between them and the monstrous creature lurking beneath them. With every strike he had delivered, the demon only appeared to grow stronger and more ferocious. It was time for Oriana to step in, for she was the fiercest being he knew, and this beast would be no match for her other half.

"What is happening?" Atlas breathed.

"We will explain everything after the creature is dead and we are safe through the storms," Garren promised.

An ominous low growl came from Oriana. The change had begun. The bloodlust unleashed.

II
ORRICK

Something was smacking Orrick repeatedly in the face. He swatted it away with an annoyed curse, but when it didn't stop, he gripped it, preventing its next attack. It was warm and soft beneath his grip and smelt of lavender and honey.

"Orrick," it whispered in his ear, and he groaned, releasing it and rolling away from the irritating thing. All he wanted was to sleep. It seemed like an eternity since he had last experienced as restful a slumber as the one he was currently enjoying. The air was warm and slightly damp, it wrapped around him like a comforting embrace. The gentle, rhythmic sound of dripping water provided a soothing melody, lulling him into a deeper sleep.

"Orrick!" the infuriating voice said again, and this time, it followed its shout with a stinging slap, a smack that felt identical to the one he had received barely a day earlier.

Sighing, he cracked open an eye to see Honoria peering down at him, "Wake up."

"Way to ruin a perfectly good dream," he grumbled.

"I think our present circumstances might change your mind about that."

He frowned and sat up, "What the fuck?"

They were in what seemed to be a dimly lit prison cell. The only light was coming from a single flickering lantern suspended high above them. Its feeble glow revealed a narrow door made entirely of steel, located along the far stone wall, bordered by two additional walls of rough-hewn stone, their surfaces jagged and sharp. But the fourth wall, directly opposite the door, was shrouded in impenetrable darkness, obscuring whatever lay beyond it.

Orrick stood, curiosity urging him to inspect the void of black. Cautiously, he walked toward it, the dim light barely illuminating his path as he reached out a hand, fully expecting to encounter some form of barrier. To his surprise, his hand passed through, plunging into the pitch-black, and he almost lost his footing, falling forward. It was only then, as he peered down into the abyss, that he realized it was a long, dark tunnel with no apparent end in sight.

He quirked a brow, nudging a stone teetering on the edge into the enveloping gloom, raising a hand to cup his ear, listening for the faint echo of the stone hitting solid earth. But no sound came.

"Damn, that's one deep pit."

A hand grabbed the back of his too-small vest and yanked him away from the black hole. "Cosmos Orrick, do you want to fall in?"

He turned to her, and a smile crept across his face. For the first time since he woke in this world—honestly, for the first time in what felt like centuries—he erupted into laughter. It was boisterous and full-bellied, the kind of laugh that brought warmth to his cheeks and tears to his eyes in genuine delight.

"What at this particular moment could be so funny?"

He wiped the tears away with the back of his hand, gasping for air between fits of giggles.

"I—I'm impressed," he chuckled. "No, that's not the right word. I mean, I am impressed, but I think I'm more so—proud."

Honoria furrowed her brow, "Proud? Of what?"

"This is exactly the kind of fucked up prison I would create," he snorted. "Maybe a little more extreme, but this isn't something I put into the Elementalist's heads. They came up with this all by themselves, and it's—well, it's amazing."

Honoria just stared at him, her nose wrinkling in disgust, arms folded tightly over her chest.

"This is wonderful." He laughed again, spinning in a circle to take it all in. "I mean, the fact that they also snuck up on us like that and were able to capture us? Impressive. They've come so far since the last time I visited."

"You have issues."

Orrick turned to her, opening his mouth to say something snarky, but didn't get the chance before the door was thrown open, and several spiked shards of stone flew toward them, stopping mere inches away from their heads. Three large Gnomes followed the rock spikes.

"Welcome to Gnomeic," the one in the center said with a smile that did not reach his eyes. "Who are you, and what were you doing on our land?"

Orrick said nothing, just cocked his head to the side, studying his magnificent creatures. The man stepped closer, "What ruler do you spy for?"

"We aren't spies," Honoria stepped in. "We are just travelers passing through. We aren't a part of your war."

"You're lying. It would be in your best interest to cooperate with us." The hovering spears of stone inched slightly closer to them. "Who do you spy for?"

Orrick grinned from ear to ear, "Might I start with how incredibly impressed I am with this setup you have. I mean," he walked to the dark edge and stuck an arm out into the void. "This is real artistry. What's at the bottom?"

The Gnome on the left stepped toward him, coming so close that Orrick could feel his rank breath on his face. "Your death," he said, and the ground beneath Orrick's feet began to rumble, threatening to throw him off balance and into the endless pit.

Orrick barked out a laugh at the Gnome's words, "See, now that's where you're wrong."

In one swift movement, Orrick lunged forward, seizing the nearest man and yanking the Gnome into the abyss behind him. The man's shrieks echoed around them but were abruptly silenced as Orrick unleashed a whip of emerald flames that coiled around the second Gnome's torso, searing through cloth and flesh as he screamed in agony. Orrick dragged the man closer and gripped his throat, squeezing until the man's eyes bulged, and he gasped helplessly for air. With a sickening pop, Orrick's fingers pierced through the man's skin, snaking around his esophagus and tearing it free. The Gnome's lifeless body collapsed to the ground, and with a kick, Orrick sent the corpse into the bottomless pit. Blood and torn flesh littered the cell as Orrick lifted his gaze to the last man, a sinister grin twisting along his features.

The final Gnome threw out several shards of stone that Orrick dodged with ease. The ground of the prison cell began to crack beneath Orrick's feet, falling away into the chasm. Honoria squealed, reminding him of her presence, and he grabbed her arm just before she fell into the deep hole.

The last remaining Gnome's eyes went wide as he turned and fled to the door in an attempt to escape, but Orrick was quicker. He snarled, and a stream of flames erupted towards the man, engulfing him with fire. His cries of agony echoed through the hollow cell as the flames melted his armor to his skin, burning away all flesh and muscle until he was nothing but a pile of smoking bone and ash.

He pulled Honoria through the open door to find a long tunneled stairway that led up.

Honoria followed numbly behind him, blessedly silent for once. He knew what he had just done might have shocked her, but they needed to get out of this place. There was no time to waste. They should have never been captured in the first place. Maybe Honoria was telling the truth that she really didn't have powers.

They made it to the surface, where they found a large wooden door with a small circular window at the top. Orrick peered through it, seeing the dark blanket of night and what appeared to be a makeshift war camp. Lanterns spread around the encampment, illuminating small tents. To the left of the door was a single guard, but other than that, he saw no other signs of life.

"Are you just going to kill him like you did the others?" Honoria whispered behind him.

Orrick turned and glared at her. He knew she didn't like what he did to those people, but what else could he have done? He would be no one's prisoner.

"I don't see many other options, do you?" he whispered back through clenched teeth.

It was dark, but he could have sworn Honoria rolled her eyes at him. "Let me handle this one."

He raised a brow but moved aside, allowing her access to the door. She brushed past him, picking up a rock just beside the door. Gently, she pulled it open, and the guard turned instantly, catching sight of Orrick, who brought a hand up and wiggled his fingers in greeting. The man's eyes went wide, and he jumped up, but before he could do anything, Honoria sprung out from behind the door and smacked him on the side of the head with the large rock.

He stumbled sideways from the blow, gripping his head where blood began to seep through his fingers, turning murderous eyes on Honoria.

"Shit," she breathed, backing away as the man took a wobbling step toward her.

"Well, that didn't work out exactly how you planned, I'm guessing." Orrick leaned against the door frame, arms crossed over his chest as he watched Honoria begin to panic.

The ground beneath her feet trembled, and she turned to him with pleading eyes, "Do something!"

He snorted, pushing away from the door and stepping between Honoria and the Gnomeic man.

"Don't kill him."

Orrick half turned his head in her direction, letting her see his annoyance before turning back to the man. "Fine."

The Gnome charged at him as the earth under Orrick's feet cracked open. He ran as the ground began to fall away, leaping to the right at the last possible second as the man barreled past him. Orrick swung back around with lethal precision, wrapping an arm around the man's neck from behind and hoisting him off the ground.

He struggled in Orrick's grip, loose rocks shooting for him, hitting him in the head and arm as the man tried to use his gifts to dislodge Orrick's arm, but he held firm until the man finally stopped squirming and the earth stilled once more.

Orrick let go, the man crumpling to the ground. "Happy?"

Honoria nodded, breathing heavily.

A chorus of shouts erupted from the tents as men began to file out, scanning the shadows in search of the commotion.

Orrick sighed and grabbed Honoria's hand, "Come on. Your approach to doing things has drawn too much attention. We need to go."

She nodded and allowed him to pull her into the darkness of the forest that surrounded the camp.

They ran until the shouts and commands of the Gnomes faded in the distance, and Orrick finally slowed, dropping her hand. "I think we are far enough away now." He said through labored breaths.

Honoria huffed and collapsed to her knees on the forest floor, placing her head in her hands.

"Are you crying?" Orrick scoffed, "It wasn't that far of a run. I mean, I didn't enjoy it one bit, but it wasn't more than a couple of miles."

She glared up at him, tears sparkling in her eyes. "You didn't have to kill those men. None of them deserved to die. We were the ones on their land. They were only doing what they thought they needed to protect their people."

Orrick took a deep breath, bringing his thumb and forefinger up to rub circles at his temples. "I did what I thought of at that moment to get us out of that situation."

"Does your mind always go to murder first?"

He narrowed his gaze at her but didn't answer.

She laughed suddenly, a rough, humorless sound and stood, "You really are the most horrid person I know. If only I had seen this side of you all those months ago, I wouldn't be here. You would be all alone."

"I would prefer that," he mumbled under his breath, and luckily, she didn't hear him, only continued on with her rant.

"First, you weasel your way into Verhaven. Then you convince me to help you gain access to the most sacred place in my home, then you get me stuck here and somehow get my mother to come and speak with you without me, and now this! I'm done." She roared, fits balled at her sides as she turned and stomped away from him, yelling over her shoulder, "I can't take you anymore. I'm leaving."

"Good luck," he called back to her. "Have fun being captured again and probably tortured."

She stopped, and Orrick smirked, watching as her shoulders rose, tensing with annoyance. He knew she was aware that she couldn't navigate this chaotic world without him, and he took immense pleasure in seeing how much that fact angered her.

"Unfortunately, we are now further away from where we need to go." He said, her back still turned to him. "I say we walk another few miles, gain even more distance from the Gnomeic camp, and then rest for the night."

She finally turned, stomping toward him, not looking him in the face.

He grinned and led the way as she begrudgingly followed.

In the tranquil stillness of the night, the forest was alive with the soft call of birds across treetops, the scurrying of rodents through the leaves, and the quiet rustle of their steps through the dense undergrowth. The canopy overhead, a thick tapestry of intertwined branches and leaves, blocked out most of the moonlight, allowing only a thin, silvery glow to illuminate their path, guiding them through the shadows. But Orrick didn't need much light to navigate. Though it had been a considerably long time since he last set foot here, the sensation of the damp earth beneath his feet and the cool, whispering breeze that caressed his skin felt as familiar as if he had walked this path just yesterday. Little had changed in these woods during his time away. This forest seemed to have maintained its serene beauty, presenting him with a place of peace, just as it had for him so long ago.

Even so, Orrick kept his senses keenly aware of their surroundings, listening for any new sounds or signs of movement around them. Luckily, none came.

When he was satisfied with their distance from the Gnomeic camp, he halted abruptly, turning to Honoria, who had wordlessly followed behind him the entire way. She looked tired. A deep sadness hunched her shoulders, and her arms hung loosely at her sides.

"We'll camp here."

She only nodded and found a lovely tree to lean up against as Orrick gathered a few dry logs and twigs to start a fire. At least he didn't need to try and create fire from the materials of this place. He simply set the wood aflame before them with a quick flick of his wrist. He was getting the hang of the fire sorcery; the gift came to him as easily as his old powers had, and he gained control in just a matter of days. He couldn't help feeling smug at how quickly he mastered it.

Honoria held her hands out over the dancing flames, warming them against the sudden drop in temperature that the evening had brought. She stayed silent and Orrick knew that she was still upset over what happened back at the camp.

He closed his eyes, taking a deep breath before opening them again and saying, "I—I don't hate them, you know."

"Who?"

"The people of this world. My creations."

"You could have fooled me," she scoffed. "Seeing how you just killed three of them with barely a second thought."

He brushed a hand through his hair, "I know you don't understand. My view of them, it—it's different in a way. All of my creations, each of them in some way, are a small part of me, and I'm—well, I'm proud of them and what they have become. It's strange to say that now. I found them not good enough for a long time, but it wasn't because of them. It was me. I was angry at myself for not being powerful enough to make them better. But in my own strange way, I love them." He looked at her to gauge her reaction, but she was unreadable. "Especially these people." He added.

She said nothing, but her eyes remained intently on him as she listened to his words. He found himself grateful for her silence and attention, for it urged him to continue. Memories swam to the surface of his mind and the words tumbled from his lips.

"Long ago, before I truly knew what I could do with my gifts, it was just my sister and me, along with the Six Eternal

Gods. We lived out our beginning years as nothing more than pawns, used and controlled by the Gods for their own purposes. We were never treated as equals or given any ounce of respect. Our lives held no value to them. They didn't care if we continued to live or die." A heaviness settled in his chest as he looked down at his palms.

An annoying emotion began to bubble in his chest, but he pushed it down, clenching his hands into fists, "When I finally discovered the true extent of my gifts, I created this world. It didn't look like this at first. Over the centuries, it has transformed and evolved into what it is now, but this world was my haven—a safe space from the Gods and a place that didn't want me. Here, I was wanted and these people became something to me. They are my first born children in a way, and I realize now that I have treated them more like play things than my own flesh and blood. I've treated them no better than the Six External treated me, as if their lives mean nothing."

Honoria's eyes darted to him a few times, her face stuck in a frown, arms crossed over her chest.

He put his arms up in the air and yelled in frustration, "All I'm saying is that I'm trying, okay? Can't that be enough for you right now? I'm trying."

Her brows relaxed slightly, and the corners of her mouth softened. "I hear you, but it might take me a while to forgive you for all you've done."

"That's fair. I'll take it." He said, shaking his head and chuckling nervously at the vulnerability he had just shared with her. "We should both get some rest. We will have a longer journey now that we are further from our destination."

She nodded, finding a soft, moss-covered piece of earth, while Orrick found his own soft patch of ground as far away from her as he could get while still being able to see her. He lay on the forest floor, looking up at the starlit midnight sky through the canopy of trees. Each of those shining specks was a world. A creation of his own making with beings large and small, good and bad, and everything in between. He didn't visit them all—he had forgotten a good portion of what he created over the years. Maybe it was time to change that and visit each of his worlds to see what had become of them. It was entirely possible, no, probable, that many were in a worse state than Emmoria.

Orrick frowned and his shoulders slumped, a sudden wave of despair washing over him, pressing down with an invisible weight. Honoria was right. He was the worst kind of evil in this Cosmos. He was a creator who didn't care.

His eyes were growing heavy with exhaustion, but as he drifted into sleep, he made a deal with himself. When he got his powers back, he would go to each and every one of the worlds he created to see what they were like now, and he would make them whole, functioning worlds, fixing any wrongs dealt by his hand.

12

GARREN

"Bloody skies," one of the crew breathed.

Garren stood on the deck, heart pounding as he watched Oriana transform into the embodiment of her bloodlust. He hadn't witnessed the shift in many months. Her features, twisted and monstrous, were now on display for everyone to see, yet he noticed subtle changes since the first time he'd seen her this way. Her eyes had softened, retaining their deep green hue instead of the predatory yellow they once were. She was present, fully aware and in control despite the ferocity of her appearance.

She grinned at the crew, her lips parting to reveal a set of jagged teeth, sharp and menacing, before she turned, focusing her attention on the creature looming towards them. Growling, she stepped off the ship onto the ocean's surface as if it were a solid sheet of glass beneath her.

"What's wrong with her? How is she doing that?" All of the men's eyes were wide.

"It's nothing, we'll explain everything later, just focus on fighting the storm and getting the ship closer to breaking out of this God's forsaken place." Garren's eyes stayed locked on Oriana.

All four heads of the creature locked in on her, following her every move. He could see her watching them just as intently, anticipating their attack.

One of the heads took its chance, snapping at her, but she dodged it with ease, digging her claws into its flesh. The creature shrieked, pulling back, but Oriana held on firm, now securely latched to the back of its neck.

An angry hiss escaped the demon's gnarled maw, and then suddenly its three other heads lunged for her with renewed fury. She quickly clawed her way down the long neck of the beast, the three attacking heads biting down onto the fourth's neck, shredding the flesh.

Suddenly, Oriana disappeared beneath the waves, and the sea beast with her.

Garren glanced back at the men. They were all still fighting the storm, but at a weaker, less hurried pace. He looked past them to the churning seas beyond, and to his surprise, he could see the edge of the funnel of storms. They were almost through.

He turned back to where Oriana had been moments ago, but she was still nowhere to be seen, and Garren fidgeted worryingly with his sword still gripped tightly in his hand, feeling suddenly useless and unsure of what he could do to help.

One of the men, Steg, was trying desperately to calm the churning sea. Sweat mingled with the rain and ocean spray on his face, his muscles trembling with exertion just before he collapsed onto the bench beside him, gasping for breath as if he had just sprinted for miles on end.

For a split second, Garren contemplated trying to use his powers, but he slapped the thought away as soon as it popped into his head. He didn't know what would happen if he tried, and he wasn't going to use this instance to test it out.

"Hold strong, men!" Atlas called out, seeing his men waning.

With every move Steg made against the howling wind, the storm seemed to rage harder, agitated by the battle. Just then, a gust of wind surged, rocking the ship so hard to the right that it almost capsized. They all rushed to the port side of the vessel just in time to save it. Steg was no longer able to fight the wind; his abilities drained, and he slumped alongside Jespin on the bench. That blow from the storm had now moved them off course.

Garren grunted and took a seat, sheathing his sword and taking an oar in each hand. He might not be able to use magic or his godly gifts, but he still had the strength and speed to rival thirty mortal men.

He took a deep, steadying breath and began to row as fast and hard as he could, turning the ship back toward their destination and onward through the raging storms, all the while keeping an eye on the waves behind them, searching for Oriana.

Garren grimaced as he moved the oars through the swirling waters. It felt as if the water was physically trying to rip them from his hands. It only made him grip tighter and push harder as he made steady but slow progress to the light on the other side of the storms.

Atlas took a seat behind him and helped him row, brow furrowed into a hard line, his eyes fixed on the end of the storms ahead, while the blue man continued fighting as best he could against the monstrous waves coming at them from all sides.

Rain pelted them, stinging with the force of the whipping winds as wave after wave threatened to capsize the ship, only to be blocked by Jespin as he pushed the water back.

Steg had fully passed out on the deck. His absence was a gaping void as the ferocious winds attacked the ship from all sides, and Garren yelled out, straining with every muscle as he battled to row against the relentless storms. It was like trying to move an entire building through quicksand.

As they rowed ever slowly away from where Oriana had jumped into the sea, Atlas glanced back to the spot they had left her and yelled, "Will she be alright with th—that thing?"

"She's gone up against worse," Garren grunted back.

"Bloody..." Atlas began, but was cut off as a cyclone of air and rain spun, reaching a tendril out toward them.

Garren braced himself for what would surely destroy their vessel, sucking them all up into its swirling grasp, but Atlas jumped over him, dipping his hands into the ocean over the front of the ship. The water rumbled violently beneath them, shaking the vessel as a mountain of sand erupted from the sea, arching over them and forming a protective cave around them. The raging cyclone slammed into the wet earth, showering sand over them all. Atlas bellowed in desperation, his voice nearly drowned out by the howling tempest, as he used all his might to fight against the raging storms until his strength finally failed him and the sand cave shattered, falling back into the ocean once more. But it had given Garren enough time to row them closer to the edge, toward freedom.

Just then, Oriana emerged from the water along with the creature, which was now rolled onto its back, floating atop the sea. Oriana growled a hellacious sound and dug her way into the monster's belly. It thrashed, several heads snapping for her, but she continued dodging them easily, the beast's skin now flayed, revealing the ivory of bone beneath. The creature's shrieks of pain had turned to tired wheezes as a few of its heads fell, slapping against the water's surface, sending even more waves towards their ship.

Garren watched as Oriana cracked the beast's ribs, ripping them from its body, to reveal a large, slowly beating heart beneath. With a ferocious snarl, she wrapped both clawed hands around the slippery organ and tore it free of the beast's body. The final heads of the sea monster gave one last thrash before slumping lifelessly into the sea and slowly sinking beneath the waves, leaving only dark blood in its wake.

Atlas coughed, gagging behind Garren, "I think that was the most disturbing thing I've ever witnessed."

"Believe me, that was nothing compared to what she can really do."

"I hope I never find out what she can *really do,* then."

The other sailors all breathed heavily with exhaustion, leaning against the sides of the vessel. Jespin's face was a pale blue, resembling a cloudless sky, and he looked as if he might vomit. Steg's nose scrunched, and his brows knitted together in disgust.

Oriana swam quickly toward them, and Garren stopped rowing momentarily, reaching a hand down to pull her up. By the time she climbed into the vessel, her features were completely settled back into the stunning Goddess she was, the bloodlust nowhere to be seen.

"I would have never thought about going for the heart," he snorted. "That was clever. What creature can regrow something as vital as a heart?"

She smiled, "If it makes you feel better, I fought with it that entire time beneath the water, and it grew about ten more flippers and heads before the idea came to me."

"What even was that thing?"

"I have no idea. I've never seen that particular one of Orrick's creatures before."

Garren shivered, "Well, I hope we never come across one again."

"You and I both," she said with a wink, just as a wave struck the starboard side of the ship and they both almost went crashing back into the water.

"Shit," Garren grunted, looking back at the blue man who was now slumped in the front of the vessel, completely spent. "We have to get out of here. Grab a set of oars and help me! We're so close."

Oriana, Garren, and Atlas, together, rowed harder than they ever had until finally, with one last push, they were free from the funnel of storms. The sunshine and flat seas were a welcome relief as they all collapsed exhausted onto the deck and Atlas let out a deep, thunderous laugh into the calm, salt-tinged air as he said, "Bloody seas, I thought we'd never break free."

PART TWO

REUNITED AND IT FEELS...
NOT GREAT

13
ORRICK

Orrick didn't sleep well. He tossed for hours, falling into a restless sleep before waking at dawn. He lay there looking up at the early morning sky through the canopy of trees above him. As the sun rose, its warm rays filtered through the leaves, casting dancing shadows across his face. The dawn began as a muted gray, slowly shifting through varying shades of purple before settling into a brilliant clear blue. It was a peaceful, quiet moment, a serenity that he hadn't experienced in ages—being in the moment, content to just be in this creation of his.

Honoria shifted across from him, pushing herself up as she woke, rubbing sleep from her eyes.

"Good morning," Orrick said, following suit and sitting up. "I hope you slept well."

She smiled softly and nodded, "I did. Much needed after yesterday."

"If only I could conjure us a delicious breakfast, it would be the perfect morning." His stomach rumbled at the very thought, and he sighed. "If we continue our trek, we might get lucky enough to find some berries along the way, but I think that's the best we can expect until we make it to the next town."

They both stood, brushing dirt and leaves from their clothing. There was an awkward silence between them, and Orrick felt a prickle of embarrassment crawling up his neck from his confessions the previous evening.

"Listen, about last night," he began, rubbing a hand along the back of his neck.

Honoria held up a hand, stopping him mid-sentence. "I let you speak, tell your story last night, Orrick, and I'm glad you opened up to me about your past."

He smiled softly at her, but she didn't return the gesture.

"But, none of that rights the wrongs you've done. We all have a past, including previous traumas, that shape us into who we are now. You have done nothing but let that past turn you into an angry, conniving bastard."

Orrick's face fell at her words, mouth forming a thin line.

"You have used and abused everyone around you. Just because you feel bad about those things now, doesn't mean they go away and everything is forgiven." She said, taking a step closer, her gray eyes shining like silver spikes aimed at his heart.

Orrick swallowed back the retaliation building on his tongue, allowing her to finish her onslaught of accusations.

"However," she continued. "I understand how hard it must have been for you to open up like you did last night. I can see that you really do want to try and change, become something better."

He arched a brow at her sudden shift in speech and tone.

"I haven't forgiven you yet, but I do hope that in time, we can form a friendship of sorts...or tolerance."

She was glaring at him with those large silver eyes, but her face softened slightly, and she wasn't exactly smiling at him, but she wasn't looking at him with murder in her gaze any longer, either, which was an improvement, he supposed.

He nodded at her and then did something so unlike him in every way that he even surprised himself. He reached out, squeezing her hand in his and said, "I would like that very much."

And with that, he was finally gifted with her genuine smile. A sort of mutual understanding formed between them, possibly an acceptance and an agreement to move forward no matter their prior animosity.

Was this a new him? How long had it been since he was actually this authentic with someone? When was the last time he considered someone a friend?

Something eased within him, melting away the layer of frost that had encased him, the shield he had constantly kept up. He suddenly didn't feel so alone.

He smiled, authentically, realizing that it was loneliness that he carried with him everywhere. Loneliness turned him into the cruel-hearted, uncaring God he had been for too many years to count. He could feel his heart swell, beating a bit more intensely than it had before. Was this... happiness?

Without warning, the forest around them grew still, a hush falling over everything as a swirling heat wrapped around them.

"Fuck," Orrick said, releasing her hand and spinning around, surveying the forest, before pushing Honoria away from him. "You need to hide."

"What?" she scowled, "Why?"

"Go! Now! As far away as you can!" Orrick snapped with a growl.

Honoria swallowed, her features growing concerned, but listened, fleeing into the shadows of the wood.

Mere moments later, a voice cut through the quiet, sharp as a knife, piercing Orrick and causing a hatred so hot and searing to travel through him.

"Orrick."

"Father," Orrick breathed into the night.

"What has become of you?" Anthes prowled through the brush of the forest, red eyes glowing like molten lava.

"Banished to your own world." He laughed, a cruel sound that made Orrick cringe.

"Why were you in the land of the Zydells?"

"Who said I was there? It is forbidden. I've never stepped foot there in all my existence."

"Do not insult my intelligence, Orrick. You make me sick. Cast into this wasteland, with this filth you created. You've lost your godly gifts, haven't you?"

"No."

"You were never a good liar. What knowledge did you gain while you were there?"

"Wouldn't you like to know?"

Anthes' arm shot out, gripping Orrick around the throat, lifting him off the ground. Orrick choked, grabbing his father's arm and twisting in an attempt to loosen his grip. When it didn't work, he pulled flames into his hands, letting the fire burn his father's flesh. Anthes released him with a growl.

Interesting. It seemed that the Gods, even one of the Six Eternal, were not impervious to his elemental abilities. Good to know.

"What is this? Your gifts have changed."

"I've become one with this world." Orrick's smile was malevolent, and he continued siphoning his fire sorcery along his arms and into his fists. "Why are you really here, father?"

"You know why I've come." He came close enough for Orrick to see that his father only carried a sword. His axe, Balthar, was missing from its sheath. That brought a smile to Orrick's lips. "After I broke my way out of the Dark World, that atrocious hole you cast me into, I set out to look for you. And what do I find out but that you've been slithering your way through the Cosmos as always, getting yourself entangled in things that are far above you. I'm disgusted even to think you are my son."

Orrick just smiled at him, ignoring every comment. Oriana had always been their father's favorite, the one with the gifts he desired to use. He always hated Orrick, and Orrick hated him right back.

"Where is Balthar?"

"I don't have it."

Anthes took another step closer, power emanated from him in waves, pulsing outward. Orrick gritted his teeth against it, standing his ground.

"That's not what I asked, Orrick."

"I don't have it," he said again.

Anthes swung faster than Orrick had time to register, fist colliding with Orrick's jaw, his head whipped to the left just before his father's other fist came out from below, hitting him in the stomach. Orrick doubled over, and Anthes' knee met his face with a bone-shattering crack. Orrick could barely comprehend the agony that seared through him, a torment unlike anything he had ever endured. His father only continued to pummel him, pounding him deeper and deeper into the unforgiving earth.

"I will find Balthar," Anthes bent down to where Orrick was lying in a bloody heap on the forest floor and whispered in his ear, "and when I do, the first thing I'll do is cut off your head."

The air swirled around him in a powerful rush of heat, and then his father was gone, and Orrick couldn't move.

Orrick lay there for how long he didn't know until Honoria's wide eyes came into view above him.

"Orrick," she breathed. "What happened? Who was that?"

"My father," he coughed, he could feel the blood dribbling from his mouth.

She kneeled next to him. "Can you sit up?"

He tried, but everything hurt, and he fell into a fit of painful coughing.

Honoria placed a hand on his chest, pushing her other arm beneath his back, and slowly helped him up into a sitting position.

"Thanks," he said, feeling extremely vulnerable and weak. Never in his life had he needed help with anything, especially not something so little as sitting upright. He felt frail; he felt like one of his creations.

Suddenly, he heard movement in the forest, and Honoria peered through the trees. "There is a group of people coming this way. The blue people."

They were currently on Gnomeic land, halfway to one of the largest cities in the area. If the Undinaam people were here, they were trespassing and ready for war.

"How many?" Orrick grunted, it fucking hurt even to talk.

"I can't see the end of the group."

"We need to hide," Orrick croaked, falling into a fit of coughing. "If they see us, they will attack. This is not their land; they are most definitely headed for an attack on one of the Gnome cities."

Honoria glanced at their surroundings. "I-I don't know where, there isn't anywhere covered or hidden."

Orrick could see a small boulder a few paces away behind some sparse bushes. "There," he tried to point, but couldn't quite raise his arm high enough, so he nodded in its direction. "Behind that boulder. It will be good enough.

Honoria gripped Orrick beneath both arms and yanked in an attempt to raise him to his feet. The pain tore through him, and he involuntarily yelled out from the surprise of it.

Honoria froze with Orrick half raised. He turned to see several of the Undinas leading the charge, looking right at them. *Shit.* He clambered the rest of the way to his feet, leaning on Honoria for balance, as the army marched right at them.

"We are here in peace. We come from Mitstab, we are Gnomes with no allegiance in this war." Orrick said, holding up his free hand, nudging Honoria to do the same.

The front man yelled out a command, and the company stopped at once. He and two other men came toward them, each with a ball of water levitating above their hands.

"Mighty seas, what happened to that one?" One of the Undina said.

Orrick glared at the man, nostrils flaring. He could burn the man alive in the blink of an eye, but then they would know he wasn't actually a Gnome and that they were trespassing as well. That would pose too many questions. And for some reason, he didn't want to kill the entire battalion.

"Tie 'em up, we'll take them with us to the Gnome Capital City. Use them as bait to open the gates."

Honoria made a small noise beside him, and he squeezed her shoulder in an attempt to reassure her that they would be okay.

"That would be a mistake. We don't come from there. As I said, we are from Mitstab; we have no allegiance to the Gnomeic people. We wouldn't be any good as bait."

The one in the center, the commander of this water legion, raised a brow, "Well then, maybe you are better dead."

Orrick laughed, "I wouldn't try that if I were you."

"Is that a threat?" The water orb grew in size, and Orrick tried not to roll his eyes.

"Listen, we honestly could not care less if you attack the Gnomeic people. Destroy the whole city if you want. We are just trying to get to my sister."

"Well, let's take you to her then, shall we?" The man gave a nod, and two Undinas stalked toward him and Honoria.

Orrick sighed, releasing Honoria, and instantly regretting it as pain laced through his torso at having to hold himself up. "You really seem not to understand. Let me explain..."

He didn't have time to explain further because he suddenly became encased in a ball of water, unable to breathe. Unable to use his fire magic. He watched as they took Honoria prisoner, helplessly unable to stop them. He choked, desperate to draw breath, darkness closing in on his vision, and thinking that this exact moment was the most helpless he had felt since being stuck in this world. In such a short time, this place had become the creation he despised more than any other. It was with that final thought that the darkness consumed him.

Orrick awoke, bound in chains, and being dragged along the forest floor. His blue embroidered vest hung from his shoulders, torn and bloodied, evidence of the onslaught he received from his father. Soreness clung to him, stretching across his limbs and webbing deep into his muscles. His body felt heavy as if wet sand had been poured inside of him, keeping him anchored to the ground. He groaned, stumbling to his feet.

Fuck, not again.

"Nice of you to finally join us," a familiar voice huffed beside him. "How are you feeling? Because you look like death."

He glared at Honoria, holding down the extreme urge to send a stream of fire at her head. Gods, this was humiliating. If only these people knew who he was. His own creations had now taken him hostage twice. He was never going to get out of here or get his powers back, was he? This was his life now, stuck in the very first world he had ever created, being bullied by beings he had formed by hand. It was so absurd, so incredibly implausible that something like this could ever happen, that all he could do in this moment was laugh.

A full-bellied bout of laughter erupted from him, not humorous, but more disbelief mingled with exhaustion. His entire body hurt with the effort, but he continued his hysterics with Honoria giving him looks of concern, until a blast of water hit him from behind and he fell face first into a puddle of mud.

He sputtered, his laughter dying as soon as it had come, and his chained wrists were once again dragging him along the earth. Slowly, he pushed himself back up and wiped a hand down his muddy face.

"Are you alright?" Honoria whispered.

He snorted, "Perfectly fine."

She frowned at him, "What are we going to do?"

"I'm trying to work that through now," he muttered. The truth was, he had no idea how they would get out of this short of him burning the entire fleet of Undina's until they were nothing but ash soaking into the damp earth.

It was strange, but the more he thought about killing all of these creations, the more he disliked the idea. Fucking Honoria had gotten to him. He muttered a curse under his breath.

"What was that?"

"Nothing," Orrick bit back. He didn't have much time to figure a way out because the stone walls of the Gnomeic city came into view.

"We're almost there, Orrick." Honoria's voice was frantic.

"Yes, I can see that." He rolled his eyes and shook his head. "It will be fine. I'll think of something."

"You won't kill them, right?"

Orrick glared at her, and she looked away, red coloring her cheeks.

"I'm getting deja vu. Didn't we just have this conversation yesterday?"

She opened her mouth, but was yanked forward, unable to utter what she was about to say.

"Company, stop!" A soldier yelled from the front of the army.

Orrick looked up to see the towering gates of one of the Gnomeic strongholds looming above them.

"Bring the prisoners!"

Both Orrick and Honoria were yanked hard, almost falling to the pebbled ground as they were moved to the front of the army, standing just before the large iron gates. Several Gnomes were stationed along the wall up above the gates, with another several dozen just within the gate that Orrick could see through the small crack between the doors.

"This isn't going to work, you know," Orrick said to the commander of the Undina company, and he was promptly shoved to his knees by the man.

"We have come to return these prisoners we picked up along our borders. Your spies have grown clumsy and weak." The commander yelled up to the men.

"Those are no Gnomes of ours. We do not claim them."

The commander growled, and Honoria's chains began to jingle beside him. Orrick looked up at her to see her shaking uncontrollably. He reached out a hand and touched her arm; her skin felt like a blazing furnace. "Hey, it's alright, Honoria. We will get out of this."

She looked down at him, sweat trickling down her face, skin pale, "I-I don't feel right. Something is wrong."

"Just breathe," Orrick said, standing and grabbing her trembling hands as the earth and water elementalists continued their conversation. "Breathe, Honoria. Slow and steady."

"I can't!" She yelled, pushing Orrick away. He lost his balance and landed on his ass just as he watched Honoria erupt. She screamed, and the earth beneath their feet shook, cracking behind her and under the entire Undina army.

"Prepare for battle!" the Undina commander yelled out, but then the earth split in two, swallowing the entire company of men. Their screams echoed in the cavernous pit as they disappeared into the darkness.

Orrick looked up at the Gnomes guarding the wall; they were all stunned into silence, watching with wide eyes until one of them said, "Who did that?"

They looked down at Orrick, Honoria, and the Commander of the Undina, the only three remaining before the gate.

Honoria's breathing picked up speed, and she yelled out again. Orrick braced himself for what was most certainly going to be catastrophic for them all, but nothing happened. He looked back at the commander, who was staring horrified at the gate in front of him. Smoke pooled beneath it, coming out from every crack and crevice, and then the screams began from within the Gnomeic stronghold, and then the gate burst into flames, licking up its surface and enveloping the Gnomes standing guard in their deadly embrace. They added to the screams as Orrick watched them burn to ash above them. He was frozen, observing the spectacle, getting to his feet, and watching as the entire village burned with not orange fire, but green.

He turned to Honoria once again, his mouth agape and eyes wide in disbelief. Her gaze remained fixed ahead, a blaze of power glowing in her silver eyes. She gripped the chains that were still clamped around both their wrists and shattered them with a burst of energy, metal fragments scattering around them. Finally, she looked down at him, watching as the brilliant light of her power faded from her eyes, just before she collapsed.

Orrick caught her as she fell, lifting her in his arms and turning toward the Undina Commander. The man opened and closed his mouth several times, eyes practically bulging from his sockets. Orrick raised a brow at him and said, "Boo."

The man fled instantly, back into the trees from where they came, leaving Orrick to look down at an unconscious Honoria in his arms, wondering how in the Cosmos she just used his own green flames to destroy an entire city of Gnomes.

14

GARREN

By the time they rowed the battered vessel ashore, both Jespin and Steg seemed to be getting some of their energy back, but the silence between them all was heavy in the air.

These people had seen too much of what Oriana and Garren were. An explanation was necessary, but whether they believed them or not was another matter altogether.

Oriana broke it by saying, "Thank you. For allowing us to travel with you."

"It's you we should be thanking," Jespin piped up. "We wouldn't have made it through if it weren't for you." He nodded his head in respect toward her.

She smiled softly back. "I can explain what..."

"No need," Atlas cut her off. "We are indebted to you. If it weren't for you killing that thing in the sea, more of us would have been lost. Possibly all of us."

Oriana nodded, "It was the least I could do. I am sorry about your friend, Valic."

They all bowed their heads in remembrance of their fellow crewman.

Garren squeezed his eyes shut, wincing against the sharp, piercing pitch in his ears. The relentless sound had intensified to an almost unbearable screeching the moment he set foot on the beach, which he supposed was a good indication that they were heading to the correct location.

Oriana's hand rubbed along his back. "Are you okay?"

"We should get going," he said through clenched teeth.

Oriana nodded and turned back toward the Elementalists of this world, "We can't repay you enough for your kindness, but we must now part ways."

Atlas cocked his head and smirked at them, "Where are you headed in a world you have never been to before?"

"We'll be fine." Garren cut in sharply. "Come on, Oriana."

"This is a world at war. You won't be safe anywhere you go. Be ready for a fight at every moment." Atlas said, "I don't know what either of you are, but I know you can hold your own. We all saw it." The men nodded beside him. "But in this world, it's either kill or be killed."

"Are there demons here?"

Atlas frowned, "No, we do not have things like that creature in our seas. Just the Elementalists, but many can be just as brutal as those storms we battled."

It seemed Orrick had left his horrific creatures only in Svakland, then, to terrorize him and Oriana.

"You aren't easily recognizable as an Elementalist. Neither of you has the look of one. The four groups will only see you as an enemy, and if they come for you and you leave them alive, they will only come back harder and stronger." Jespin said.

Garren furrowed his brows. What a world to live in, possibly even harsher than their own. At least in Svakland, there wasn't war among one another.

"Emmoria is split into four regions, one for each Elemental King. The King's each want complete control of the realm," Steg added. "Our world has been at war for centuries. Each King has a thirst for power that can only be quenched when their kind are the only ones remaining alive." Garren snorted. Orrick had most definitely created this world.

"You're warning won't go unheard." Oriana grabbed Garren's hand and squeezed. It was only then that he realized he was chuckling and shaking his head. "Thank you again for everything." She said quickly before yanking him to follow her into the thick forest that was several paces from the beach.

"What were you laughing at?" Oriana snapped, "They have lived in a world of unrest, Garren. All they have known is war, and you were laughing at them for talking about their history."

Garren sighed, "I wasn't laughing at that. I was laughing at how much this place is like Orrick. It's as if he put his very essence into the soil. His own wants and desires into these people. Don't you see it? A place where the only thing anyone wants is to be the most powerful? To be in control?" He smirked, "Tell me that isn't Orrick."

"Orrick puts something of himself into every one of his creations, so of course some of his characteristics are in these people." She said, pausing a moment before adding, "Actually, if I remember correctly, he was quite fond of this continent."

Garren rolled his eyes. "I wonder why."

Oriana shook her head in annoyance. "Oh, shut up and come on. The sooner we find the source of the sound you're hearing, the sooner it will stop," she said, then added in a barely perceptible whisper. "Hopefully."

"Oriana, wait," Garren grabbed her hand, spinning her round to face him. All this talk about Orrick brought his mind back to people trapped beneath the storms—the people who were most likely there because of the God of chaos.

She looked up at him with worry in her eyes, "What?"

"I have to tell you about what I saw beneath the Storm Sea."

She frowned, waiting for his explanation.

"There is an entire city at the bottom of that sea, encased in some kind of perimeter, or a forcefield, a bubble, something, but it's an entire working city full of people."

Her eyes grew wide, disbelief washing over her features. "So they survived? The entire city for almost two thousand years. That's extraordinary." She mused, eyes darting away from him, a crease forming in her brow. "You actually saw people there? Living and moving? Not just ruins of an old city?"

He nodded, and her emerald eyes met his gaze again, curious, "Yes, and we have to save them."

Oriana pulled her hand from his grasp. "They have been living beneath the sea for over two thousand years, Garren. Did they look like they were in distress or in need of saving?"

Garren looked away from her. An argument was brewing between them, one that felt all too familiar, but he begrudgingly replied. "No, they looked fine, but that doesn't mean we should leave them trapped there, stuck in some curse your father cast on them."

"If they aren't in any danger, if they are living perfectly fine and harmonious lives, removing them from that place would disrupt everything. They might not survive as well in the world up here."

"Oh, like the people of Svakland? Are they struggling to survive now? Did they have any trouble learning and fitting in?"

"That's an entirely different situation, and you know it." She snapped, "The people beneath the storms don't have a threatening monster lurking in their town."

"How do you know?" He crossed his arms over his chest, "I saw them for barely a minute. I locked eyes with a girl there, and yes, she looked fine, but there is no real way of knowing unless we go there. They could be living in a nightmare for all we know."

Oriana ran a hand through her thick locks and growled in frustration. "We won't agree on this, Garren."

"Well, I'm going to help them with or without you."

Oriana sighed and turned away from him. "We don't even know anything about the curse or how to break it, if it even can be."

"There's only one way to find out."

She turned back to face him and rolled her eyes. "I'll think about it, but I really do believe they're better off left alone for right now."

"I know you do. We can agree to disagree on that," he frowned. "If I've learned anything about your family, it's that they enjoy seeing others suffer and couldn't care an ounce about the people in this world. So chances are the people down there aren't living a life of luxury, and there is probably something far more sinister happening there."

Oriana grunted, "How about we handle one thing at a time. Let's find this sound you're hearing first, then we can think about helping the people beneath the Storm Sea."

"Fair enough," he nodded, and he could see from the way her eyes were determined, her jaw set into a thin line, that she knew he was right. After they figured out what was going on with him, he knew she would accompany him and help those people, whether they needed it or not.

"It's still coming from that direction," He said, pointing to the endless forest behind her.

"Wait up!" Someone suddenly called after them. Garren groaned, followed by Oriana smacking him in the chest, hard. He coughed and doubled over, glaring at her. It was Atlas, trotting through the forest toward them.

"Atlas!" Oriana called out, "What are you doing?"

"I'm coming with you." He called back, "I don't feel right about you going into my home region blind. I'll help however I can."

Garren rolled his eyes, this man was a damn nuisance. Why would he leave his crew to help them? They didn't need any help; they needed to do this alone without a third wheel at their backs slowing them down. "You were too friendly." He whispered down to Oriana.

"Maybe a guide will be a good thing. Maybe Atlas can help us so that we aren't forced to kill any of these people if we come across them."

"We don't have to kill anyone now," Garren grumbled. "More than likely, we will end up having to kill to save him if we let him follow us."

He shot a wary glance at the man, only to find his clear amber eyes staring directly at him with a slight smirk on his lips. It sent a tingle of suspicion through Garren. What motive did Atlas have? There was something else to him. He gave the impression of someone who acted solely out of self-interest.

Atlas was still staring at them with that same casual, almost arrogant energy shifting around him, as if he always got his way. A thought suddenly came into Garren's mind—did Atlas know what they were? Was he aware from when he met them that he and Oriana could potentially assist them in returning to their home?

"It will be fine." Oriana sighed, "Why does it seem like we've changed personalities recently? How did I become the optimistic one and you the brooding, angsty loner?"

Garren's nostrils flared, yet he remained silent, grappling with conflicting emotions. It was true; ever since Oriana's curse was broken, she had transformed, embracing herself fully and accepting each half of her godly gifts, mastering them. Her life had changed drastically for the better, and her entire demeanor had softened as a result. But for Garren, it had the opposite effect.

While breaking the curse and seeing Oriana so happy filled him with immense joy, the process had also revealed dark secrets that had been buried deep within him. Things that kept him from delving further into himself, afraid of what he might uncover.

He walked the earth every day, worried that he would accidentally do something to hurt someone, or even worse, hurt Oriana.

The visions of Orrick's mangled arm, his screams of pain, swam in his mind. If he was able to crush a God's arm like that with the smallest use of his abilities, what else could he do? And what if he tried to use it again and couldn't control it?

It was easier to keep himself at a distance from everyone and never reach back for that power inside of him. He didn't need it, and he didn't want to know anything about it.

A stabbing pain came into his ears at that very moment. "Fuck!" he yelled out and Oriana turned to him.

"Garren? What is it? What's wrong?"

"It's getting almost unbearable. I think we are close to whatever it is."

Atlas walked over to them, standing far too close for Garren's comfort, "Is he okay? It's getting dark. This might be a good spot to camp for the night. In the morning, we can start fresh, and I can guide you around the large Gnomeic camps and cities."

Oriana nodded, "That sounds like a good idea. We should all rest after today."

"We can't build a fire, it will attract the Gnomeic scouts, and they won't hesitate to attack even with me here with you. You are strangers, and they don't ask questions."

Oriana looked up at Garren, searching, and he knew what she was asking. "Fine," he mumbled. "We can camp here." But he gave Atlas a sharp look. He didn't trust the man, and he would be damned if he didn't keep an eye open tonight while they all slept.

15

GARREN

arren couldn't sleep. He walked through the moonlit forest until he came upon a small stream. He bent down, taking the water in his hands and drinking. He sat at the bank, leaning up against a tree close behind him, and sighed, looking up at the stars winking in and out of the midnight sky. The ringing in his ears had settled slightly, which was terrific but caused him anxiety at the same time. He didn't know what it was and the way it changed made him wary. Why was it sometimes so intense and high pitched, sending shards of pain through his entire body, and other times just a low whisper like a song carried on the breeze?

"Can't sleep?" Oriana walked up from behind him, taking a seat on the bank beside him, letting her bare toes touch the cool water. The only sound around them was the rustling leaves of the forest on the swift breeze and the bubbling brook along the smooth stones.

Garren grunted in response.

"What's on your mind? You always have trouble sleeping when your mind is running."

Garren chuckled, "We spend way too much time together."

The moon sent a glow upon her face, illuminating her smile. Gods, she was beautiful. She no longer hid her Goddess features from the world. Her flowing white hair shone and shimmered like snow, her green eyes sparkling with an ethereal glow. There was no questioning her as a Goddess anymore.

"Would you rather that I spend time with Atlas? I can go snuggle up next to him instead. I'm sure he wouldn't mind." She smirked at him with a devilish look.

"Very funny," he growled, pulling her to his side.

"Tell me what's on your mind, Garren. I'm always here for you. You know you can talk to me about anything."

"I know," he whispered, wrapping his arms around his knees and pulling them to his chest. " I-I don't want to be a God." He said, with a heavy sigh. It felt good to say it out loud finally. "I don't want to be a God or a Zydell. I don't want powers. I don't want any of it."

Oriana said nothing, but looked at him, listening with understanding in her gaze.

"This beacon that is calling for me, I'm not sure I want to know what's at the end of it."

"You think it has to do with your Zydell heritage?"

"It has to." He brought a hand up and ran it through his hair. "What else could it be? You can't hear it. No one else is hearing it. The only thing that makes sense is that it has something to do with whatever my Zydell gift is."

Oriana took a deep breath, "Why don't you want to know what your gifts are? Why do you keep your heritage at such a distance?"

She had always let him have his space when it came to trying his gifts. She never forced it on him, and he loved her for it, but he knew it drove her crazy. She couldn't understand why he wouldn't at least try and see what they were. He knew a small, destructive piece of them and he didn't want to know anymore.

If anyone could understand it, he thought it would be her. She had suppressed a piece of herself for centuries just because she hated it.

"When I was with Orrick in the monastery in Sardorf, when we created a plan to help you, I—I tried to use my gifts."

"You did?" Oriana said, surprise evident in her voice. She turned fully to face him. "Why didn't you tell me? Were you able to tap into it?"

Garren picked up a stone, throwing it so that it skidded across the stream. The ripples made the moonlight dance across the surface, creating wavy reflections of themselves.

"I did. I used just a small piece of it, and I crushed Orrick's arm."

Oriana coughed, choking on air, "You what?"

"I was angry at him when he told me who I was and told me to try to use my gifts. I discovered them buried deep inside me and unleashed them on him." Garren leaned his head back against the tree and looked up to the star-scattered night sky, "You should have seen it, Oriana. His arm looked like a stampede of horses had run over it."

Garren shook his head, picking up a stick and snapping it in half, replaying the event in his mind.

"What happened? His arm is fine now. Fuck, Garren, what else can you do?"

He looked down at her, regretting that choice because he hated the look in her eyes. It was intrigue, mingled with the slightest hint of fear. That is what he didn't want. He didn't want her to be afraid of him. He should have kept his mouth shut.

"I put his arm back together, and then I didn't use my powers again."

Oriana furrowed her brows and looked away from him, "You're scared to try again, aren't you? That's what's holding you back. You don't know what you might do if you try again."

He gave a small nod and sighed, letting his head fall into his hands. "If it only took a small pool of that power that's hidden deep inside to mangle a God, an immortal being of omnipotence, then what might I do if I pulled too much? I don't know the extent of my gifts. I don't even know what they are. Maybe they are specific like yours. Or are they unlimited, are they more vast due to my Zydell half? I don't even know what a Zydell's powers are, so how can I explore it when I have no idea what might happen?"

Oriana's eyes took a distant look, she was thinking, considering his fears, "A Zydell is powerful in a different way to a God. They are keepers of time and space, able to bend reality, even alter the timeline of everything. You have blood from both powerful lines, which could mean your gifts are a melding of both, in one proportion or another."

Garren frowned, so there was no knowing what he could do unless he tried to use it.

"We know you are impossibly strong and that you have put at least a piece of your power into your blade. Maybe your gifts lie in your fighting abilities. Maybe you use a small piece of your power each time you fight a demon, you just never knew it." She reached over, placing her small hand on his arm, "You said you crushed Orrick's arm, right? How did you do it? By force?"

"No," he shook his head, the memory materializing in front of him. "I—I just thought about breaking his arm, I focused solely on that thought and felt a cold rush run through me just before it happened, and his bones snapped."

Oriana rubbed soothing circles along his arm, looking over at her, he noticed her brow furrowed in contemplation. "And how is his arm fine now? Were you the one who fixed it again?"

He nodded, "I just did the same thing, but thought the opposite, of putting the bones back together."

"Interesting," she mused, dropping her hand from his arm and bringing it up to rest under her chin. "I think your power might involve the manipulation of objects around you. Almost like my enchantments, except you can permanently alter them, where I only create an illusion that will fade or disappear in time."

Garren looked out over the stream, watching the clear water dance over the stones beneath it.

"In a way, you may have the Zydell gift of alteration, but instead of time and space, it's with tangible objects around you, whether that be people or things. You can break and rebuild them, or alter them completely." She spun in the dirt toward him, eyes sparkling with excitement. "That's so fascinating."

Garren thought about that for a long while, and wasn't sure he liked it, but thinking back to that day with Orrick, it made sense. "Well, I don't want to test it to see if it's true or not. I won't use it and accidentally crush someone close by. I don't know if I will be able to control it."

Oriana was quiet as she looked at the moonlit stream bubbling along the smooth stones. Suddenly, she stood, "Do you hear that?"

Garren couldn't hear much of anything right now with the damn ringing in his ears, but there was just the small slip of movement in the brush through the forest on the other side of the stream. "What is it?"

"Quick behind those bushes."

They both shuffled behind a thicket of green by the stream, and just in time because several absurdly pale people with varying shades of light colored hair moved toward the stream. They were wearing strange, yellow, armored chest plates and carrying what looked like triangular shields. Garren frowned and whispered, "They are ready for battle. Those are fighting leathers."

Oriana just nodded, continuing to watch as several of them filled their waterskins up in the stream before continuing in the direction they came from, toward the beach. There had to be hundreds of soldiers; they stretched further through the forest than even Garren could see.

"They look like Steg, the one who was able to manipulate air," Oriana whispered. "They are going to fight. It's like what Atlas said: this world is at war. And something big is brewing for that many soldiers to be marching."

"Good thing we are heading in the opposite direction, then. I don't want to get caught in whatever territorial shit these people are caught up in." Garren grumbled, "I want to find this damn sound and go home."

Oriana huffed a laugh, "Come on, lets get your grumpy old ass back to camp. Try and get some sleep before sunup."

16

ORRICK

He would be lying if he said he wasn't jealous of the fact that Honoria possessed all the elemental gifts. Not only did she have the same green fire sorcery as he did, but she used earth sorcery as well. It seemed that Ada had given her much more, which wasn't surprising. She was her daughter after all, and he was nothing but a tool in her master plan. A plan he wished she would have told him more about, not that it mattered—he wouldn't have listened. No one told Orrick what to do. He followed his own set of rules.

Orrick looked out at the damage around him. Through the Gnome's gate, smoke billowed, and the chasm she created cut their entire city almost in half. He hadn't realized how far her use of the earth sorcery had gone. People screamed, blood could be seen dripping from half-destroyed buildings, and burning piles of bone and flesh littered the ground. In under ten minutes, she had practically annihilated an entire company of Undina's and destroyed half of a major Gnomeic city. Whatever her powers were before, they must have been immense.

They needed to leave quickly. Orrick glanced down at Honoria, still unconscious in his arms, her face was pale yet serene, contrasting the chaos that surrounded them. Gritting his teeth, Orrick limped them away from the city and into the copse of trees just west, each step bringing sharp pain that ricocheted through him, an annoying reminder of his father's attack.

The burning city faded behind them as the sounds of wailing were replaced by the soothing rustle of leaves and crunch of fallen twigs beneath his feet. Hoisting Honoria over his shoulder in the hopes of being able to move quicker, Orrick pressed on until night began to hover along the horizon like a shadowy veil. Exhaustion clung to him, weighing him down with every movement forward. He forced himself to go as far as he could until the relentless ache of his battered body wouldn't let him carry them both much further.

He trudged as best he could through the dense, darkening forest until they emerged at the edge of a small lake nestled deep within the heart of Gnomeic. Gently, he laid Honoria down onto the soft sand at the lake's edge before allowing himself to collapse beside her, utterly drained.

Night had fully fallen, wrapping the quiet, tranquility of this lake in a blanket of darkness, the sliver of the crescent moon casting its pale light over the landscape. The moonlight sparkled along the water's surface as the wind blew, sending ripples lapping toward them on the bank.

Honoria's words from earlier about how he treated his creations replayed in his head. To him, they had always been mere playthings, intricate toys he took pleasure in crafting and manipulating at will. Yet, something in Honoria's words triggered a deep emotion, awakening things he had never allowed himself to feel before.

She was right, his creations weren't just objects, they were living beings with their own free wills, living independent lives. Most of them were blissfully unaware of his presence. That truth often fueled his frustration. These beings he had meticulously crafted were utterly ignorant of who their maker truly was. But it wasn't their fault. The true culprits were the Six Eternal, the glory-hungry Gods who lacked the ability themselves to create worlds and living things. They were jealous of his talents and hated him for what he could do.

His gifts had long been a contentious topic within the counsel of the Gods, a constant reminder of their limitations. He took great pride in the fact that his power was both envied and feared.

But perhaps it was time for a change. For centuries, Orrick indulged in mischief, spreading chaos throughout the worlds he spun into existence, purely for his own amusement.

A shift had begun within him over the past several months. The discovery of the triplets had consumed him. He needed to know who they were and what they could do. That obsession spurred him forward even now. He was certain they were the key to ending the Six Eternal's reign. And with them dead at last, his creations would finally know the truth of who their creator really was. *Him.*

For centuries, the Six Eternal inserted their own stories into each world in the Cosmos. Stories that he tried to erase, only to realize there was no use. The Six Eternal had slithered their way into the minds of every one of his creations until they began to worship them, and build statues and temples in their honor. They offered them sacrifices, and Orrick could only sit back and watch as it unfolded. His gifts alone weren't sufficient to challenge them. They were simply too powerful.

Yet it was their presence in this world, in Fellhaven, that unsettled him the most. This was his most cherished creation, the one he took the greatest pride in. He didn't want their hands influencing a single piece of this world. He wanted them gone, better yet, dead.

Garren and Honoria's powers were immense. He had witnessed only a fraction of their capabilities. He also knew where the final triplet was and believed that once he regained his powers and escaped this realm, he could gather them all and persuade them to help him destroy the Six Eternal once and for all.

He lay staring up at the starlit sky, letting his thoughts run rampant, his ire building with each passing moment, until the early tendrils of dawn caressed the treetops.

"Orrick?" Honoria groaned beside him, pulling him from his thoughts.

He winced, rolling onto his side to face her. "How are you feeling?"

"Okay," she said, sitting up. "Where are we? What happened? My head is killing me."

Orrick sighed, "Much farther away from where we were originally headed. I figure we can stay here for the day, get a fresh start tomorrow morning."

She nodded, "I guess there is no rush. We are stuck here for the foreseeable future."

Orrick's temper was already high from his thoughts of the Six Eternal and all they had done to him, causing him to snap at Honoria, "You might not have places to be, Honoria, but I do. I have many things I need to do, and I need to get back home and restore my Gods-given gifts. So you might not care about our current predicament, but I didn't fucking make these worlds to live in them. I made them to show my power to the infuriating Six Eternal who sit on the throne of the Cosmos, thinking they are the most powerful beings in existence." He turned away from her, "I will show them that they should not have cast me out as some lowly God. They will see the truth of what I can do."

"Your thirst for power is insatiable." Honoria huffed. "Is that what you were looking for in Verhaven? For a way to overpower them?"

Orrick narrowed his eyes at her, "Never mind what I was looking for. It's no concern of yours, and it doesn't matter right now."

"It is, seeing as I've been banished because of it. You made it a concern of mine when you roped me into your foolish scheme."

Orrick closed his eyes with a sigh and raked a hand through his hair. "Honoria, I..." But he stopped short, the words clogged in his throat like rotten meat.

He *had* roped her into this. If it weren't for him, she would still be safe in Verhaven, a place where Anthes couldn't touch her. Now she was vulnerable, all because of him. He knew his father wanted the triplets, too. He wanted the same thing Orrick did, and Orrick vowed to beat him to it.

Orrick groaned, shaking his head as he scooted closer to Honoria and couldn't quite believe the words tumbling from his lips, "I'm sorry to have dragged you into this. I should never have used you the way I did."

Orrick thought he might vomit. What was happening to him in this place? Was he turning soft?

Honoria narrowed her eyes at him as if she didn't quite believe what he was saying, and Orrick floundered for a way to change the topic. "You're very powerful, you know."

She frowned, "What are you talking about?"

"You—you don't remember what happened?"

Honoria looked out over the lake. It was a pristine indigo, the cresting sun revealing its true beauty in the early morning light.

"I remember getting captured by the blue people and being practically dragged through the forest," she looked down at her wrists, rubbing them, remembering the chains locked around them. "Then I just remember feeling overwhelmed, like I was going to pass out, but that's it. How did we get here? And how did we get away from that army?"

"You decimated that entire army." He said, "In a single blow, you broke open the earth and swallowed them whole."

"What?!" Honoria pushed herself to a standing position. "You're lying."

"Honoria," he said, standing up slowly beside her. "You used all the elements. You destroyed one of the major earth Elementalist cities. Your gifts are... well I don't exactly know what they are, but you used the Elemental gifts to extreme lengths. What you did would have taken hundreds of Elementalists together to do."

Honoria's eyes were wide, mouth ajar. " I-I don't remember any of it." She looked away from him and down at her trembling hands. "I've never had any gifts. I've never felt even an ounce of power flowing through me. How is it possible that it would only now appear in this mortal world? You must be mistaken. It wasn't me who did those things you say. It must have been someone else."

"It was you, Honoria." Orrick stepped closer, taking her trembling hands in his, and she looked up at him again. "I'm not sure why it didn't appear until now. Maybe something about this place made that power come alive, but you might be one of the most powerful beings in the Cosmos."

"How would you know that?" She pulled her hands from his, taking a step back from him.

He sighed and brought a hand up, raking it through his hair. "It has to do with what I was looking for in Verhaven. What I," he stopped, grimacing at his next words, "used you for."

She furrowed her brow, her entire face darkening as she said, "What do you mean?"

"Honoria, you are..." but he stopped abruptly, Honoria cutting him off as she stammered.

"I–is the water glowing purple?"

Orrick frowned and looked out at the lake, raising both brows at the sight, "It does appear to be, yes."

The strange waters began to bubble as if boiling, and something rose to the surface. Both Orrick and Honoria stood, moving closer together just as something broke through the surface.

"Huh," Orrick huffed. "Not what I was expecting."

A beautiful woman stood on the water's surface, her naked body shimmering and wet.

"Well, this is quite a pleasant surprise," Orrick mused, and Honoria smacked him on the arm.

"You're absolutely infuriating."

He turned to her with a smile and a wink as he smacked her back on the ass. She jumped with a yelp and moved away, glaring at him.

The woman on the lake walked toward them. Her brown skin was flawless, her figure absolute perfection, and her hair was in braids so long they fell to her waist, covering her breasts. It was a bright red, her eyes matching the shade, glimmering like rubies.

"Orrick," she said. "You've come back."

He furrowed his brow, opening and closing his mouth, before taking a glance at Honoria, whose arms were crossed over her chest, a single brow raised, lips pursed. He looked back at the woman who had stopped just a few feet from the beach.

He smiled at her before saying, "Have we met?"

Her ruby eyes turned molten. "What do you mean, have we met?"

"Yeah, I'm not remembering who you..." He stopped short, turning his head slightly as he studied her further.

There was something so familiar about those eyes and those hips. He narrowed his eyes, studying her in depth until. "Holy shit, Vala?"

Her nostrils flared, and she growled, low and lethal.

"Fuck, have you been here all this time? How long has it been?"

"A thousand years," she said through clenched teeth.

Orrick whistled, "Wow, listen, I gotta be honest, I completely forgot about you. You were only supposed to be here for a week, tops."

Suddenly, the water began to ripple around her, and he could have sworn she grew several feet. Had she been that giant a second ago?

"I would stop talking if I were you," Honoria said in a hushed voice, her lips barely moving.

"Nonsense," he quipped back. "Vala. I think the years here have done you well actually; you are looking exceptionally stunning."

Was her skin turning red?

"Orrick," Honoria grabbed his arm as she slowly backed away toward the forest, trying to pull him with her. "Shut up."

"It's fine. We are fine." He yanked his arm from her grasp. "Everything is fine. It's all just a little misunderstanding, Vala. I'm sure we can..."

"Misunderstanding?" Vala growled, her voice several octaves deeper and more guttural than it had been moments before. Large red spikes began to grow from her flesh, her entire body shifting into something not at all human or elemental, for that matter.

"Yes, yes. Just a misunderstanding, is all. I can fix it."

Her face began to elongate, black scales emerging along the surface of her skin, as she transformed into a serpentine creature, enormous and menacing. A beast that Orrick had forgotten about entirely: she was a Haltifca, a temptress, a water demon who could shapeshift into the beautiful form she had just been.

"A thousand years is not a misunderstanding, God," her fangs snapped as she spoke, and she struck before Orrick had the chance to open his mouth again.

She was fast, powerful, and she grabbed Orrick with her clawed hand, pulling him into the lake and beneath the surface.

He shot flames into the water at her, but they extinguished as soon as he conjured them. Brute force it was then.

Orrick was still in pain from his father's brutal beating, and Vala's grip around his chest was practically suffocating. He didn't think he had ever felt as much agony as he had these past two days in this world. He punched a fist into a weak point on her hand with all of his strength, feeling the bones snap beneath, and then he dug with finger and nail into her scaled flesh, right where the bones had cracked. He clawed his way through her inky black hand,

Vala wailing as dark blood seeped, pooling into the water around him. Yet her grip only tightened, unrelenting to the pain, until he reached the remnants of the bones he'd just broken and wrapped both hands around one of the thick shards of her skeleton and pulled the entire thing free from her hand.

She roared into the water and released him. Bone still in his hand, he swam to face her, but she was too fast, agile in her element, and her teeth bit down just as he dodged her attack. They bore into the flesh of his shoulder, tearing through muscle and cartilage.

Orrick gulped in lungfuls of water at the sheer pain that burned through him, his arm falling limp at his side. He choked on the lake water, pushing his way to the surface until he broke through, spitting up water as he gasped for breath.

The bone was still gripped in his hand, and he yelled out in complete torment as he moved his mangled arm to swim back beneath the water's surface.

Vala was swimming straight up from the bottom, mouth opened wide, revealing the rows of sharp teeth ready to rip him in half.

This was his chance; he had this one shot, or well, he didn't know what would happen. She couldn't kill him, but he was able to be injured in his current state, so she could make his life a living hell of torture. He definitely wasn't about to let that happen.

He kicked his way down toward the monstrous serpent as fast as he could, straight into her wide-open mouth, and just before she could snap her jaws closed, he stabbed her own bone straight down into her brain.

Vala went still and twitched several times, blood clouding Orrick's vision of the damage. He pushed himself from her slackened mouth and watched as she sank to the bottom of the lake, nothing more than a sack of bone and flesh. *What a pity,* he thought. She had been such a beautiful creation.

Orrick swam slowly to shore, his mangled arm floating limply beside him. When his feet made purchase with the sandy lake floor, he used the rest of his strength to wade through the water until he made it to the beach and promptly collapsed face first into the sand, shaking uncontrollably as he coughed a bit more water from his lungs.

Honoria came to his side, placing one hand on his back and the other beneath his armpit as she helped him stand. "Cosmos, Orrick." She breathed, staring at his shoulder.

"I need to stop creating such powerful and angry creatures. Is it as bad as it feels?" Orrick ground out.

She hesitated, scrunching her nose slightly as she looked at it again. "Well, it's not great."

He finally peaked a quick look at it, "Fuck, please tell me that isn't bone I see."

Honoria looked away from it, putting a hand up to her mouth as if she was about to vomit before she said, "Okay, it's not bone."

"Fuck."

"Orrick?" a voice suddenly broke through the shadowed edge of the forest. He looked up to see three figures come into view, one of them with hair and eyes that matched his own.

He snorted, shaking his head at his luck, "You couldn't have shown up ten minutes earlier?"

17

GARREN

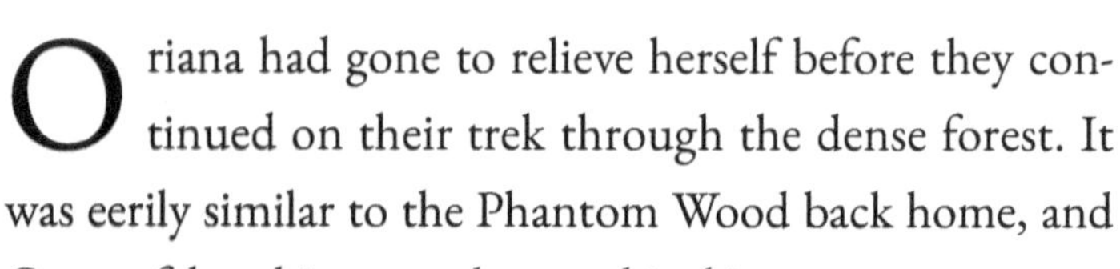

Oriana had gone to relieve herself before they continued on their trek through the dense forest. It was eerily similar to the Phantom Wood back home, and Garren felt a shiver crawl across his skin.

Atlas was beside him, watching him with great interest. "You alright there, warrior?"

On second thought, maybe his skin had been crawling due to the way this strange purple-haired man was looking at him. Garren opened his mouth to respond, but instead a guttural cry escaped him. His hands instinctively moved to cover his ears even though he knew it would do nothing to help block out the sound that had been plaguing him these past few days. It screeched, intensifying with each pulse. It felt like sharp needles piercing through his skin and scraping at his skull. The gnawing sound was worse than before, almost tenfold, and Garren crumpled to the ground in agony.

Atlas quickly knelt in front of him, concern etched across his features as he placed a comforting hand on Garren's shoulder. He seemed to be saying something, his lips moving, but Garren couldn't hear a single word over the deafening noise that consumed his senses. It felt like being trapped, locked inside his head, and unable to escape. Tears welled in his eyes as he suddenly knew how Oriana felt for all those centuries, caged within herself.

As soon as it had come, the sound was gone, and Garren sighed in relief, finally able to hear what Atlas was saying.

"Come on, get up, big guy. Fight through it."

"I'm alright," Garren said, grabbing hold of Atlas' outstretched hand and allowing him to pull him off the ground. "Thanks."

Atlas nodded. "So I take it that you are here because of whatever that was?"

Garren grunted in response.

"There is something powerful in this forest," Atlas said, cocking his head to the side with a smirk that made Garren take a step away from him. "Can you feel it, warrior?"

He didn't respond, but Atlas didn't seem phased; he just continued on as if in a daze.

"Something that hasn't been in these woods for hundreds of years. Something I've been waiting for," he mused, looking off into the distance.

Garren frowned. The man had gone daft. Why the fuck was Oriana taking so long?

Atlas pinned his eyes back on Garren then, and that same eerie smile spread across his lips.

Just then, Oriana came back to join them, and Garren gripped her arm, bending down to whisper in her ear, "We need to get away from this man. He's creeping me the fuck out."

Oriana shook her head at Garren, "You need to get over whatever hatred you have for him. He's harmless. Look at him."

They both turned back to look at the man who'd invited himself along on their journey to find the genuine, wide-toothed grin he often had plastered across his face. Garren glared at the man; there was something not right about him.

"Well, we best be on our way then," Atlas said, a little too cheerfully. "I don't want your brain exploding before we've had the chance to find out what the thing in your head is." He winked and motioned for Garren to lead the way.

Oriana raised her brows at Garren, "See? He's a nice guy. Harmless."

Garren ignored her and turned to lead the way. The damned pounding in his head was putting him in a bad mood, and had been since they started this journey.

They took no more than ten steps when a sudden blood-curdling scream pierced through the air, echoing between the trees of the forest, scattering birds and rodents alike. They all stopped in unison.

"What was that?" Oriana asked, her eyes wide with alarm.

"I don't know," Atlas said, his tone laced with uncertainty. "It didn't sound human."

"Someone's fighting a monster." Oriana stated, peering into the shadowy forest, searching for any movement within the brush.

"Like I said, we don't have those here," but Atlas' voice wavered slightly, giving way to his possible creeping skepticism at his statement.

Oriana chuckled, "I doubt that's true."

"It might be a battle," he suggested, and not a second after, a monstrous roar shook the ground beneath their feet, rustling the leaves ahead of them. Both Atlas and Oriana took on a fighting stance, ready for whatever was coming their way.

"See?" Oriana said, "What did I tell you? A monster."

Garren yelled out in pain, covering his ears as the most intensely searing, skull-splitting screech assaulted his head. "That's the direction the sound is coming from," he ground out, through clenched teeth.

"Well, what are we waiting for? Let's go." Oriana urged and Garren pulled out his long-sword, leading the way once again, just as the sound died completely.

"I swear if we came all this way just to find out that this is one of Orrick's sick games, I'm going to—" Garren began, but Atlas suddenly grabbed his arm, halting him mid-sentence.

"What did you just say?"

Garren frowned at the purple-haired man, "If this is a monster, I'm going to—"

"No, that name. What name did you say?" Atlas pressed, with a strange urgency.

"Orrick?"

Atlas furrowed his brow and looked away from him as he breathed, "I knew it."

"Do you know Orrick?" Oriana questioned.

"I—no, it just made me think of someone I used to know. Sorry, that just...the name sparked a sudden memory, is all."

Garren narrowed his eyes at him. There was more happening here, but the ringing in his head picked up again and was honestly the only thing he really cared about at the moment. He wanted it to go away once and for all. He couldn't live with its incessant nagging any longer.

He exchanged a glance with Oriana, who seemed just as put off by the brief interaction, but she just shrugged her shoulders, and they all set off through the dense undergrowth of the wood, pushing aside branches and vines as Garren led them toward the noise pounding like a beacon in his head.

Garren's heart pounded wildly as they drew closer, each step amplifying the ringing in his ears until it morphed from a piercing shriek into an enchanting melody, like a stunning and ethereal lullaby. It was oddly soothing and only spurred him forward with renewed urgency.

He sprinted with relentless determination, leaping over fallen limbs and dodging tree trunks until he burst through the edge of the forest. Oriana and Atlas were hot on his heels, their feet pounding onto the sand with a thud before they halted beside him. A vast, shimmering lake spread out before them, and suddenly the sound ceased its assault, and the renewed silence was an instant relief.

Garren observed their surroundings desperately, trying to find its source, until his eyes landed on the one person he had never wanted to see again.

"Orrick?" Oriana gasped as Garren growled.

The white haired bastard turned to face them, bloodied and battered, gripping his side and doubled over, practically heaving to draw breath. The sight of him so beat up gave Garren immense pleasure until the urchin opened his mouth and said, "You couldn't have shown up ten minutes earlier?"

"You dirty fucking, bastard!" Garren yelled.

"So thrilled to see you too, halfling," Orrick wheezed.

Garren glared at him, listening for that ringing that had brought him here, but it was gone entirely. "It was you this whole damn time, wasn't it?"

"Normally," Orrick coughed, wincing at the effort. "I would love for the chance to banter with you about whatever you're talking about, but now isn't the best time." It was then that Garren noticed how pale Orrick was, his skin a strange gray hue. Blood poured from a grotesque wound on his shoulder and didn't seem to be stopping. His breathing was shallow and labored, and he fell to the beach onto his knees. *Good.* Garren was going to finish him off. He took a step forward, ready to rip the slimy, malicious God a new one, but Oriana put an arm out, stopping him.

"Wait," She said softly, "I don't think it's what you are thinking, Garren. Something isn't right here."

Garren grumbled, but consented, standing firmly in his spot even though his fingers were tightening around the handle of his sword. Seeing Orrick this way suddenly had his mind flashing back to the temple, Orrick yelling for Garren to fix his arm. He quickly shook those memories free from his mind. Oriana was right, something wasn't right here.

Oriana knelt next to Orrick, and Garren sighed, sheathing his blade, "What happened?"

"He fought a creature in the lake," a dark-haired woman said from beside him. It was only then that Garren even noticed her standing nearby.

"Honoria," Orrick coughed again as Oriana helped him gently down to the sandy earth to lie on his back. "Meet my sister, Oriana, and her beefy companion, Garren."

Oriana nodded at the women, putting her attention back to Orrick, but Garren stared at her. He could have sworn they had met before, but how was that possible if she was in this world across the Storm Sea?

"Do I know you?" Garren cocked his head to the side. The woman said nothing, only shook her head, staring at him unblinking. "Are you sure?"

"Why aren't you healing?" Oriana said to Orrick beside him. "How did one of your own creatures do this to you?"

He wheezed a gurgling laugh, "It wasn't all the creature. Father got in several shots first."

Oriana opened and closed her mouth several times, many questions were obviously churning their way around in her mind, "But why aren't you healing?"

"He's not exactly himself right now," the woman, Honoria, finally spoke, coming closer. Garren was acutely aware of her presence. "H—he doesn't have his godly gifts."

"What?!" Oriana whipped her head toward the woman. "How is that possible?"

"Ada," Orrick whispered.

Oriana's mouth dropped open, her face frozen in shock.

"Ada?" Garren frowned, "Why does that name sound so familiar?"

"Because she's your mother, Queen of the Zydells," Orrick said before nodding his head toward Honoria. "And her mother, too."

Garren blinked several times before looking over at Oriana, who looked just as stunned as he was, if not more so. She cocked her head to the side and moved her eyes back and forth between Garren and the woman named Honoria. "There is quite a resemblance there. Honestly, they might look more alike than we do, Orrick."

Garren looked over at Honoria. She was staring directly at him, her face a blank, unreadable slate. She had the same coloring as him, the same eyes, even their hair was practically the same unusual shade of dark blue, shifting to black.

He knew there were two siblings out there, beings just like him that he might never meet, but now, standing here, meeting his sister for the first time, he didn't know what to do. If he was being honest with himself, he hadn't really thought about them at all over the past few months since Orrick told him. It didn't seem much use thinking about people he might never see. Orrick said they were hidden away in the Cosmos, just as he was, so the thought of actually coming face to face with a brother or sister hadn't crossed his mind.

But now he was face-to-face with one—a sister. What was someone supposed to say to a sibling they had never met before? Should he hug her?

She just kept staring at him, not even blinking, and Garren felt himself begin to fidget under her scrutiny. So he finally broke the silence that fell all around them and waved at her, "Hello." He said awkwardly.

Orrick barked out a laugh that quickly turned into a wheezing groan. "Wow, this is so intriguing to watch. This is how I know I didn't make either of you. Two such lumbersome individuals could never come from my hand."

Oriana smacked him on the shoulder, and he cursed at her. "What? You agree with me, I know you do."

Oriana just rolled her eyes, but there was humor dancing behind her eyes that made Garren glare at her in annoyance.

"How about you two newly discovered siblings go and get better acquainted with one another? I want to speak with my dear sister alone."

Garren opened his mouth to tell Orrick exactly what he thought about that idea, but Oriana gave him a piercing glare that had him biting his tongue and growling profanities under his breath as he walked over to Honoria.

"So," he said, bringing a hand up to brush through his hair before holding it out for her to shake. "Nice to, uh, meet you."

She stared at his hand before cautiously placing her own in his. She looked up at him, her silver eyes like a mirror to his own. The touch of her skin against his was electric; it shot through him, bringing with it that same loud, incessant ringing he had dealt with over the past few days, but it was more lyrical, like a song he had heard long ago. It was beautiful and it brought with it a strange feeling of loss and longing that he hadn't felt since the death of his parents—the ones who raised him.

He released her hand and frowned. So it had been her all along. She had been calling out to him, but why now?

"I—um," her voice was meek, just barely above a whisper.

"How about we sit on that log there by the water's edge?" he pointed to a large fallen tree angled perfectly for them to sit and look out over the peaceful lake.

She nodded and they walked in silence halfway around the lake, Oriana and Orrick now too far away to hear their conversation.

Honoria sat, her hands gripping the wood beside her so tightly that it crumpled beneath her hands, and she gasped almost as if she was shocked.

Garren smiled, "I forget my own strength sometimes, too."

She looked up at him with a furrowed brow, her silver eyes churning like storm clouds. "I didn't know my mother had any other children. I–I didn't realize I had a sibling."

"Neither did I until a few months ago, when Orrick told me who, or rather what I was."

"What do you mean?" she narrowed her eyes, glancing over to where Orrick lay in the sand.

"I grew up in this world, on the continent across the sea. I never knew my true heritage." A heavy weight settled in his chest as he thought of his parents. "I was raised by wonderful, loving people there, but a few months ago Orrick told me who I truly was, one of a set of triplets born to both a God and a Zydell."

Honoria whipped her head to look at him, pushing quickly up from the log, horrified shock etched on her face. "What did you say?"

"You didn't know?" Garren frowned, surprised by her outburst. "Supposedly, we were born not only to your mother, but also to the King of the Gods, Zanos."

She closed her eyes, and her face paled to the point he thought she might faint. Her limbs were shaky as she took a seat back down on the log beside him and rested her elbows on her knees, looking down at the white sandy beach. "No," she whispered. "I didn't know."

" I-I'm sorry," Garren placed a reassuring hand gently on her back. He knew exactly how she felt. Her whole world was probably crashing down at this moment; she was questioning her entire life. He had been in that exact situation months ago and still hadn't fully comprehended it.

In fact, he had simply been ignoring it, but at this moment, he couldn't fully push it aside. This woman was his sister, one of the half-God, half-Zydell siblings that he hadn't even known existed. She was real and sitting right next to him. "If it's any solace, I'm thrilled to meet you."

She lifted her gaze to meet his, studying his face so intently that he let his hand fall from her back, an awkwardness rising within him. His instinct was to shift his eyes away, breaking their eye contact, but then she raised a hand to his cheek and gently brushed her fingertips over the uneven ridge of the scar that marred the right side of his face, the touch both tender and curious.

As soon as her finger touched it, a searing pain shot through it, burning his flesh, and he was suddenly no longer on the beach but looking up at a figure looming above him, a blade glinting in the dimness above him as it slashed down toward his face. Pain erupted at his temple, and he saw a flash of red eyes and a white braid before the entire vision vanished just as soon as it had appeared.

"Anthes," Garren gasped, and Honoria dropped her hand away.

"Wh—what was that?"

"You saw it too?" his eyes widened as she nodded her head to say yes. " I-I think it was a memory." He brought a hand up to touch the scar. "About how I got this." Oriana had been right all along. Someone had carved the jagged scar into his face. Anthes. He would know those eyes anywhere, as red as the blood moon that had trapped Oriana for centuries.

"Can we try that again? Whatever just happened, maybe we can see more, understand better who we are."

Honoria was gripping the log on either side of her again, and just as before, it crumpled beneath her grasp.

She sprang to her feet, eyes wide and darting as if trying to make sense of a sudden nightmare. Hugging herself tightly, she rubbed her hands along her upper arms and began inching slowly away from him.

He stood, putting up his hands, "It's okay, don't worry about the log. You've just discovered something significant and life-changing. I get it, sometimes our powers take over when we're stressed."

Honoria shook her head, "I don't have any powers, though. At least I never thought I did."

Garren raised a brow, looking back at the crumbling log quickly and then back to her, "Um...I hate to break it to you, but no ordinary person in this world can do that with their bare hands."

"You don't understand, I've never been strong. I don't have some kind of super strength or anything. I—I—I..." she stuttered, and Garren could see the tears begin to well in her eyes. "I just want to go home. I want to leave this place!"

Out of nowhere, a sharp wail pierced Garren's eardrums, sending shards of pain through his head like tiny daggers, and he doubled over, clamping his hands tightly over his ears, agony contorting his features.

Honoria was by his side in a split second, a hand on his back, "Are you okay?" And just as soon as it had come, the sound was gone again.

Garren dropped his hands and stood tall, looking into Honoria's eyes. "How long have you been here?"

"At this lake? Maybe a few…"

"No, in this world. Away from your home."

"Three days."

Garren's eyes widened. "It was you. You led me here."

" I-I don't even know you, how could I have done that?"

"For the past three days, I've been hearing a beacon, a strange ringing that continued to get louder as I followed it. It led me across the Storm Sea, all the way to this spot where it stopped when I found you. But it just rang out again when you said you wanted to go home." Garren took a step closer to her; she was too close to the water's edge to take a step away. "I think you called me here somehow without knowing it, because you wanted home and in this world, I'm the closest thing to home—your brother."

She turned her head slightly to the side and stared into his eyes, studying his face and features, and then she huffed out a meek laugh, "You look so much like her—our mother. Your face looks like home." She swiped at the few wayward tears that trailed down her cheeks. "Why did she never tell me about you?"

Garren shrugged, "Probably for the same reason she separated us, spreading us throughout the Cosmos—to protect us."

Honoria frowned, "And there is one more sibling? We are a set of triplets?"

"As far as Orrick has said."

"Protect us from what, though? What was so terrible that she needed to separate us, rob us of growing up with one another?"

"Orrick said it was to protect us from the Gods." That flash of Anthes standing over him suddenly came back to the forefront of his mind.

Honoria scowled at Garren's words and then looked over at Orrick and Oriana, who were, to Garren's surprise, huddled close together in an affectionate sort of way. "I would have liked to have grown up with siblings."

Garren smiled down at her, "Me too."

"I think we might need to sit and talk with that devious little bastard of a God. He has some explaining to do. He owes us at least all the knowledge he has about who we are and why mother has trapped me here with him."

Garren barked out a laugh. He quite liked this sister of his. She seemed to hate Orrick just as much as he did. "Agreed."

18
ORRICK

A peculiar figure stood at the edge of the shadowed forest, his gaze fixed intently on Orrick. It unsettled him, and he furrowed his brow, squinting at the man to get a better look. He was a Gnome, and an odd, unsettling sense of familiarity washed over Orrick at the man's presence.

"Who is that?" Orrick asked Oriana, gesturing towards the figure. "And why is he lurking in the shadows like a creep?"

Oriana glanced behind her, "That's Atlas, he helped us get across that cursed Storm Sea and has been our companion on this journey. I think he's just trying to give us all some space."

Orrick grunted, but he couldn't shake the feeling that there was something more to his presence.

He wasn't able to give it much more thought because Oriana was close beside him, inspecting his wounds, the ones he still refused to look at.

"What the fuck happened to you?" She demanded.

"It's fine. I'm already starting to heal." He could feel the flayed skin of his arm knitting itself back together, although slower than it might normally. Honestly, he was relieved he was healing so quickly. For the past few days, he couldn't shake the nagging feeling that Ada had turned him into one of the Elementalists completely. The looming threat of death had haunted him since he arrived. Now, after surviving the attacks from his father and Vala—both capable of inflicting harm on him even before his powers were stripped away—he knew that he was still a God. Why he had made any of his creatures capable of actually hurting him was an oversight, that was for sure. When creating the Haltifcas, he wanted to make a being that could actually go up against the Gods, but he hadn't imagined one would ever go up against him.

"Will you tell me what's going on?" Oriana's voice was soft, and it sparked fond memories of peaceful moments with her in this place.

A sudden wave of sadness and longing washed over him, and before he could stop the words from spilling free, he said, "They're dying, Oriana."

She frowned at him, at his vulnerability.

Maybe it was the loss of his power, or perhaps it was the pain of his injuries, but he knew it was most likely being back here, in this place where it all began—his first creation.

She placed the back of her hand on his forehead. "I know you are injured, but is your head okay? Do you have a fever?"

He swatted her hand away, "Stop it, I'm fine. I—I just..." he sighed. "I don't know what I'm doing anymore. I don't know what I want."

Her face changed to one full of sympathy.

He looked away from her, "All I've wanted since father banished me and the Six Eternal cast me off as nothing, is to see them all dead. I've wanted nothing more than to sit on their thrones with their severed heads on spikes, bowed before me."

"Fuck, Orrick. That's gruesome, even for me."

He ignored her. He had struggled with these feelings ever since returning to this world, and Oriana was somehow the only person he could voice them to, the one he thought might be able to understand. They had been friends once, when they were young.

"This world was the first of my creations. Did you know that?"

She nodded, lips turning into a brief, solemn smile as she watched him intently.

"Of course you did, you were there when I made it." She had been in awe of his gifts; honestly, it made sense why she loved this world so much. She had been there at the start, had been the one to oversee and look after this place for thousands of years. His mind flashed back to a vivid memory of them in this very forest when it was only just created.

Oriana's laughter echoed toward him as she darted her way between the small saplings, not even as tall as either of them yet. Orrick chased after her with playful determination, tackling her to the moss-covered ground, lush and soft like a welcome embrace.

"Orrick!" she screamed, squealing as he tickled her until she could no longer breathe, and then he stopped his assault, laughing along with her.

They lay there under the vast obsidian sky, heads resting together, staring up at the pitch-black canvas above with no other worlds yet twinkling in and out. Fellhaven was the only world in existence, Orrick's first experiment with his gifts. It was then, while they lay in darkness, that he crafted the moon to be a light in the night, choosing Oriana's favorite color of green. It cast a gentle glow around them, bathing the world in an emerald haze.

Oriana beamed at him, her smile wide upon her lips, and she wrapped him in her arms, bone-crushingly tight.

"I love you, Orrick," she said. "But I'm not sure green is the right color to light up this world."

He smiled back at her and said, "I think it's just right, but maybe it should be saved for the rarest occasions."

Orrick shook away the memory, meeting his sister's bright green gaze, filled with the same warmth and affection she always gave him. He didn't deserve it.

"It's been several centuries since I've been here, on this side of the world, in Emmoria." A strange burning sensation climbed up his throat, and he swallowed, trying to get rid of the foreign feeling, but it only traveled up to his nose and then behind his eyes, where he suddenly felt moisture begin to well. "They are all killing each other," he breathed. "Something catastrophic is coming. I can feel it. They are on the verge of extinction. I fear that soon these people, my Elementals, will wipe themselves from this world."

Something wet rolled down his cheek, and he swiped at it, fingers glistening with the salty liquid. *Was he crying? Fuck.* Orrick frowned.

Oriana grabbed his hand, rubbing her thumb along its back. "It's okay to love something. You know that, don't you, Orrick?"

He looked up into her green eyes, almost an exact match to his own. She was quite possibly the only person in the Cosmos who knew him—the real, true him. The only person he ever confided in and the only one who had gone through the same painful upbringing as he did.

"I don't know what's happening to me," He whispered. He couldn't stop the second, nor the third tear from breaking free and streaking down his face.

Oriana pulled him into an embrace, and he sagged against her, resting his weary head on her shoulder. He wrapped an arm around her, keeping her there in this embrace. She felt like better, happier times. She felt like the past, present, and future. She felt like his childhood.

"I'm sorry, Orrick, for what the Gods did to you. To us." She said, "I'm sorry that you never felt love."

He blinked away the remaining wetness in his eyes and huffed, pushing away from her. "You have nothing to be sorry for. It's them who need to pay a price."

Oriana's gaze traveled across the gentle rippling lake to where Garren and Honoria sat deep in conversation. "How did she end up here?"

"It's a long story." Orrick huffed, rubbing his eyes. "Do you remember when we were children and mother used to tell us stories about the Zydell Queen, Ada, and how she was able to see things before they happened?"

"Yes," she said, raising a brow in interest.

"Well, I think I read one of those predictions."

"What? How?"

"I went to Verhaven."

Oriana's eyes went wide, her mouth moving to speak, but nothing came out until she finally screeched, "You did what? It is forbidden! When? How? Why?"

"Shhh..." Orrick placed his hand over her gaping mouth to quiet her outburst. "Calm down, I don't want them to hear. They can't know anything about this."

Oriana's breathing began to mellow out, and Orrick released his hand from her mouth. She took one deep, calming breath, crossing her legs in front of her and leaning an elbow on each knee, her face only a few inches from his, "Tell me everything."

He snorted and shook his head before taking his own deep breath, "When I learned about Garren and what he was, I couldn't get it out of my head. I had to know who the others were and what they could do. I snuck into the Zydell world, gained access to their vault of archives, and..." Oriana drew in a breath about to speak, but he placed a finger over her parted lips. "*How* isn't important, *what* is all that matters."

She grumbled something under her breath, "Fine, what did you find?"

"I discovered who his siblings are. Honoria is one of them, but there was a piece of parchment within the pages. It was written quickly by hand, almost in a shaky manner. It was a poem or rhyme of sorts, and it told of the end of the Cosmos, and its connection to Garren and his siblings."

Oriana went still and very quiet, "Do you remember what it said? Was it like one of father's riddled curses, or was it clear and plain? Are you sure you read it correctly?"

Orrick ran a hand through his hair and sighed, "I don't remember the whole of it, but it was fairly obvious that they were the ones who would either save or destroy the Cosmos. Oriana, they have the power to destroy us all."

"So they could either be our saviors or our annihilators? But what would even set the event in motion? It's just a tale about them, a random chance. I'm sure the Queen Mother has seen many futures of the Cosmos, and that was just one of many possible outcomes."

"No, you don't understand. There was more to it than that, much more. Their being here together is not good."

Oriana wasn't paying attention to him anymore; she was looking across the lake, watching the siblings caught deep in conversation. "I mean, she looks pretty harmless to me."

"Oriana! This is serious. Them being together isn't good, they need to be separated, far across the Cosmos."

"Until your memory gets better and you actually can think of what the damn random piece of paper in a book said, then I don't think it's that serious, Orrick. Think about it, if it was important Cosmos ending information, wouldn't it make sense for it to be something more legitimate? In a history book, a book of prophecies, maybe? Not on a small scrap with a scribbling scrawl stuffed into a book?"

Orrick looked away from her; frustration was clouding his vision, his memory felt fuzzy, and he needed to be alone. Needed to clear his head and remember everything about not only what that page said, but what Ada herself said to him.

He pushed himself up shakily, wincing as pain sliced through him, but he bit down, breathing through it. He could take a little pain to finally have some peace and quiet.

"Where are you going?"

"Away," he growled. "Just keep your eye on them, and where the hell did that other guy with you go?"

"Atlas? I'm not sure, actually," Oriana got up and looked around the perimeter of the lake. "Maybe he left to give us some privacy for our sibling reunion."

Orrick snarled, "Whatever," and stormed into the forest with as menacing a stride as he could muster. His fists were engulfed in green flame, licking up his wrists. The fact that he couldn't keep his fire sorcery at bay, as he had so often over the past few days, was a true testament to the depths of his seething anger.

PART THREE

Fuck... again

19
ORRICK

Orrick walked until he couldn't anymore. He wasn't sure how far he'd gone; his mind had been spinning at a dizzying speed. The last few days had provided him with little time to think or truly understand all that he had learned about the siblings, the prophecy, and what it all meant.

"Ada!" he yelled, into the canopy of trees above him. "Get your ass down here and tell me what the fuck is going on!"

He knew that she could hear him; he was certain she had, but only the soft rustle of leaves responded. The silence was deafening. He was on his own then, forced to figure it out alone. If only he could remember what exactly the prophecy was. Why hadn't he stolen the wretched thing? The only certainty he knew was the undeniable reality that the two of them together wasn't good. He needed to get Honoria out of this world, away from Garren, and safe once again in Verhaven. But if that were true, then why had Ada done this? He was obviously missing a key piece of information, and it was maddening.

Suddenly, the hair on the back of his neck stood on end; there was someone behind him. Orrick spun, throwing a stream of flames at the assailant, but before it hit its mark, a wall of packed earth shot up from the forest floor, his fire extinguishing on impact.

The rock wall crumbled into thousands of pebbles, revealing the man who had been with Oriana and Garren, watching him from the shadows.

"Have you been following me?" Orrick growled. How did he not notice this Elementalist was following him?

"What if I was?" A sly grin spread across his lips as he tilted his head.

Orrick bristled at the man's stark tone. It was playful yet laced with something almost deadly. His ebony skin glistened in the streams of sunlight pushing through the treetops. There was a gleam in his violet eyes that seemed to say come and get me.

"Who are you?" Orrick took a step back, narrowing his eyes. There was something off about him, yet so familiar.

The man snorted, then laughed outright, his twisted purple locks bouncing with the effort. "Of course you've forgotten. I wish I could say I'm surprised, but it has been an exceptionally long time."

Orrick rubbed at his eyes. He was so tired of these games. Why was everyone trying to play with him? "Listen, I've been hearing that a lot lately and it's honestly just becoming more annoying than anything, so how about we cut all the secrecy and you just tell me who the fuck you are."

"But what fun would that be?" The man cocked his head with a lazy smile that made Orrick want to burn his face to ash.

Now he was really annoyed. "Don't test me."

"Oh, but Orrick, testing you is always my favorite part of our interactions."

Fuck, this man sounded exactly like him. If he didn't know any better, he might think he was speaking with a clone of himself. It was infuriating, but also arousing? What the fuck? He was losing it. This place was making him go insane. He shook his head, letting out an annoyed huff before saying, "Well, I think I'm done. Goodbye."

He turned to walk away, but the man moved fast, gripping his shoulder and spinning him back around. Orrick's face fell, who the fuck was this Elemental, and why was he so fast?

He leaned in close, whispering next to Orrick's ear. "Come on. I've missed this. Lash out, I dare you." His hot breath on Orrick's face sent a shiver down his spine.

Orrick pushed the man away as hard as he could. He stumbled back several steps, but remained upright, smiling a bit more widely. Fuck, the man liked that. What kind of sick Elementalist was this? And how the hell did he know Orrick's name? He wasn't about to give this man the satisfaction of more questions, so instead he said, "Alright, but when you are dying in a smoldering heap, just remember you asked for it."

Flames erupted from Orrick like the tentacles of a massive squid, lashing out like whips towards the earth Elementalist. Packed earth and stone shot up, blocking each one of his attacks. The man's purple locks spun around him as he dodged and dove, sending spikes of rock at Orrick. He fell onto his back, one of the daggers of stone just skimming his cheek. Orrick raised a hand to the spot, his fingers coming away with blood, and snarled, kicking himself back up to a standing position.

"You drew blood, you fucking Gnome."

The man just laughed again as if it were the funniest thing he had heard all day. "You've lost your touch, God of Chaos. What happened to you?"

That sent Orrick's skin aflame, literally. He was a roaring ball of fire, and he sprinted for the man, throwing out punch after punch and kick after kick. The strange Gnomeic man turned his damn hands into large rocks, blocking his every blow with a fucking toothy grin on his face the whole time.

Orrick knew he wasn't quite himself at the moment. His godly gifts were somewhere out of reach, but he still had his strength and speed for the most part, yet this Gnome was taking each blow as if it were nothing.

"Come on, Orrick, you remember me. It's Atlas. Doesn't that ring a bell?"

Atlas? He had no idea who this man was, and he wasn't even particularly worried about that; what he wanted to know was how this man was so strong.

Orrick sent out a roaring yell, extinguishing the flames that engulfed him, smoke rising from his skin. "Enough!"

"There's that spark I love."

Cosmos, this man was insufferable. How had he created something so utterly defiant, so deranged, completely exasperating, surprisingly flirtatious, mischievous, and stronger than any other Elementalist in this world? This man was somehow different, like every piece of himself put into the body of a Gnome. He was closer to a God than... Suddenly, it hit him, just like a solid rock smacking him right between the eyes.

Orrick's mouth dropped open, then closed, before dropping again, and for the first time in his entire existence, no words came out.

"Ah, and recognition dawns," Atlas winked at him, and Orrick punched him in the face, finally catching him off guard. Atlas hit the ground hard with a grunt.

Orrick watched as he pushed himself up, shaking his head from the blow, and then stood laughing and grabbing

Orrick by the shoulder, bringing him in for a suffocating hug.

"I didn't think I'd ever see you again." Atlas began, "When I met your sister in Svakland, I knew I needed to find a way to stay with her, hoping it would lead to you."

Atlas held the hug for too long, and it began to turn into something more intimate, and Orrick pushed him away.

"I—I..." Orrick stuttered. He didn't know what to say, what to think. Atlas was the very first creature he ever created. His first living, breathing masterpiece. Atlas was him, in mind and soul. Atlas was home.

Orrick grabbed Atlas, and this time it was his turn to hug him too tightly, for too long. An emotion crept to the surface, threatening to spill, but he pushed it down and withdrew the embrace once again, more gently this time.

"I don't know what to say."

Atlas smirked, "'You look fantastic for your age' would be a good start. I mean, I don't look a day over thirty, am I right?" He spun around, then flexed his biceps and struck a pose.

Orrick just continued to stare at him, truly at a loss for words.

Atlas smacked him on the shoulder, "Oh come on, snap out of it. What has it been, five hundred, maybe a thousand years? I do lose track of time these days."

"Eight hundred and seventy-three."

Both of Atlas' brows rose and then that damned smirk was plastered on his face again and he winked, "So you did miss me."

"Don't flatter yourself," Orrick snorted, finally finding his voice again. "That's the last time I've been to Emmoria, that's all."

"Sure, whatever you say, creator." Atlas bowed, and Orrick rolled his eyes and began walking away from him.

He was feeling overwhelmed, and this had tipped him over the edge. This wasn't something he could deal with right now. He just wanted to be alone so he could think and figure everything out.

He needed space.

"Where are you going? We have so much to catch up on." Atlas jogged after him.

Orrick closed his eyes and took a deep breath. "Not now, Atlas. I—I just, I can't do this right now. I need to be alone. Please leave."

He didn't look back, lest he see whatever dejected, sad expression was now on Atlas' face; he just kept walking, satisfied to hear no one following him.

But that small victory was short-lived as hot air swirled around him, and Orrick groaned before looking up from the mossy forest floor.

Anthes stood before him, and Orrick held back the urge to run. He didn't have the patience or the ability to handle this right now. And even worse, not more than a mile away, both Garren and Honoria sat, two of the most powerful beings in the Cosmos, and the very ones that Anthes wanted.

"What do you want, father? I've already told you—" Anthes threw a dagger, it sliced through Orrick's shoulder, pinning him to the tree just behind him. Taken off guard, he yelled out in pain. How the fuck had the blade pierced his skin? Had Anthes created a second God killer? Putting more of his power into a weapon?

Orrick gritted his teeth, nostrils flaring as he breathed through the burning that shot through him and glared at his father. "It seems you've been hard at work, father. Do the Six Eternal know you've created another God killer?"

Anthes snarled, "That's none of your concern, boy. The blade in your shoulder can't kill a God; only one weapon can truly do that."

Two, Orrick thought. Garren's blade was also a God killer, but he wasn't about to let his father in on that little secret. Orrick grabbed the hilt of the knife and pulled, biting his lip against the pain, but it didn't budge. Blood trickled down his arm, dripping from his fingers to the solid earth.

"Where is Balthar, Orrick?"

He rolled his eyes with a grunt of annoyance, "Like I said, I don't have it." He held his breath, waiting for the next blow from his father, but it never came.

Anthes' face changed into something far more terrifying as a smile spread across his lips, "I know you went to Verhaven."

Orrick didn't move, didn't even flinch at his father's words. His heart picked up speed, beating faster and faster. Not wanting to hear his next words.

"I know what you were looking for. I've been looking for them far longer than you could know."

Orrick just stared at his father, face unmoving even as his breathing quickened.

"It took me a long time to realize something, but I finally figured out who the boy with Oriana is—what he is." Anthes took a few steps closer to Orrick. "I cut that scar into his face long ago when he was no more than a babe. I can't wait to cut more scars into his flesh."

Did he take him? Honoria and Garren are together at the moment. Did his father know? He shouldn't have left the lake. He needed to go back. Were they even still there to go back to? "What have you done with Garren?"

"Garren? Do I sense a hint of adoration in your tone, Orrick? So unlike you." Anthes smirked maliciously. "I'll come for him soon enough, but I've found another of them—a woman."

Orrick held his tongue; he would not fall into his father's game and give up Honoria's name or her whereabouts. If he didn't have Garren, then he didn't have

Honoria either. They were safe for the moment with Oriana.

The blood trickling along Orrick's arm began to dry, growing sticky and dark. "How good for you father. Now, can you please remove this blade from my shoulder?"

"Not until you tell me where Balthar is."

"No, I don't think I will."

Anthes pulled another glittering dragger from its sheath and threw, Orrick turned his head, closing his eyes and tensing for the pain that was to come, but it never did. Instead, he heard a clink as the daggers impacted and then a thump as they fell to the ground.

Orrick cautiously opened his eyes to see a wall of stone in front of him. He frowned and heard Anthes curse on the other side.

A loud bang echoed around him, and the wall crumbled into several large pieces, revealing Anthes' seething face several feet in front of him.

"So this is who messed you up so badly, huh?" a voice came from Orrick's left, and both he and Anthes turned to see Atlas standing there, arms crossed over his bare chest.

"Who—" Anthes began to growl, but Orrick didn't give him the chance to finish before he lashed out with a flaming whip that wrapped around Anthes' wrist, the one that was mere centimeters from the blade at his hip.

"I think it's time you left, father."

Anthes glowered at him, wrapping his hand around the whip of green fire, smoke rising as his skin sizzled and he yanked. Orrick yelled out as his shoulder slid along the blade, his father agonizingly pulling him away from the tree. The blade was now fully to the hilt within his arm.

Sweat coated his skin, and his vision blurred from the pain. He had never felt anything like it.

"How dare you," Anthes spat in his face.

Orrick was on his knees, panting, the whip evaporating into thin air as he lost control over it. He looked up into his father's red eyes just in time to see a massive boulder fall from the sky directly onto his head. Anthes' knees buckled from the surprise of it, and he almost lost his balance, stumbling backwards, away from Orrick.

Then began the onslaught of sharp, dagger-like rocks as they speared for Anthes, one after the other, with such speed and accuracy that Anthes didn't have enough time to dodge them as they hit his chest, face, and legs, shattering upon impact, but pushing him farther and farther back. He pulled the sword from his back and swung at the onslaught of stone knives.

Orrick glanced over to Atlas, who now stood beside him, pushing forward as he continued his relentless attack on Anthes, until Atlas was standing directly in front of Orrick.

"In case you didn't hear him correctly, he doesn't have what you are looking for."

Anthes' eyes glowed like burning embers, and he took a step toward them, but before he could take another, two massive boulders slammed into him from either side, crushing him between their girth.

Anthes grunted, pushing against the rocks encasing him, and glared at Atlas until the stone began to crack, finally shattering into several large boulders.

"Pathetic," Anthes snarled, breathing heavily. "You're so helpless that you need this creature's help." He sheathed his sword and snorted. "You'll see me again, boy." And then he was gone with a swirling hot wind, the dagger in Orrick's shoulder vanishing with him, causing a fresh squirt of blood to spray from the wound.

He fell forward, catching himself with his good arm. Large, strong hands came around his waist, pulling him up to his feet. He groaned, gripping Atlas's waist

"Are you okay?" Atlas asked, his hazy violet eyes sparkling brightly in a beam of sunlight.

"Why did you do that?" Orrick breathed against the pain that still seared through his shoulder.

"I would do anything for you, Orrick."

"That was stupid, you know that, right?"

Atlas huffed a laugh, his breath stroking Orrick's cheek. "It was worth it." He came closer, whispering into Orrick's ear, "For you."

Orrick shivered as Atlas placed a gentle kiss along Orrick's jaw. He felt a warmth spread through him, a different kind of sensation, one that he had forgotten, one he hadn't felt in a very long time. Something that sat deeper, that filled him to the brim with not only lust, but what could only be considered affection. This Gnome was unlike any of his creations; he had made Atlas for himself in the beginning, crafted him for his very own purposes.

He was powerful, cunning, fearless, and intelligent. His abilities were far greater than any other Elementalist in this world, and he was immortal, just like a God. He was able to sneak up not only on Orrick but on Anthes. He was, in a way, the closest being to himself that he had ever made. They were one and the same, and there was something entirely enticing about that.

Orrick couldn't hold back any longer; he brought a hand up, hooked it behind Atlas' neck, and pulled those plump, waiting lips to his.

20
GARREN

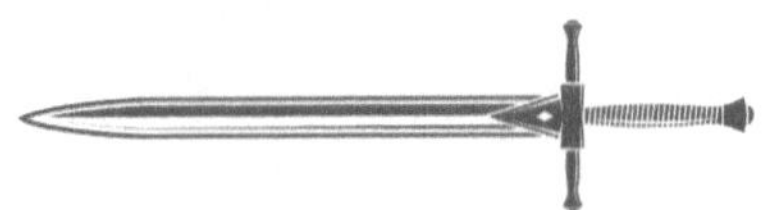

Orrick had, of course, disappeared, nowhere to be found. So Oriana, Honoria, and Garren sat on the beach building a fire as night closed in around them. A quiet awkwardness between them.

"Where did Orrick even go? He's been gone for hours." Garren grumbled, poking the small fire with a stick.

"He does that a lot," Honoria said, hugging her knees to her chest, resting her chin atop them. "He left me alone for half the day when we first arrived, and just last night I found out that he had gone to call upon my mother, without me."

"Ada was here?" Oriana frowned.

Honoria huffed a laugh, "Supposedly, Orrick spoke with her. So glad she's trapped me here with him and hasn't even bothered to visit me or tell me if I can come home."

"Why did she trap you here?" Garren asked.

"Because of Orrick."

"That's not surprising. He ruins everything." Garren snorted.

"I hear you all talking about me, you know." Orrick and Atlas came from the bushes.

"Gods, Orrick," Oriana was instantly by his side. "How is it that you look worse?"

"We need to talk privately, again," he tried to whisper, but it came out as more of a wheezing groan.

"No," Honoria cut in. "No more secrets. Whatever it is, we all have a right to know. I want to get out of here and go home just as badly as you, Orrick! Tell me what's going on!"

Garren raised a brow; his sister was feisty, and she was facing off against Orrick, completely unafraid, as if she were the one who could snap his neck with a single flick of the wrist.

Orrick's face dripped with exhaustion and annoyance as he glared at her.

"Fine," he wheezed. "But can we please sit down?"

The ground beneath their feet began to quake, and Garren reached for his sword just before the sand swirled up into the air, clouding all of their vision until it settled, revealing a sand-carved chair for each of them to sit on, circled around the fire.

Atlas gently helped Orrick sit down in one of the seats he had skillfully created. Garren didn't miss the intimate way Atlas's hand brushed against Orrick's, lingering too long for a new acquaintance. He frowned at the exchange. Did they already know one another? He knew that Atlas was from this world, so obviously one of Orrick's creations, but there seemed to be something more there.

Garren took one of the seats across from Orrick, eyeing Atlas with keen interest as the purple-haired Elementalist took a seat beside Orrick.

He looked up to Oriana, noticing how her head was cocked at the exchange between Orrick and Atlas as well. He grabbed her hand yanking her down into the seat beside him, and whispered, "What the fuck is going on there?"

Oriana shrugged, shaking her head.

Honoria was the last to sit, taking the final seat between Garren and Atlas.

A hush settled over the group, each person lost in their own thoughts, as the fire crackled softly and the logs shifted, sending sparks into the air. The tiniest sliver of light barely illuminated the sky, as stars began to emerge for their nightly appearance. A chill moved around them at the lack of light; Honoria shivered beside him. She was wearing a thin top and practically see-through pants, an outfit that left her midsection completely exposed. It was clothing that would have worked if they were farther south, but in these dense northern woods, it was no wonder she was cold. He felt the sudden urge to offer her his shirt, even though it would leave him exposed to the elements.

He opened his mouth to offer the strange gesture, but suddenly a stream of green flames erupted from Orrick's hands, and the fire grew, instantly warming the air around them.

"What the fuck was that?" Oriana asked in disbelief.

"Oh, I didn't tell you? It's my new ability. I no longer have my Godly gifts, but I'm a Salamander."

Oriana raised her brows, "That's...unfortunate."

"Indeed," Orrick said, sounding dejected.

Honoria was beginning to breathe heavily beside him; he could practically feel the heated rage emanating from her.

"Why would Ada take away your God gifts, but then give you fire sorcery? That seems so strange." Oriana continued, "I mean, what is her aim? What is her goal in all of this?"

"She's just pissed I was fucking her daughter. She wanted to show me how much more powerful she is than I am. Teach me a lesson, I suppose."

Garren's head swung from Honoria to Orrick at that, "What did you say?" His chest welled with anger. How dare he so callously say that about his sister, no matter that he only just met her. Orrick was vile, and he defiled his sister. It was about time the former God of creation and chaos learned a lesson from Garren's blade.

He stood, glaring at Orrick when a low growl suddenly sounded beside him. "What was..." he began as he turned to what used to be Honoria. Garren's eyes went wide. No longer was she the beautiful, smooth-skinned, delicate-featured woman he had met. Her face had transformed into a grotesque malformation: bumped out ridges along her brow, a hooked nose, long needlelike teeth that snarled at Orrick, and her eyes were no longer the sparkling smokey grey that were so similar to his own. Instead, they were a monstrous yellow.

He knew instantly what was happening. He had seen the same thing happen many times in the past months; Honoria had become the bloodlust.

"Orrick," Oriana anxiously said, "What is this? What is going on?"

Orrick's eyes were just as wide as their own, his mouth agape as he stared at what Honoria had become. "I-I don't know," he began, but stopped short, some realization washing across his face as the breath left his lungs. "Ada," he said suddenly. "When I met with her in the desert she told me Honoria *'has been asleep for far too long, but here she will awaken'*. I didn't understand it then, but now...my Gods..." he breathed, just as Honoria attacked.

Claws reached for Orrick as she lunged. If Garren were a better person, he might have stopped her, but the thought of his sister taking a few chunks out of the God gave him far too much delight.

Orrick fell from his sandy chair, dodging Honoria's attack. Garren watched, stunned, as Honoria's yellow eyes fixed on Orrick with a predatory focus. A low growl hummed around her as she stalked toward him.

Grains of sand clung to Orrick's already blood-soaked clothing as he backed away, pushing himself through the sand as she prowled closer.

"Honoria!" A familiar, grizzled voice said beside Garren, a voice that sent a shiver down his spine. He turned to see Oriana's bloodlust in full view, wiping his head back and forth between Honoria and Oriana. They looked the same, both had become Oriana's bloodlust incarnate, but how?

Honoria turned toward Oriana with a snarl, and then the two women became nothing but a tumbling ball of hair, nails, shrieks, and growls as they fought, each desperate to overtake the other.

"Am I the only one aroused by this?" Orrick was now standing beside Garren, intently watching the two women brawl. Garren bit back a retort and instead brought his elbow back hard into Orrick's stomach. The chaos God let out a pained sound, making Garren smile.

"Understood," Orrick coughed as he bent forward, trying to catch his breath. "I'll keep my mouth shut next time."

Oriana had Honoria in a chokehold, her clawed fingers digging into her neck. She squealed, struggling to get free, but finally began to settle, coming back into herself. The bloodlust dissipated, as her features settled back into soft, rounded cheeks and silver eyes, her claws retracted, replaced by dainty fingers. Oriana released her, and she collapsed onto her knees, hands digging into the sandy earth, her breathing labored.

"W—what happened?" she breathed. " I-I don't know what that was."

"It was me," Oriana said, crouching beside her and rubbing soothing circles across her back. "My bloodlust. Has that ever happened before?"

"No, never."

"She's a siphon," Orrick said, standing beside the fire, green flames casting a glow across half of his face, the other half hidden in shadow.

"What do you mean?" Garren frowned, coming to Honoria's other side and helping her stand.

"She mimics the powers of those around her. I had my suspicions, but this proves it. Honoria draws on the powers of others and uses them as her own."

Oriana's brows went up, "So she drew on my powers to become the bloodlust? But I don't feel depleted or like any of my power is being pulled from me."

"She doesn't take them from you, she mimics them." He repeated. "So right now she could use your enchantments too, and Garren's strength and his..."

Garren cut him off, "So she, at this moment, is more powerful than us all, because she is all of us combined?"

"Correct."

Honoria was breathing heavily, "Why has this not happened until now? I've lived my entire life surrounded by powerful beings, and I've never been able to do anything."

"Sometimes we don't truly know ourselves or what we are capable of until we are away from those who have kept us from being ourselves." Atlas' voice came from the sandy seat he was still sitting in. Garren had forgotten entirely about the Elemental in their group. What must he think of all this?

Orrick snorted, spinning toward Atlas, a look of annoyance on his face.

Garren frowned. There definitely was a strange connection between the two. They knew each other. Atlas glared back at Orrick, unflinching and unblinking. Garren narrowed his eyes and was about to question them on their strange interaction when Orrick cut back in.

"We need to get out of this world, all of us, but especially Honoria and Garren. They are vulnerable here together."

"Why?" Honoria asked, "Please, Orrick, just tell us what's going on."

"The Gods want to use you to essentially destroy the universe. "

"Well, we won't let them." She frowned.

"It's not that simple. There is a prophecy, one that foretells the end of everything, and it clearly mentions both of you along with your other sibling and the Gods. Whether you want to or not, you will be used by them if they get their hands on you."

"I'd like to see them try," Garren grunted.

"So, how do we stop this prophecy from happening?" Honoria asked.

"We kill the Six Eternal Gods," Orrick said.

The entire company fell silent at that.

"There has to be another way," Oriana finally cut in. "We can't kill them, our family."

"Who's family?" Orrick snarled, "There has been no '*family*' between the Gods for centuries."

Garren stepped forward, "I for one am completely fine with killing Anthes. He does nothing but harm from what I've seen."

Orrick smirked at him, "Out of everyone, I didn't think you would be the one to join my side."

"Oh, I'm not joining your side. I don't want to kill all of the Six Eternal, only Anthes. I've seen what his power can do firsthand, more than once, and it's nothing good."

Orrick snorted, shaking his head. "Well, all of that doesn't matter right now. All that matters is they know something is going on here, and they are close. We need to get Honoria and Garren away from them until we are ready to strike."

"And you can't do it yourself in your current state," Oriana continued. "So you need me to try."

"Yes," Orrick sighed. "Exactly."

Oriana's face fell slightly, and Garren knew she was thinking about when the Storm Sea had stopped her, but she still nodded, grabbing Garren's hand and reaching for Honoria with the other. "Alright, it's a little jarring to go from one world to the next, so hold on tight and close your eyes."

She squeezed tightly onto Garren's hand, and he felt an energy wrapped around him, but nothing else. It was a tingling that seemed to crawl across him. He cracked an eye open only to find Orrick cross-armed and glaring at them.

"Well?" He said, "Are you going to do it?"

"I just tried," Oriana said, dropping both Garren and Honoria's hands. "I couldn't do it. It was like something was pushing against me, keeping me from moving into the next world. The same thing happened when I tried to get us through the Storm Sea. Is there a curse over this place?"

Orrick brought a hand up to rub at his temples. He sighed and then tilted his head, his hand falling to cup his chin as he narrowed his eyes. "Can you try only with Honoria?"

Oriana furrowed her brow but nodded, grabbing Honoria's hand.

"Ready?" she asked. Honoria gave a quick nod, and they both closed their eyes, but went nowhere for the second time.

Orrick growled, "Now try only the halfling."

"Orrick, I don't understand—"

"Just do it! I'm trying to figure something out." He yelled, and Oriana huffed, sticking her tongue out at her brother before grabbing Garren's hand.

The same tingling sensation rushed over him, but this time it was tenfold, and he felt his stomach lurch as suddenly everything fell away around him, as if it were becoming sand falling away into nothing. His body almost went numb, losing all feeling before his feet were back on solid ground again, and his body exploded into a million pins and needles, the weight of being back in a world slamming into him. He toppled forward, landing in a puddle of purple liquid.

"Fuck!" He yelled, standing and trying to wipe the purple goo from his knees and hands. "What was that?"

"We jumped worlds," Oriana said beside him. "I'm sorry, I didn't think anything would happen since, well, since it didn't work at the Storm Sea or with you and Honoria. I should have taken it a bit slower for your first time."

Garren was gasping in lungfuls of air as he heaved, almost losing the contents of his stomach completely before standing up straight and looking around at their surroundings. "Where are we? And why would it work with me and not her?"

"We'd best get back and find out. I brought us to the first world I could think of, but it isn't one I would want to stay in. This is where the Cherlkur resides."

"Why the fuck would you bring us here then? Let's go! I don't want to face one of those again."

Garren braced himself for another trip through time and space; luckily, this time it wasn't as bad. He still had that feeling of weightlessness and when they landed back in front of the waiting company, he held the vomit back, letting his body ease itself back into the world, the pins and needles becoming only a minor annoyance as he opened his eyes and took in Orrick, Honoria, and Atlas' faces.

"Well shit," Orrick said. "That leaves us right where we started. It seems that your dearest mother made it so that we are well and truly stuck here. Lovely. We'll move to plan B then."

"There is a plan B?" Honoria said.

"Well, sort of," Orrick shrugged. "I honestly thought that Oriana would be able to get us out of here, so I hadn't really thought we needed another way, but technically, there might be one. It may still not work, depending on what exactly Ada did to us, but it's worth a try."

"Well," Garren raised a brow. "What is it?"

"Balthar."

"Father's axe?"

"The axe?"

Garren glanced at her, both of their eyes wide and filled with a mixture of surprise and curiosity. Slowly, they turned their attention back to Orrick.

"Why would you leave his axe here? In the same world that we disarmed him of it?" Oriana questioned.

"Because it's one of the only places he wouldn't look. He wouldn't think us daft enough to leave it where we took it from him."

Oriana snorted, "I can't believe I'm saying this, but he's right. That was a smart idea, Orrick."

"Why does everyone always have such little faith in me? I have good ideas most of the time."

"Because you're an asshole." Garren chimed in, "And we all hate you. Except for Atlas over there. Weirdly, he doesn't seem to hate you at all."

Atlas flinched at the comment, looking out over the lake, pretending as if he hadn't heard the comment.

Orrick completely ignored it as well: "You might find your hate of me fading slightly when you hear what I did to the axe."

Garren narrowed his eyes at Orrick, but Honoria took the bait.

"What is this axe? And what did you do to it?"

"It's my father's battle axe, which he has imbued with his own Godly power, and we stole it from him several months ago. After I put him in the Dark World, I took his axe and had mother put a spell on it," Orrick said, smirking at Oriana.

"You did? How did you get her to do that?" Oriana raised a brow in question.

"I told her everything father did to both you and me. It was fairly easy to make her angry towards him. I mean, he is awful," Orrick sighed lazily. "But I had her put a spell on it so that if he did find it, as soon as he grips the handle, the axe will transport him to a new location of mother's choosing. It will continue throwing him through worlds until he realizes all he must do to stop it is pick the place he wants to go himself, and the spell will end."

Oriana laughed, and Garren frowned. "So where did you put it?"

"In the center of a volcano."

Garren pinched the bridge of his nose, "Like in the lava? Or...."

"Honestly, I don't understand why you all go straight to thinking I'm dumb. No, Halfling, I did not put it *in* the lava. It's simply magically suspended above the raging pit of fire."

"Oh, above it, even better. So you have to jump into the mouth of the volcano to get it, landing in lava." Garren snorted

"Does anyone ever listen to me?" Orrick threw up his hands and walked away from them.

Atlas finally spoke up for the first time and said, "Once you grab the hilt of the axe it will transport you to a place of your choosing, so yes, you will probably have to jump into the mouth of the volcano, but you won't land in the lava, you'll land in the place you are thinking about."

"Thank you!" Orrick yelled, "At least someone listens to me."

Honoria sighed, "I'm not sure I'm fully following, but I would do just about anything to get home, so when do we go and get this axe thing?"

"We should all have one more good night's rest before heading out," Oriana suggested.

"It's settled then. We will leave at first light." Orrick nodded his agreement.

As everyone settled in for the evening, Garren watched the love of his life and the bane of his existence catching up as if they hadn't seen each other in centuries. He snorted, finding amusement in the fact that just a few days before, he had said he never wanted to see Orrick's face again, so of course that's the person they find at the end of their journey. At least the ringing in his ears had stopped.

That thought had him looking over at his sister, sleeping soundly several paces away from him by the strange green flames of the fire. He found himself wondering what her life had been like, how different it was from his, having grown up with their mother. He sighed and closed his eyes, trying to sleep at least a few hours before sunrise.

Whispers from Orrick and Oriana's direction drew him, keeping him from slumber. They were talking in hushed tones that he was too far away to hear, so he slowly scooted himself closer to eavesdrop and heard Orrick whisper, "Listen, getting Garren and Honoria out of here and hidden from the Gods until we can figure things out is our only chance of saving the Cosmos. We need time to make sure that the triplets fare on the right side of fate. On our side."

"They will," Oriana said back.

"We don't know that, yet, which is why we must hide them from the God's until we know. So if anything happens on our way to the axe, get them out, Oriana. Leave me behind, just get them out."

"You would sacrifice yourself?"

Quietly and hesitantly, he replied, "I would do anything to save my creations."

Garren furrowed his brow. It seemed Orrick might not be exactly who Garren thought he was after all. Maybe, just maybe, the God of chaos had a heart, or at least some beating ember in his chest. As he drifted off to sleep, he wondered if it was time he gave Orrick a chance.

21

ORRICK

T he moon hung low overhead, glowing with a sage hue, marking the impending green moon that was probably just a day or two away. It was a time when the Elementalists' powers surged to unparalleled heights. He had crafted the unique moon at the beginning for Oriana, making it only to grace the night sky on rare occasions, bringing with it a potent energy.

"Can you feel it?" Atlas came beside Orrick, sitting next to him in front of the fire.

"Feel what?"

"The power growing in your veins?" Atlas clenched his fists, the ground beneath them rumbling before he opened them, and the sand stilled. "I've always loved the night of the green moon. Although I think this one might be different."

"What do you mean?" Orrick frowned.

"This is the most restless the Elementalists have ever been. War is inevitable, and what better time for it than during the green moon?"

Orrick rubbed a hand down his face and shook his head. "What happened over these last centuries, Atlas?"

"This has been building since the beginning, Orrick." His tone was harsh, nearing accusatory.

There was a heavy silence between them. Atlas was correct, of course. This place was born from his own selfish ambition. Orrick's life with the Gods had never been easy. He wanted them so badly to recognize his immense ability, to accept him as one of their own. So, when he created this world and they only laughed in his face, calling this place nothing more than 'a good effort' and 'a cute trick', he lost it. All that seething anger and hatred had been poured into these beings, his original children, molded to populate this world. That venomous loathing had not left him since that fateful day. It only festered, carving a permanent mask of indifference and cruelty that clung to his features.

"Why did you leave?" Atlas's voice pulled Orrick from his thoughts.

He looked into Atlas' violet eyes and could feel the pain in his gaze. Orrick quickly looked away. "It's complicated."

Much of his life lay hidden, veiled from all those around him. He never had anyone to share it with, never allowed anyone in, keeping his true self locked away deep in the labyrinth of his mind. It was better that way—safer. The closest person he had was Oriana. He almost snorted at that, realizing how sad his life really was. He had dwelled in a constant state of loneliness, enacting his own agendas into the Cosmos, but to what end? Was it all even worth it if he still ended up alone once the Gods were dead?

"It's been eight hundred and seventy-three years," Atlas said beside him.

"I—I didn't mean to stay away so long." He breathed.

"I've been trapped here, forced to live in this hellhole, stuck in the middle of countless wars, surrounded by Elementalists... without you." Atlas said, "And then when you finally come back, you don't even remember me."

Orrick looked back at Atlas, the green flames dancing, sending a glow that illuminated the haunting sadness on his face. He reached out to touch Atlas' face, but he batted Orrick's hand away.

"Atlas, it wasn't like that..." He tried to grab his hand, but Atlas yanked it away, the green glow showing the frown etched on his face.

"I just need to know why."

Orrick sighed, letting his head fall into his hands. "I didn't forget you. I could never forget you."

"Then what happened? Where have you been, Orrick?" His voice cracked with emotion, and Orrick's heart lurched. He couldn't take it any longer. Orrick grabbed Atlas and pulled him into an embrace, just before the tears spilled free.

"I'm so sorry," Orrick sobbed. He didn't even try to stop the emotions as every single bottled-up feeling poured out of him. He couldn't stop it; the floodgates were open. Everything he had held inside was coming out in this moment, with the one person he had missed the most, the one he had shared everything with once upon a time. He had lost sight of everything, blinded by his need to be in power. His mind recalled what Honoria had said to him, *'Your thirst for power is insatiable'*. She was right.

Atlas softened against him, returning the embrace, tightly.

"I wanted to kill the Gods," Orrick whispered in Atlas' ear.

Atlas pulled again from him, his face a blank slate, "You left me for nearly nine hundred years for that?" He shook his head with a huff. "Did you even succeed?"

"No," Orrick breathed, looking away from him. "But I'm close."

Atlas was quiet, and Orrick looked back up at his face. There was no anger there, no annoyance; there was only longing and acceptance.

Why had he left Atlas for so long? He should have come back for him.

"Will you help me?" Orrick suddenly blurted, and Atlas' brows rose in surprise.

"I—do you want me to help you?"

"Yes," he sighed. "More than anything."

Atlas's smile lit up his entire face, and his eyes twinkled with excitement. "I will go with you anywhere, Orrick. Forever and always."

Orrick grabbed him and pulled Atlas into his waiting lips, kissing him soundly before breaking away and saying, "You are perfection. You know that, right?"

Atlas only smirked, "Well, you did create me to be."

Orrick snorted, "I created you to be me, so yes, *we* are perfect."

He leaned his head on Orrick's shoulder, and they stood there enjoying the peace of being together, the only ones awake.

"You should sleep. Tomorrow will be a long day for us all."

"Will you lie down with me?"

Orrick smiled softly at him and gave a gentle nod, and Atlas pulled him down into the sand, wrapping his arms around his waist and settling his head in the crook of Orrick's neck.

The warmth of Atlas against him sent a wave of contentment through Orrick. Something he hadn't felt in a long time. His life had been long and full of loneliness, but he was realizing for the first time that the cold that surrounded him, seeping into his bones and icing over his heart, was self-inflicted. He had alienated himself from everyone who had ever tried to get close, even the one being he created for himself, Atlas.

Orrick pulled Atlas closer, holding on to that warmth, the peace of being with someone who, after everything he'd done, still cared. He listened to Atlas' gentle breathing as he drifted off to sleep, and with a sigh, placed a kiss on his forehead.

How had everything gotten so fucked up? The weight of everything at play pushed against him, making his head throb relentlessly from the buildup of pressure. If not even Oriana's power could get him and Honoria out of this world, then what had Ada actually done to them? And the nagging question, the one that burned into the back of his mind, was why? Why would Ada trap both Honoria and himself in this place together? He was missing something. He didn't know much about Ada, but he could venture that she always had a reason for what she did. Was she trying to force the prophecy to fall in her favor somehow?

There were just too many unknowns. Too much was being left to chance, and he was caught in a web of in-decision, paralyzed by uncertainty, not knowing the right moves. His instincts were all he had to rely on, but with Atlas and Oriana by his side, they could navigate the un-known together.

Even though countless questions remained unan-swered, drifting in the ether to taunt him, two crucial tasks demanded immediate attention. They needed to retrieve Anthes' axe, and they needed to find the final Zydell sib-ling—Ari.

Orrick did not sleep for the rest of the night. The creeping feeling that tonight would be the last quiet, peaceful night he would have in a long time hung over him like a noose. He wanted to savor every moment of it, with Atlas warm and secure in his arms and everyone sleeping soundly around him. So he stared up at the sky, watching as light crept into darkness and gave way to dawn. Watching until the green moon was nothing more than a barely perceptible blip in an ocean of clear blue, and the sun shone brightly as it peaked over the treetops.

Atlas stirred at the morning light, and everyone else began to rise from their slumber. Orrick sighed and got up, extinguishing the dying green flames of the fire with a single wave of his hand. His final night of peace had gone by too fast. He turned to everyone and said simply, "It's time to go." Before walking into the dense landscape of trees, ready to fight for not only himself but for the people at his side and the creations that surrounded him.

22
GARREN

Travel—it was all they seemed to do lately. In fact, it was all Garren ever really seemed to do, even before meeting Oriana. Garren wasn't just tired, he was physically and mentally exhausted.

The past months had been a whirlwind of discovery and emotion, and now he had come halfway across the world to find a sister he never thought he would meet in a million years waiting for him. Why was life getting more complicated every day?

He longed to go back home, to the place that Oriana created for them. He wanted to smell the fresh pine of the forest, swim in the warmth of the bay, just relax and stay in one place for once in his life. Was that too much to ask for?

There was a strange energy that hummed through the air here, and the trees were a paler green, shorter than those in Svakland. Their leaves were large, causing them to spread out more above them, and Garren hated them.

He suddenly had an overwhelming feeling of anxiety and dread crashing over him. It felt as if he were drowning on land, the weight of everything ahead was heavy, and he suddenly wanted nothing more than to leave it all behind. To hide away forever somewhere remote where no God, and no demon could get to him.

"Would you stop moping?" Oriana said, elbowing him in the ribs. "You're literally grumbling under your breath. What is wrong with you?"

"I think it's time for me to retire."

She choked on her own spit, half coughing, half laughing, "What do you mean, retire? From what?"

He frowned at her, "From this."

"Hiking?"

He let out a heavy sigh, slumping his shoulders, "Never mind, Oriana."

"Stop," she grabbed his hand, pulling him away from the group as they continued on ahead of them. "What is going on with you? Is it Orrick? Or is it Honoria?"

"It's everything. It's Orrick, it's Honoria, it's your father, it's the demons, it's all of it."

"Hey," she whispered, her face softening with concern, her hand lifting to rest on his cheek.

Garren closed his eyes, leaning into the touch, turning his head to kiss her palm before grabbing her around the waist and pulling her against him. "I just want you and me together, in peace."

She stood on her tippy toes, wrapping her arms around his neck and leaning her forehead against his. "We are together and always will be."

He sighed, "Yes, but I don't want to do any of this anymore. I just want to be at our home, no monsters, no siblings, no... nothing. You and I together, in our home with no more fighting, but with... a family."

Oriana startled slightly, "Garren, I... I don't know what to say."

"Say you'll go back with me. Let's forget all of this and just go." His words came out as a plea, "We don't even have to go back to Elscar. We can find a place for just us, and be blissfully alone, and one day build a family together there."

She looked away from him, shaking her head as she pushed away, but he held on tightly, not letting her go.

"It's a wonderful dream, Garren, but our lives will never be peaceful. They will never be normal, because of who we are."

Garren finally released her, running a hand through his hair as he turned his back to her.

"Where is this coming from all of a sudden? Just days ago, you wanted to go save the people trapped beneath the sea, and happily fought several monsters." She touched his shoulder, urging him to spin back and face her. "What happened?"

He let his head fall, looking down at the moss-covered earth with a humorless chuckle, "I realized it's never going to end. There will always be something pulling us this way and that. A demon here, a God there, a curse that threatens us all, a new discovery at every turn, and a strange world-ending prophecy that shows up out of the blue." He looked back up, locking on her green eyes, showing her the tiredness in his gaze. "It's a loop, an endless loop that brings nothing but misery."

Oriana stared at him, silent, her face frozen in a mask of disbelief.

"I didn't have anything to live for before, Oriana. Demon hunting was my life, everyone I had ever loved was gone, and the only purpose I could find to keep living was to save others from the same heartache I experienced." Garren walked closer to her again, "But now I have something. I have you, and I don't want to lose you."

Tears welled, making her eyes almost glow in the sunlight before spilling free. Garren reached for her, wiping them away with his thumb.

"I'm not going anywhere, Garren."

"But if the prophecy your brother speaks of is real..."

"Garren," she grabbed his hands again, kissing along his knuckles. "The Gods won't stop, they will come for you and your sister at every turn. The only way to find the peace you speak of is to end the prophecy. They know who you are, they know you exist, so the prophecy can be fulfilled. If we hide, they will find us. We would be on the run forever. What kind of life would that be for us?" She paused before adding, "For a family?"

"Hey, you two!" Orrick yelled through the trees, his white hair a mere speck in the distance. "Are you coming or not?"

Oriana took a deep breath as she rose up to her tippy toes and placed a gentle, lingering kiss on his lips. He closed his eyes, sighing at the contact, at the taste of her, and deepened it as he pulled her flush against his chest.

"Eww, gross! Get a fucking room." Orrick's voice echoed through the forest, "Let's just leave them. They can catch up when they are done."

Oriana giggled against his lips, breaking their kiss and looking up into Garren's silver eyes, her face growing serious, "Listen, I hear you and once we figure out this prophecy and how to help your sister and my brother, we can come back to this. But what's happening now, in this moment, is far more serious than you or I, Garren. This prophecy is something that has been intertwined with your fate; you can't run from it. No one can. The work of the Cosmos is at play here, and we have to see it through."

Garren kissed her once more before letting her go, but he held on tight to her hand as they continued walking along the path to catch up to the others. He knew she was right, but he didn't want her to be. Whatever this prophecy was, it involved not only him but also his siblings. It was something big enough to have Orrick spooked. Garren had never seen the God of chaos so panicked. He wasn't acting like himself. Even what Garren had overheard him say to Oriana last night. *Get them out, Oriana. Leave me behind, but just get them out.* There had been fear laced in his words. Garren still didn't fully understand what the prophecy meant. It seemed that it defied one's own free choice, at least the way Orrick had spoken about it. He made it seem like Garren and his siblings wouldn't be able to say no to the God's when the time came.

"You should talk more to Honoria, you know." Oriana said, pulling Garren from his circling thoughts, "You've been given a gift by her being here. She's your family."

He simply grunted, and she squeezed his hand before letting go and running to catch up to Orrick and Atlas, who were at the front of the group.

Garren glanced at Honoria, who was walking several paces in front of him. She was a part of this too, and it seemed like they would be stuck with one another for the foreseeable future, or at least until this prophecy was dealt with. It couldn't come soon enough.

He watched as Honoria's hair shifted to a dark blue beneath the rays of the sun that filtered in through the canopy of leaves above them. It turned from the darkest black to a deep blue just like his own.

She stopped and looked back at him with a brow raised. "Are you staring at me, Garren?"

Heat rose to his face, and he smiled awkwardly, "I–It's just I haven't seen someone else with that shade of hair before."

"Well, we do come from the same parents," she smirked. "So it would make sense we have similar features."

He caught up to her and they continued, pushing away brush and vines as a cool breeze whistled its way around them, chasing away the heat of the sun high overhead.

"The dark hair must come from our mother, then."

"Dark hair is a Zydell trait. Everyone back home has varying shades of onyx and midnight blue hair."

"What is she like?" Garren asked, "Our mother."

Honoria's brows drew together, and she slowed her pace. "Powerful, severe, and serene."

Garren frowned at her answer; none of those things were tender or loving. They were simply facts, random traits.

"What is life like in your home?"

"It's," she bit her bottom lip and closed her eyes, "lonely."

Garren was surprised by that answer. He had assumed the Zydells to be more endearing, nurturing, a far better, powerful race than the Gods, but possibly the Zydells were more like the Gods than anyone really knew. Honoria was quite literally the only one in their group who knew them.

"I'm sorry to hear that," Garren offered, not knowing what to say.

Honoria took a deep breath, exhaling with a weak laugh, "It's the whole reason I'm in this mess. I was lonely, and Orrick took advantage of that. I knew there was something off about him, but I didn't care. I was so desperate for any tiny bit of attention that I welcomed his advances with open arms." She swallowed back the emotion Garren could see welling on her face. "I am a fool."

A fiery rage welled in Garren's chest as his heart ached for her. She was in pain, stuck in a strange place, with people she didn't even know, and it was all Orrick's doing.

"I'll kill him for you."

"What?!" she squealed. "I don't want him dead. Cosmos, you're very violent, aren't you?"

"I'd say that's also Orrick's doing." Garren grumbled, "If it weren't for him, my parents would still be alive and I wouldn't have spent my life hunting down and killing every beast I could get my hands on."

"We're quite the pair, aren't we?" Honoria smiled, eyes crinkling at the corners. It was so genuine that he found himself smiling back. "Neither of us seems to have had an easy life, even so far apart. I wonder how our supposed other sibling fared, wherever they are."

Garren snorted, "Probably better than us if they are lucky enough to have never met Orrick."

Their laughter rose together, intertwining like a harmonious melody that soothed him. He could feel a bond forming between them, binding their spirits into some-thing tangible—a sibling connection.

Orrick turned and glared at them from up ahead, "What are you laughing at back there?"

"Nothing!" they said at the same time and then turned back to one another, laughing again.

Garren smiled at the kinship settling between them as they continued in companionable silence, just happy to be in one another's company.

The sun was now low in the sky, hitting them through the trees just in their line of sight. They had walked for many hours, stopping only for brief breaks to relieve themselves and fetch water. What little food Garren and Oriana had with them had now dwindled to a mere three apples after the group had gotten into their supplies. Garren's stomach grumbled. He could use a hot meal, preferably some meat, right about now.

"What are your gifts?" Honoria suddenly pulled him from his wandering thoughts, "Besides the super strength, of course. When Orrick brought it up before, you interrupted him."

Garren blew out a quick huff of surprise. "Caught that, did you?"

She smiled softly in response.

"To be completely honest, I don't really know. I've only used it once."

"Really?" Honoria tilted her head, curious. "Now that I know about mine, all I want to do is practice, perfect it until I can control it." She grew quiet before continuing, "My entire life, I was known as the one Zydell with no gifts. I grew up as an outcast, unable to participate in anything related to power. It's funny how it took coming here to discover my gifts. Maybe this trip was a small blessing after all."

Garren smiled weakly at her, "I think mine is more of a curse."

"What do you mean?"

"The first and only time I tried to use it, I completely crushed Orrick's arm beyond recognition. It looked like an animal had chewed it up and spat it back out."

Honoria's brows rose as her eyes widened, "That doesn't sound like a curse to me. What I wouldn't give to crush Orrick's arm, or any part of him, really."

Garren snorted, "Yeah, well, at least it was only him, and I was able to put it back. But I've been too scared to try again. I don't want to hurt someone I love accidentally. I don't really know much about it or truly how to use it."

She nodded, "Why don't we go somewhere far away from the others and try? Maybe we can help each other to understand our gifts better."

"I–I don't think that's a good idea," Garren rubbed at the back of his neck.

"Why not? If you don't try, you'll never learn to control it."

Garren sighed, "I don't want it."

"Don't want it?" Honoria frowned, "But you could..."

A massive explosion echoed around them, cutting off their conversation as a wave of air almost knocked all of them to the ground. A plume of flame and smoke rose above the trees up ahead.

"What the fuck was that?" Garren growled only to look up and see Orrick, Atlas, and Oriana running to the edge of the forest. The force came from the direction of the beach several paces in front of them.

"Come on," Honoria said, grabbing his hand and running to follow them.

Garren grumbled as twigs and leaves smacked him in the face, snapping as they rushed through the brush, but he didn't let go of Honoria's hand, not until they made it to the forest's edge and looked down at the beach below.

Laid out before them was a smoking wasteland of blood and ashen sand.

Every element was thrown through the fray of war. Fire blasted, water hovered encircling other Elementalists like a raging storm, whipping at them like snapping snakes. The wind howled as Elementalists were swept into the air by large gusts only to be dropped from high above, crashing to the earth below. The ground continually shifted beneath them like tremors in the earth, swallowing entire groups of people as large boulders were flung out, crushing anyone in their path.

"Bleeding skies," Atlas breathed. "War has finally come to Emmoria."

Thousands upon thousands of Elementalists were locked in battle. The war stretched farther down the beach than Garren could see.

"I didn't think this day would come so soon, and in this same spot," Atlas murmured, his eyes sweeping the scene below, as if he were hoping it wasn't truly there.

"What do you mean?" Garren questioned.

"This has happened before, two centuries ago. We call it the great purge." Atlas' eyes were glazed, staring off into the distance, as if lost in a faraway memory.

"What happened?" Honoria asked, brows drawn together.

"The Salamanders burnt through entire Elemental armies, making this place what we call the Scorched Lands. It's a dead piece of earth, a graveyard of our ancestors." His voice was quiet as he continued, "And now the purge continues."

"We need to help them," Honoria whispered. She was watching the battle with horror in her eyes. "This has to be stopped."

"This war has been brewing for centuries; there is no stopping what's to come," Orrick said. There was a strange tone to his voice, almost as if he were sad.

"You could do something," Honoria snapped, and Garren could have sworn Orrick flinched at her words.

"What exactly am I to do without my powers?" He growled back. "I am no help to them now."

"I must go and fight with my brothers," Atlas suddenly interrupted, taking a step forward, but Orrick grabbed his arm, pinning him with a pleading gaze. Garren couldn't see Atlas' face, but he could hear his grunt as he ripped his arm from Orrick's grasp and sprinted down the sandy slope in front of them using his earthly gifts the entire way. He threw out rock and stone, shooting spiked earth up from the ground with each step to spear those in close range.

"Well, that's probably the last we'll ever see of him," Orrick drawled, looking down to inspect his fingers. "Damn, I knew I broke a nail back at the lake."

Garren narrowed his eyes at him, noticing the way his jaw clenched. He was putting on a front; there was some bond between him and Atlas that meant more than he was letting on.

Honoria smacked him on the back of the head, the sound of it so loud it echoed in the forest behind them.

"What the fuck?" Orrick groused, rubbing at the back of his head.

"You're an ass. I'm going down to help," Honoria huffed.

"Try not to kill them all, won't you? We wouldn't want that on your conscience."

"I'm not going to kill any of them," Honoria bit back. "I'm going to stop them from killing each other."

"Honoria," Garren cut in. "It isn't your responsibility. These people won't stop fighting. Listen to what Atlas said; this war has been brewing for centuries. There isn't anything to be done."

She turned her glare on him, and tendrils of her power seeped out; he could feel the energy begin to wrap around him. "I can't just watch as an entire civilization massacres itself, Garren. They need help."

Garren swallowed hard at that, because wasn't that what he had done his whole life? It's quite literally what he wanted to be doing right now by going and helping the people locked beneath the Storm Sea. She was right; even if these people were bound for war, the casualties would be innumerable, and if he could help save even one, he should.

Honoria sent Orrick a parting glare that made even Garren back away, wearing her power like a cloak. It felt strange, though, like something he knew. Orrick said she was like a siphon for the power of those around her, and he literally saw her turn into Oriana's bloodlust. Was it possible that she was using his gifts right now? The ones he himself refused to use. Garren shuddered at the thought and watched as she stormed straight down the slope and into the elemental war.

23

ORRICK

The air crackled around them with a pulsing energy. Sand sprayed as flames danced across the beach, only to be swallowed by water as it moved like a serpent, weaving through the battlefield. It sliced and snapped as it went, until it became a shimmering ball of liquid, picking up several Salamanders that tried desperately to break free.

Rocks flew like spears, fast and lethal, blood spraying in their wake. A raging wind swirled along the beach, scattering Undina and Gnomes as it flung them into the sky. The acrid scent of burnt flesh and the metallic smell of blood were heavy in the air.

The war had only just begun.

A low rumble shook the earth beneath their feet, spreading out across the shore, halting the fighting as Elementalists attempted to regain their footing.

Orrick could only watch as the ground split in two, swallowing hundreds of his children, the rushing waves of the ocean following them into the abyss before it closed back up, trapping them beneath rock and sand.

"Honoria's right," Garren said beside him. "This is more than just a war. They are going to annihilate one another."

Orrick stayed quiet.

"They've always been this way," Oriana's voice was low as she watched the battle with sadness in her eyes. "Since the beginning."

"I made them this way," Orrick whispered. "Full of hatred and desire. This is what happens when that's all there is."

"Why am I not surprised?" Garren shook his head. "So they'll never truly stop, will they?"

"Not unless something changes inside of them. War is woven into their very essence."

"You should never have been given the power you possess." Garren spat, his eyes narrowing with disdain. The words hit Orrick like a sack full of rocks, but instead of anger, a bark of laughter burst from his lips. The irony was just too much because that power was gone, stripped away, and he wasn't sure if he would ever figure out how to reclaim it.

Oriana sighed, placing a gentle hand on his back. "We'll try to help them, Orrick. We will save as many as we can."

Orrick looked away from her, swallowing hard against the heavy emotions clogging his throat. All he could do was watch as Oriana threw out her enchantments, confusing the Elementalists on the edge of the battle, Garren's sword singing as he unsheathed it, and they both charged into the battle.

A heaviness settled deep within Orrick's center, squeezing the air from his lungs as he gazed into the chaos. His body refused to move, and he struggled to swallow the knot in his throat. These were his children, his creations—his responsibility, and he failed them. This was all his fault. He was not a great creator, not even a good one. Who made living things and then just left them to be on their own, hoping they wouldn't kill themselves?

A figure suddenly pushed through the edge of the battle and came right up to him. Orrick's eyes were glazed with the reality of what was happening in front of him, but he blinked, and there was Atlas. He was blood-soaked and breathing heavily, but his presence was somehow a comfort. It was like a tangible thing that Orrick was now acutely aware of whenever he was near.

Atlas shifted in the sand until he stood beside Orrick, looking out at the scene. "Why did you make the Gnomes so powerful? They have always had the upper hand in these centuries of wars."

"You know why," Orrick said, not looking at Atlas' face, not wanting to know his reaction.

Just then, a group of Salamanders charged a waiting group of Sylphs, throwing sparks and flame, attacking from the higher ground. However, several of the Salamanders were not wielding fire, but instead, rock and stone were flung like darts into the backs of the charging Salamanders. They were Gnomes in disguise. Atlas was right; the Gnomes were a force to be reckoned with. They were the strongest of the Elementalists on land, but their one weakness was water. It was why they lived in the north, within the mountains, away from any large water source. Not only could they literally move the earth, but they could shapeshift, taking on the appearance of any Elementalist.

Atlas had been the first. Not only the first Elementalist, but the first walking, talking, magic-wielding being he had ever created. He wanted someone to be a companion, someone who could change and move the elements of this world with him, so he had given Atlas the power to do so. He was a Gnome, but he was far more than that. He was the first Elementalist, more powerful, more Godlike than the rest. He could do so much more than any of them, and yet he often didn't.

As if sensing Orrick's thoughts, Atlas grunted, "I should go help my brethren. I was hoping you would come with me."

Orrick's eyes lingered on Atlas, etching every detail of his face into his memory, yet he remained rooted to the ground. Atlas, knowing Orrick more intimately than anyone else, understood the futility of asking again. With a heavy sigh, Atlas bowed his head in reluctant acceptance and turned away, leaving Orrick where he stood to watch Atlas as the melee swallowed him up.

Orrick gazed up at the sky. It was clear and vast, as the last traces of sunlight slipped beneath the horizon. The green moon loomed, growing bright as night descended, casting an eerie glow across the landscape. The emerald moon appeared only once every four hundred years. To Orrick, it symbolized creation because it was the moon he painted into the sky when he first created the Elemental-ists. It was meant to be a beacon of hope and joy, but it had shifted into a harbinger of death and war.

He looked back at the brutality in front of him, where chaos reigned and the violence intensified with each heart-beat. Blood sprayed, raining down and covering the battle-field as heads burst like overripe fruit. The bitter scent of charred earth rose into the air, mingled with the anguished screams of his children. Orrick simply watched, unable to tear his stare away from the scene as his creations tore each other apart mercilessly.

He had made a mistake. This place, these people—it was all a mistake, one that was tearing at the organ beating rapidly in his chest. He had to do something, he needed to change things. He needed to save them, to fix it.

Clenching his fists into tight balls at his side, until he could no longer bear what his eyes were witnessing, Orrick yelled out as flames licked up his arms and legs, spreading across every surface of his body until he was a living, breathing, raging ball of fire. His vision went green and the only thing going through his mind was—*save them.*

Orrick charged into the Elemental war, and this time, instead of killing everything in his path, he built up walls of flames around them, dividing up Gnome, Undina, Sylph, and Salamander into groupings away from one another. He was stopping the killing. Just like with the Elementalists, the emerald moon in the sky was strengthening his power, and he wove himself throughout the entire battle, trying against all hope to stop this war.

There was just one small problem in his plan—the Salamanders. Even though his fire sorcery was different from the other fire wielders, marked by its green hue, it was only fire, and the Salamanders simply walked through his maze of flames directly into the convenient pockets of trapped Elementalist that Orrick had stupidly set up for them.

"Fuck," Orrick whispered, halting halfway through the mass of Elementalists, realizing his error. The world around him faded away until the only sound that pierced through the void was the blood-curdling screams of his children as they were set on fire by the Salamanders. Their cries tore something in his soul, something that would haunt him for eternity.

"Orrick!" Someone called from the dunes beside him, it was Atlas. "What have you done?"

"I was trying to help." His voice came out like a plea. He had unknowingly given the fire wielders the upper hand.

"Do you see this earth beneath our feet? Black and charred, dead and useless?" Atlas said in a guttural tone. "This is what happens when the fire cannot be contained. It envelopes everything, burning until there is nothing left. You've just helped the Salamanders in their goal to burn every last Elementalist to this ashen ground and join their ancestors beneath this cursed place."

A lump formed in Orrick's throat, and he was unable to utter anything but, "Help me. Fix it."

Atlas growled, closing his eyes and lifting his head up to the darkened night sky, soaking in the green beams of the moon.

Orrick could practically feel the energy building within Atlas; it was like a tangible thing pressing against him.

When Atlas opened his eyes again, looking back at the labyrinth of fire streaked across the beach, his eyes glowed purple, and he grunted, his nostrils flaring before he stomped a foot hard onto the beach. The sound reverberated violently around them, resembling the explosive cracking of rock and the roar of thunder as the dark sand rose above everyone. For a moment, the chaos of battle halted, as the Elementalists stared in awe as half of the beach hovered threateningly above them. With the snap of Atlas' finger the sand fell, smothering the flames as quickly as Orrick had set them ablaze.

"Don't do that again," Atlas bit out the words before disappearing once again into the frey of blood and bodies, leaving Orrick only to watch, paralyzed by the weight of helplessness that threatened to crush him where he stood.

24

GARREN

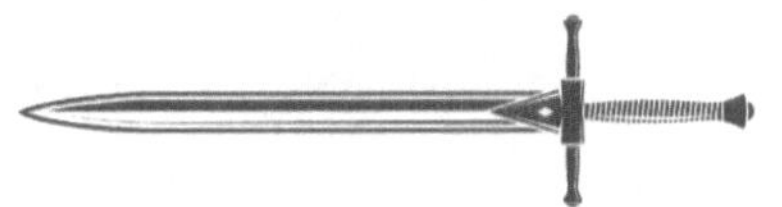

The air hummed with an electric force around them, charged by the swarms of Elementalists whose power was thick in the atmosphere. It felt almost tangible, like he could reach out and pluck a thread of their power from thin air. Flames licked across the battlefield hungrily, swallowing everything and everyone in their path. Surging waves of water crashed down upon the expanse, smothering the fire before it could spread too far. A fierce gust of wind slammed into Garren, knocking him hard onto the blood-soaked earth, his sword slipping from his grasp and clattering several paces away.

Gritting his teeth, Garren pushed himself back up, but a hand of jagged rock and dirt erupted from the ground, clamping tightly around his leg. He strained against its grip, trying desperately to break free, but the solid earth held firm, remaining intact.

Beside him, Oriana let out a feral growl that echoed above the battle. He watched as she tore through the Elementalists, a mere blur of teeth and claws, not even blinking an eye at the destruction she left in her wake.

Garren grunted, his jaw clenched as he grabbed the stone hand, forcing it to crack and crumble beneath his strength. Freed at last, he jumped up to his feet, retrieving his blade just in time to deflect a barrage of razor-sharp stones hurtling toward him.

A man with bright purple hair coiled atop his head and pure rage in his violet gaze pushed through the crowd straight for him. Garren backed away, sword poised for battle.

A shard of earth shot out of the sand, and he dove to the side, rolling back up to his feet just before another spike erupted from the ground with lethal intent, narrowly missing him.

Garren had fought against monsters, demons, every creature thrown at him, hell he had even faced Gods, but he had never faced the elements in a battle. This style of fighting was foreign to him. These people wielded the elements as their weapons. Garren didn't spot one sword or hear a single clang of steel through the fray of war. Only water, fire, earth, and air, all things that his sword was no use fighting against. He wasn't able to get close enough to anyone to land a blow. He had never felt so helpless, so underprepared for a battle in his life.

For the first time, his blade was failing him, and he didn't know what to do, or whose side he was even on.

Wind howled like a ferocious beast, pushing against him, bringing with it the scent of the sea. He held firm, planting his feet into the sand as it slammed him with gust after gust of cold slicing air, until suddenly it stopped, and he watched the earth Elementalist who had been attacking him moments before get yanked backward and flung far out into the ocean.

Garren took the opportunity to sprint back to a spot at the forest's edge, several paces away from the battle, regain his focus, and figure out a game plan. His breathing was labored, adrenaline thrumming through his veins as he scanned down the beach for Oriana and Honoria.

Something caught his attention. Honoria was in the very center of the battle, and she wasn't holding back. Fire, water, earth, and air, all of the elements were at her fingertips, and she was throwing them out like a vicious storm. Bodies were thrown and picked up in a torrent of wind, as a ring of fire surrounded her, blocking any Elementalist from getting close.

She was syphoning their powers, using her gift to fight against them.

Garren sheathed his blade along his back. It was no use to him against these people. The only way to fight them was to use his power. He glanced down at his hands, where they trembled with the thought. How could he possibly control the force within him? He didn't want to kill the people, only stop them from being able to fight and use their gifts.

When he tapped into his power in the monastery with Orrick, he had crushed the God's arm. Garren frowned, wrestling with the knowledge of what his abilities were. He knew that he was extraordinarily strong and capable of incredible feats, such as holding his breath underwater for nearly an hour. His skin was nearly impervious to being cut, and he healed almost instantly, but that seemed to be only a fragment of his full power. The other half, he didn't understand. It somehow involved change or alteration. He was torn; he never wanted to uncover the mystery of his gifts, but maybe now he had no choice. Could he avoid inflicting the same harm he had on Orrick's arm, and instead find a way to change these people somehow? The thought unsettled him, leaving him caught between fear and necessity. He couldn't bear to stand here helpless.

Orrick's face, twisted in pain, suddenly swam in his vision, and he shook it away.

Garren groaned with a heavy sigh, turning away from the battle, leaning his back against a tree. His mind was a whirlwind of thought as he tried to figure out what he should do. A part of him longed to walk away, to escape the chaos and forget about his unwanted gifts altogether. But he couldn't leave Oriana and his sister. He was no coward.

It wasn't in his nature to abandon those in need. He had to help. It was like a compulsion, an active force pushing him forward. No matter how much he tried to shake it off and turn a blind eye, the urge to help those who couldn't help themselves felt like both a burden and a destiny—one he couldn't escape.

He thought back to his conversation with Oriana earlier in the day. At that moment, everything felt so bleak, like his world was ending before it had even begun.

Garren snorted, inhaling deeply as he tried to concentrate on the task at hand. There was one thing he knew for sure—Oriana was right. There was a prophecy in the works, and if they were to stop it, he needed to accept who he was. He was both God and Zydell, and it was time he started acting like it.

Garren straightened, his chest swelling with an unfamiliar sensation, a mixture of clarity and peace that was both strange and comforting. With renewed vigor, he turned back to the battlefield where each of the elements were being wielded into deadly weapons, striking with lethal precision. He concentrated on the Elementalists' movements, on how they manipulated the elements, and on the way their energies flowed, imagining how he could alter those movements. If he could focus on a single group and keep his intentions clear in his mind, then perhaps he could use his gifts and change the elements themselves without harming anyone.

A surge of renewed energy coursed through him, and he locked onto a group of the blue Elementalists who were using water like whips, slicing and cutting into the flesh of retreating air Elementalists. He honed in on them, steadying his mind until all he could see were the five water users and their whips. A bitter cold welled within him. It was familiar, the same frost that had moved through his blood, latching onto his bones in the monastery with Orrick. He didn't flinch at the feel, but instead welcomed it like an old friend. His nostrils flared, and he thought of exactly what he wanted to do to the Elementalists. With a single breath of air, each of the whips of water that were spilling blood vanished, replaced by bubbles that floated up above the water sorcerers, shimmering green under the moon's light.

The Elementalists yelled out in confusion, and Garren watched as they continued to pull water from the sea and try to use it as a weapon, but every time, the water only turned to bubbles in their hands.

Garren sighed in relief and looked down at his hands, still tingling with power, before shifting his gaze back up to the battle. A slow smile spread across his lips as he unleashed his power on the unsuspecting Elementalists below.

25

ORRICK

Darkness had finally beaten out the light, descending like a thick, suffocating blanket around them. The moon was now at its peak, full and looming, casting an eerie emerald glow over the battlefield like an omen as the Elementalists only grew stronger beneath its gaze. Each of the elements only continued to clash like an unrelenting symphony of chaos and destruction, with no end in sight.

A gruesome tapestry of blood and lifeless bodies now sprawled across the sand, transforming the beach into a horrific landscape. Exhaustion bore down on Orrick like a crushing weight, pressing against his back, squeezing his shoulders, and pounding relentlessly inside his skull. He stood helpless, a mere spectator to the carnage as they annihilated themselves into oblivion. His heart throbbed with a searing agony, feeling as if it were being ripped mercilessly from his chest. It had to stop, but in his current state, without his Godly gifts, he was powerless against the tide of destruction.

Lightning shot down from the sky, drawing Orrick's attention. A figure walked from behind the smoke across the battlefield—Honoria. She looked feral with a focused determination on her face. Another bolt of lightning speared the ground near her, forcing the advancing Elementalists to back away. It was her; she wasn't hitting them with the bolts but using the lightning to make them retreat. Her pants were in taters, blowing behind her as she strode toward him. When she finally reached him, he didn't know what to say other than, "It needs to stop."

She cocked her head to the side, eyes boring into him with an intensity that he felt in his bones. She reminded him of Ada in this moment, her Zydell half on full display before him.

"You said it before, Orrick. You created them to be this way, to fight. It's never going to stop."

"Use me," he breathed, desperation climbing up his throat, constricting his lungs. "My gifts. It's the only way to stop it. The very fabric of their being must be altered—balanced."

Honoria threw out a gust of wind, knocking two attacking Elementalists several feet away from them, all the while frowning at Orrick, "But you don't even have your powers. How could I siphon them?"

"Just try!" He practically cried out, "Your mother told me they aren't truly lost. I just don't know where they've gone or how to retrieve them. But somehow, they are still with me. I know it. I just can't reach them."

Honoria looked past his shoulder, and Orrick almost jumped toward her when lightning struck the ground just behind him.

"Honoria," Orrick grabbed her hand, pulling her gaze back to his. "Please, help them." He didn't hold back the tears that welled in his eyes and fell, trailing through the gore coating his face.

Her nostrils flared, mouth thinning into a hard line before giving him a quick nod. He nearly sighed in relief, watching as she turned away from him, walking into the center of the battle. Wind swirled around her, lightning continuing to strike the ground in her wake, keeping everyone at bay. She was like a walking storm, commanding the elemental gifts with the ease of a seasoned warrior—like she was born for it.

Air seemed to be her favorite of the four gifts, as it was the one she kept in constant use throughout this battle.

Honoria stood perfectly still in the center of her storm, and then she began to rise. The sand built into a large dune beneath her, pulling away from the beach and climbing up the slope until she was high above them all. He met her eyes briefly from her peak, glimpsing the fiery intensity burning in her gaze. Orrick gave her a nod in return, motioning for her to do what she needed.

The ground under the entire expanse of the battle began to shake. Orrick frowned. What was she doing? He told her to use his powers, but these were not his. These were still the elemental gifts. He took a step toward her, but suddenly, a hand pushed through the sand, grabbing hold of Orrick's ankle. He yelled out, trying to shake free the charred, blackened hand without success.

Orrick growled, looking up to find a sea of bone and burnt flesh rising from the beach, sand coating their limbs. Screams echoed around him, ones not of pain but of fear as thousands of corpses rose from their resting place. Their skeletal hands grabbed hold of the Elementalists, stopping the fighting. Ash from centuries past broke away from their burnt remains, floating into the wind-swept night air. An eerie silence descended across the moonlit beach, the harsh gaze of the green moon blanketing the scene in its milky glow.

"Look around you!" Honoria yelled out from her spot above them all. Her voice carried on the wind to reach every Elementalists ears. "These are your ancestors, those who fought in this very spot for the same reasons you are today. Power."

The silence hung heavy in the air, all eyes pinned on Honoria. The emerald moon reflected in her eyes, glowing with an unnatural brightness.

"Your thirst for power, for control over one another, is killing you." She continued, "It killed them, and for what? What will you do when everyone you've ever cared about is dead? What will happen when only one element remains? Will you live peacefully, or will you grow restless and begin to kill your own people just to feel again? This path you are on is fruitless. It will only end in extinction. Are you not tired of this life of war?"

Murmurs began in the crowd around him, but Orrick couldn't take his eyes away from Honoria. She turned, her glowing eyes boring into him, and then her voice was in his head, and he almost jerked out of the ivory bones that wrapped around him. That was his power. She had siphoned it, using his own gifts on him. Relief washed over him at what it meant. His gifts were still with him; he just had to figure out how to access them again.

"*Orrick,*" her voice caressed his mind. "*I will not take away what you have given them, but a balance is needed for these people to survive. Hatred and desire do not create balance, so I am giving them love, joy, and wonder, but also sadness to create the balance they need in this life. So that they can thrive for many more centuries to come.*"

He couldn't speak, not even in his mind. She was doing what he should have done long ago. Orrick had let them suffer for so long, not caring what happened to them. All he could do now was smile up at her, a fresh set of tears welling in his eyes at what she was doing for them—saving his children. She simply smiled back and then raised her palms into the air as a surge of power shot forth, rocking into every single Elementalist in this world, not only the ones on the battlefield.

The army of the dead released their brethren, crawling back into their holes, covered once again by the ashen sand. All of the remaining Elementalists fell to the ground as Honoria used Orrick's power to alter their very being. The pulse of power was immense, and Orrick could feel it nuzzling against him as if a pet to its master. He tried to reach out and grab it, pull it back into himself, but his fingers only slipped through the air.

Honoria stood at the top of the dune until it was done, and the power was gone just as soon as it had come, stroking across Orrick as it dissipated.

Slowly, the Elementalists began to rise, confusion smeared across their faces, followed by a new emotion, one he hadn't seen on their faces before—sadness. Many fell to their knees, overcome with remorse and disbelief. This battle was over, as was the war that had molded these people since their creation, and now they needed to build something new. The Elementalists could finally find peace after so many centuries of strife, and it was all thanks to Honoria. She might not know it yet, but she was quite possibly the most powerful being in the Cosmos.

26
ORRICK

"You're their hero now, you know," Orrick said. He joined Honoria at the top of her sand mound as they watched the Elementalists collect their dead and perform their burial rituals. "They will sing sonnets about what you did here."

"I'm not even sure how it worked. I didn't have a plan, but I could somehow feel the presence of death pulsating beneath this place. It was as if the spirits of those who perished centuries ago for the same senseless conflicts were calling out to me. And then the idea began to weave together in my mind. What better way to confront them with the brutal reality of their actions than to unleash the wrath of their own ancestors, who lay in silent judgment beneath their feet?" Honoria sighed, taking a deep breath. "Your power is truly remarkable. I—I'm not sure if I like holding that type of ability in my grasp. It feels too great a responsibility."

Orrick smirked, putting an arm around her shoulder, "Honestly, I think you might be better at wielding it than I am. You used it for good, while I only ever used it for amusement. You fixed what I fucked up."

Honoria shook her head, "You didn't fuck it up. You just need to stop letting your emotions control you while you're creating. You told me you were in a certain mood when you crafted these people. Perhaps you should wait to create anymore until you can manage your emotions better. It would likely be safer for everyone."

"Wise-ass," Orrick grunted just before spotting Oriana and Garren in the crowd, helping some of the Elementalists carry their dead loved ones.

They spent the entire evening on this beach, and the first tendrils of light were stretching over the horizon. "I'll be right back," Orrick said to Honoria, stumbling down the dune.

They had lingered here for far too long, and with Anthes lurking about, appearing unpredictably at any given moment, staying here any longer wasn't a good idea, especially with Honoria and Garren together.

"Oriana!" Orrick called, waving a hand for her to come over to him.

She walked to him, exhaustion and anger clear on her features. "Nice to finally see you chipping in to help."

Orrick ignored her comment; there were more impor-tant things at foot, and the Elementalists could handle it from here.

He grabbed her arm, pulling her close, "Listen, we've been here too long. Father is close. I can feel it."

"Orrick, you're hurting my arm."

He released her with a frown, looking down to see the imprint of his fingers on her skin. "Sorry," he said quick-ly. "But this is important. I didn't tell you earlier, but in the forest, Father said he knew the location of one of the triplets, a woman. I don't know if he was speaking of Honoria or the third sibling."

Oriana bit her lip and furrowed her brow, "If it's her, then wouldn't he be here now?" She said, looking over at Honoria, who was speaking to a group of Elementalists.

"If it is Honoria, then he probably thinks she's still tucked away in Verhaven with Ada, but if it's the third sibling...we have to get to them before he does." He al-most yelled the words, desperate for her to understand the urgency of their situation. "What if he's beaten us there already? What if he has them in tow as we speak?"

"Whoa, whoa... slow down, Orrick," Oriana said, grip-ping his shoulders with a firm, steadying hand, and only then did he realize he was trembling, his body a chaotic mess of adrenaline and fear.

"Oriana, if we don't beat him to the triplets and these God killers, everything is lost!" His voice rose with desperation, and his breath came out in ragged gasps. "All of my creations will be destroyed. Garren and Honoria together are too vulnerable. We need to separate them. It won't be long before Father finds them here with us."

"Okay, okay," Oriana soothed, her voice a calming force against his chaos. "Just breathe. We will separate them. We'll leave soon."

"Balthar is close by, and I think he knows it. If he gets his hands on that axe again, we lose one of the God killers, and he'll be one step closer to his goal. We have to get it now. He used it to carve that scar into Garren's face when he was just a babe. Who knows what horrors he will unleash if he retrieves it and captures one or all of them." His words spilled out in a torrent, anxiety taking over as the realization of everything he stood to lose crashed over him like a tidal wave. His creations, his dreams, all stood on the brink of annihilation. He couldn't let them die; he couldn't bear the thought of losing them all.

"I understand, Orrick. It's okay, we will do what you say. Just slow your breathing."

He closed his eyes, gripping Oriana's elbows, feeling the warmth of her skin beneath his grasp. With each deep inhale, he focused on the cool air filling his lungs and then exhaled slowly. Gradually, the frantic rhythm of his heart began to slow to a steady pace, and the pounding in his head faded.

"The Elementalists are almost done gathering their dead. It looks like they are heading back to their territories," Honoria ventured down to meet them. "We should go with them."

"No!" Orrick and Oriana said in unison.

Honoria frowned, "But this isn't over yet. They need help to enact peace. The war may be over, but they are still far from establishing a genuine and enduring normalcy of order."

"You can't," Orrick practically growled, and Honoria's nostrils flared with irritation.

"Wait," Oriana said, grasping Orrick's arm to bring his attention back to her. "It could be a good thing for her to go with the Elementalists and stay here. If, as you suspect, father thinks she is still in Verhaven, then she may be safer here for now."

Orrick squinted at his sister, irritation flashing across his face because she had a valid point. He was fairly certain their father was unaware of Honoria's presence here. She had been well hidden both times Anthes came to visit Orrick, and he was far too annoyed and preoccupied with torturing Orrick to have noticed her anyway. Oriana was right, which frustrated him immensely.

"Fine," Orrick ground out. "I agree. Staying here and helping the Elementalists hold council to figure out their new normal might be the best place for you to hide. But," Orrick added. "That means Garren needs to leave. Father knows for a fact who he is and that he is in this world. If he comes looking for Garren he might inadvertently find Honoria as well, then we would all be fucked."

"What are you saying about me?" Garren abruptly appeared behind them all.

"We have to leave," Oriana said flatly.

"You need to go get Balthar first," Orrick interjected. "It's one of the God killers from the prophecy, and Father knows it's here somewhere."

Garren pulled a hand down over his face with a sigh, "Oh right, you want us to go and get the axe that you suspended over molten lava in the center of a volcano? I think you should be the one to get it since you put it there."

"I agree with Garren," Oriana said. "It might be the only way you can get off this world. Maybe you can use it to get back to Verhaven and make Ada give you your powers back."

Orrick groaned. What was wrong with him? She was right—again. That was the logical option, considering he still didn't have his powers. Yet doubt crept into his mind, gnawing at him. Something didn't feel right. It was true Oriana could get Garren out of this world with ease, which meant he should get the axe and attempt to reclaim his gifts once and for all. But something was pulling at him to stay. It had been a long and taxing few days, leaving his mind weary and exhausted. His indecision was only delaying what needed to be done.

Orrick huffed out a small laugh and said, "Right again, sister, but one of us needs to go and find Garren's and Honoria's sibling. They are in the world of Szaro."

Oriana gasped, "Why in the Cosmos would Ada put one of her children there?"

"Your guess is as good as mine," Orrick shrugged. "But that's what the book said. Their name is Ari or something. Oh!" Orrick suddenly proclaimed, smirking at Garren. "I almost forgot to tell you your real name, halfling."

Garren grunted, glaring at Orrick, "I don't care, and I don't want to know."

"Well, too bad. It's far better than your current one."

"Doubtful," Garren muttered and walked away from them before Orrick had the chance to tell him.

"It's Alvar!" Orrick yelled back at him, and Garren gave him a crude gesture. "Right," he continued, turning back to Oriana and Honoria. "I'll go get the axe, Honoria will stay here with the Elementalists, you and Garren will go to Szaro and find this Ari person, and Atlas will...where's Atlas?"

He turned to look for Atlas, and then he felt it, heat, cloying and pulling the breath from his lungs. He knew that change in the air. Atlas appeared seemingly from nowhere next to them, and Orrick frowned, but then Atlas said, "Do you feel that?"

Orrick glanced at Oriana, and he could see her body tense at the shift in the atmosphere. Their eyes locked, and she whispered, "Father is coming."

27

GARREN

Garren groaned, and not for the first time during this trip, was second guessing getting involved with this family of Gods.

Oriana cursed beside him, her dress half singed from her body, the blood of the Elementalists covering her now exposed legs. "What do we do?"

"Hide quick!" Orrick said, "They can't see him or Honoria. Change of plans, you and Garren go get the axe, I'll hold them off and meet you there. Honoria, take the remaining Elementalists and leave now."

Honoria nodded, a sadness passing over her features, and Orrick took her hand, squeezing it gently. She smiled at him and then turned to Garren, wrapping him in a sudden hug, pushing the breath from his lungs. He tensed but then closed his arms around her just as tightly, realizing that he wasn't sure when he would see his newfound sister again.

Oriana only nodded grimly and grabbed Garren's hand, pulling him quickly to the edge of the forest.

They crouched low behind a small boulder where the forest met the beach just as two enormous men appeared on the sand, walking toward Orrick and Atlas.

Garren growled as he saw Anthes' corded white locks blowing in the breeze. His only reprieve at seeing the God who had tortured Oriana was that he no longer had his precious axe at his side. As a warrior himself, Garren knew how the lack of your blade was like missing a piece of yourself.

He let his gaze move to the man beside Anthes. He was several inches taller than the God of war, and he practically exuded power. His hair was black with silver-streaked through it, and even from this great distance, he could see the man's dark eyes. They sparkled as if the stars were held in his gaze.

Sudden recognition dawned on Garren. He had seen this man once before. It was the man he saw at the docks, the one he had felt that strange connection with; he was sure of it. "Who is that walking in front of your father?"

"Zanos, God of life and death," Oriana whispered. Garren bulked, breath catching in his throat, and Oriana reached down, grabbing his hand and squeezing it tightly.

Just like on the docks, everything around Garren quieted, falling away as if he was alone, staring his father in the eye. This was the man who had sired him. This was the man who ruled the Gods so ruthlessly. The King of the Gods.

Garren's throat grew tight, constricting with emotion. He watched his father's every step, watched as Anthes followed him like a dog on his heels. There was something malicious in the air; it wrapped around Garren, clinging to him like a thorny vine, making his skin crawl.

He finally found his voice, but it came out as no more than a strangled breath, "Something's wrong."

Oriana squeezed his hand tighter, "Yes, something is very wrong. Orrick believes the Gods have a way of enslaving you. They will use you at any cost, whether you want them to or not."

Suddenly, Zanos' head shifted to the forest, directly at him. He could see the solid black voids of his gaze narrow on him. Garren fell backward from his crouched position, smacking the hard ground with his back, breaking eye contact, and losing sight of his father. "H–he saw me."

"We have to go. Now!" Oriana scrambled to her feet, and Garren followed, sprinting behind her.

They ran as fast as they could, pushing through branches and brush until the scent of sulfur filled the air.

Oriana stopped, looking through the forest behind them. "I don't think anyone is following us."

Garren breathed heavily, nodding in agreement. He hadn't felt anyone on their trail, but he hadn't wanted to stop either. Getting as much distance from the two powerful Gods on that beach seemed like a necessity, especially if what Oriana said was correct and they had a way to use him without his consent.

"Do you smell that?" Oriana scrunched up her nose at the vile scent. "We are close."

"Come on," Garren grabbed her hand, and they walked hand in hand together, following the volcano's perfume of ash and rotten egg.

"Are you okay?" Oriana looked up at him, her eyes questioning and filled with worry.

"Yes," Garren said, frowning. "I—I don't really want to think about it right now."

She only nodded in understanding. "I'm here whenever you want to talk."

A bubble of laughter suddenly erupted from Garren, "You know, I used to think my life was complicated. How naive I truly was."

Oriana didn't respond to that, but then they pushed past the last row of trees to find themselves on a beach once more. Across the sandy stretch of land, out in the ocean, was a massive island, and in its center, smoke coiled from the top of a volcano.

"Thank the Cosmos, we made it." Oriana huffed. "Let's go get the axe. I don't know how much time we have or if Orrick can even hold them off for long."

Garren grunted his agreement, and they ran down the sand and across the beach. There was a stone bridge leading from the beach to the island, where a large door was carved into the stone of the cliffs.

"Ready?" Oriana raised a brow at him.

He simply grunted in response again. Taking a quick glance out over the sea, toward the horizon where the storm clouds swirled with relentless ire. His nostrils flared, and his mind shifted to the city locked beneath those storms and the people forced to live there, isolated from everyone and everything, just like Sardorf had been.

With the curse broken, Sardorf was thriving more than ever. They had only been surviving before, thanks to Oriana, but now their quality of life was soaring to new heights. Did the city beneath the sea have someone like Oriana to protect them? Were they only just surviving? He had to know.

Trapped with no sunlight beneath the raging storms, it didn't seem like a life worth living. Now was their chance to go there and help them break the curse. The axe was so close, only a few feet away, and he was positive that it was the key to breaking whatever curse Anthes cast upon those poor innocent people.

He sighed, shaking the thought away because it would have to wait until after this prophecy they were living was done. At least they would have the axe now and be ready for whenever the time came to help the people beneath the sea. Maybe they were safer trapped there for now, isolated and away from what was to come.

Garren and Oriana slowed their approach as they came to the large stone archway and walked into a faint orange glow that illuminated the obsidian rock. Heat surged like a wave, washing over them, searing their skin, and pulling the breath from their lungs. A long stairway climbed up the black stone. Garren looked up its many steps and could see the bright glow overhead. The axe had to be up there.

"Of course, Orrick would make this as dramatic as possible," Oriana mumbled, rolling her eyes. "Come on, we have a hundred steps to climb."

They climbed up every shallow step, the air growing hotter with every second, sweat dripping down their bodies until they finally made it to the top. It was a small ledge, and directly below them was a raging pit of lava, and hovering directly in front of them, above the pit of death, was Balthar.

"So how should we do this?" Oriana asked, pulling at the tightness of her leather corset. "Cosmos, it's unbearable in here."

"I mean, we are in the center of a volcano; it is bound to be hot."

She smacked him but smirked nonetheless, "I think we just have to time our jump perfectly together and grab the hilt at the same time."

"Seems as good a plan as any," Garren shrugged, holding out a hand to her. "On the count of three?"

Oriana laced her fingers through his, holding on tight, and nodded, "I know where to take us, so keep your mind clear. Alright, one...two...three!"

They jumped together, each making purchase with the hilt of the axe, and Garren felt a whoosh of air swirl around them until his feet suddenly landed on solid ground.

Garren's breathing was heavy as he looked around. Where had Oriana taken them? This place looked ancient, with buildings that seemed to have been in existence for thousands of years.

"What happened? Where are we?" Oriana frowned, following his gaze, looking at their surroundings. "This isn't where I thought of going when we grabbed the axe."

They both looked up at the sky above them, but there was no sun, no light blue or fluffy clouds; there was only the dark blue of the sea.

She turned her furrowed gaze at him, "What did you think of, Garren?"

"I—I was thinking of the people trapped beneath the sea."

"What?!" Oriana squealed. "Why in the Cosmos would you do that? We need to get out of Fellhaven!"

Garren bit his lip, "I must have grabbed the hilt just before you did...I'm sorry, Oriana."

He looked down at her, watching as her entire body sagged, and she shook her head. "It's alright. The spell on the axe is broken now, so we just need to get out of here. Grab my hand."

He did as she asked, and she took a deep breath and closed her eyes. Garren braced himself for the jump between worlds, but nothing happened. They were still within the shimmering orb under the sea.

Oriana cracked an eye open, and Garren could feel her begin to shake beneath his grip as she looked up to him and said what they were both thinking, "Fuck."

28

ORRICK

O rrick spun to greet the unwanted guests, clenching his jaw to keep himself from saying something that would get him blasted by Zanos' retched staff or, worse, Atlas. He wouldn't survive a blow from it. Zanos' staff would simply suck his lifeforce from him until he was nothing more than a husk of skin and bone.

He plastered a smile across his lips, one that didn't reach his eyes. Zanos' gaze locked onto him. It was like a noose tightening around his neck, but Orrick didn't dare flinch. Suddenly, Zanos' eyes shifted to the line of trees, to where Oriana and Garren had fled.

"My King," Orrick yelled down the beach, bowing dramatically and pulling Zanos' attention back onto him. "What an honor it is to have you visit one of my worlds."

"My, my, Orrick, what happened here?" The God of life and death's voice boomed, piercing the quiet of the empty beach like a clap of thunder as he walked through the wasteland of dead Elementalists, his father, Anthes, keeping carefully behind him.

Orrick said nothing, watching as Zanos pulled the energy from the death around him into the dark staff he carried. That staff was the most powerful object in this world and Zanos' claim to the throne. He was the most powerful God in the cosmos and one of the reasons that Garren and Honoria were as gifted as they were. And not only did Zanos' blood flow through their veins, but that of the most powerful Zydell as well.

Zanos stopped several feet in front of Orrick and Atlas. He could feel Atlas tense beside him as Zanos' black eyes were like endless voids pulling on their life sources with their intimidating stare.

"I've not known you to step foot within my creations, Lord King. What an honor it is for you to be here."

The corner of Zanos' mouth twitched, "Your father tells me that you have been a very bad God these past weeks and have somehow managed to extract the very knowledge we need."

Orrick glanced at his father, whose face was a mask of indifference, but there was a small second that Anthes' red eyes moved to Atlas, and a flash of some unknown reaction was there before disappearing.

Orrick frowned, looking back to Zanos, "I'm not sure I know what you mean."

Zanos smirked, "I was hoping you wouldn't make this easy."

Orrick's brows drew together before realization hit him. Zanos wanted to torture it out of him. In a split second, he was on his knees, pain lashing through his body. It felt as though the very essence of his soul was being torn from his person. He clenched his teeth, not daring to make a sound as Zanos said, "While normally I would find your show of strength impressive and an asset for any of my Gods to have, you're much better off stopping this charade and telling me where my children are."

Suddenly, it was as if his soul was slingshot back into himself, and he fell back hard onto the sand. Breathing heavily, body aching, he pushed himself back up, standing once again and glared at the two Eternal Gods standing before him.

"Well?" Zanos' tone was deep, demanding.

If Orrick had been smart and taken a moment to think before doing anything, he would not have glanced over at Atlas, but he did. Zanos' dark gaze locked on Atlas, eyebrows shooting up as if he hadn't realized the Elemental was there until this very moment.

"So," Zanos said, looking at Atlas with a frown. "This is one of them?"

Orrick had a split second to react, anticipating the move right before Zanos shot a bolt of energy from his staff. He spun, knocking Atlas out of the path of the stream of death. The blow instead hit Orrick's hand, severing it from his body. He yelled out, cradling the bleeding stump to his chest. He bit his lip against the pain just as a sudden realization sparked his memory.

He was a fool. He had it all wrong. The Gods didn't want to use the triplets; they wanted them dead. They wanted to destroy them, getting them out of the way to enact their plan to purify the Cosmos. The triplets were the God killers. There were no actual weapons of metal and power like Balthar or Garren's longsword; those were simply God-made weapons. The triplets *were* the weapons. They were the only things that could stop the Gods and save the Cosmos. The prophecy finally came fully to his mind as if a fog had been encasing his mind and finally cleared—the words forming before him like an etching upon stone.

Three bound by fate, born of both God and Zydell. They hold the power to break the Cosmos. War and death stalk them for their own means. Immortal weapons wielded hold the key to salvation. But discovery by the hungry Gods and all will be lost, the Cosmos unmade until only silence remains.

Orrick's breath grew ragged, and each exhale was pure fire fueled by his rage. A low, lethal growl erupted from deep within his chest, echoing around them. The time had come for the Six Eternal Gods to be wiped from existence. He would go to great lengths to save the Cosmos, and he would do anything to save his creations. One thing blazed clear in his mind: the Gods were the greatest threat to them all. They had to be eradicated, no matter the cost.

He looked at Atlas then, whose eyes were wide, his body shaking, and asked, "Are you okay?"

"Yes," Atlas breathed. "But your hand." He pointed to the pale, limp appendage lying discarded in the sand.

Orrick didn't even look at it; his eyes locked on Atlas. "It doesn't matter." He ground out. "That bolt would have killed you, and I couldn't—wouldn't have been able to live with myself if…" Suddenly, a surge of power slammed into Orrick, and he let go of his bleeding arm, bracing himself on the beach against the energy coursing through him. It caressed his bones, massaged his muscles, and swam through his blood, emanating from his entire being. He looked down at his bleeding stump, gritting his teeth as the skin knit back together, a new hand growing in its place.

He wiggled his new fingers, clenching them into a fist, feeling the electric flow of his dear old friend. His power was back.

Before Zanos or Anthes could try anything else, Orrick grabbed Atlas' arm, turned toward the two Gods, and said, "Tootles," with a grin and a wink. He waited for a single moment, watching as realization dawned on their faces, and then he let his power soar. The two God's yelled out, running toward them just before Orrick transported himself and Atlas from Fellhaven to the one place he needed to go—the home of the third and final halfling sibling.

The world shifted, the stretch of beach and vast ocean replaced in the blink of an eye by harsh mountains, dirt, and brown buildings.

Mud splashed, covering their clothing as a team of horses pulling a carriage full of what Orrick called Trolls passed by. Towering structures loomed overhead, and Orrick realized they were directly in the middle of the busy main street in the city center. He grabbed Atlas, pulling him over to the side of the road just before another carriage almost ran them over. Beside them were a pair of fighting goblins. Across the street were several other creatures, all beautiful in their own way. *His* creatures, including fairies, orcs, dwarves, griffins, dragons, elves—the list went on. This world was covered with his experimental creations, but ones he loved nonetheless.

He looked over at Atlas, who was gazing around at their surroundings, completely stunned by what he saw.

Orrick smirked, "Welcome to Zsaro, Atlas. Home of the magically insane."

ACKNOWLEDGEMENTS

Thank you for reading this book! I appreciate you more than you know. Readers are what makes writing and telling stories worth it. So, thank you.

Troy – Thank you for being my biggest cheerleader. You always let me know how proud you are of me, and I am forever grateful for you. I love you.

Cass – Without all of our writing sessions over the year I don't think this book would have gotten done. Thank you for being the best friend and keeping me motivated!

Katelyn – You are always there to read the earliest (sometimes unfinished) drafts of my writing! Thank you for being the best friend and helping me by being another set of eyes on those early drafts!

Tatyana – Bestie! Thanks for listening to all my talks about this book and helping me work through plot holes. You are the best cheerleader! Love you!

Tank – My cutest pup and constant companion. Thank you for keeping me company during those late writing nights. You're the sweetest puppy doggy.

Arc Readers – All of your support, enthusiasm, and encouragement keep me going. Thank you for reading and helping me spread the word of this book! I adore you all.

About the Author

K.C. Smith developed a love for fantasy at a young age, which only grew as she got older. Katelyn works as an Accountant in Baltimore, Maryland where she lives with her husband and their chihuahua, Tank. Writing allows her an escape from the corporate world at the end of the day. When not writing she can be found rock climbing and traveling the world.

Visit her on the web:

https://www.instagram.com/balancingbooksandcoffee/

https://www.facebook.com/kcsmithbooks

https://www.tiktok.com/@balancingbooksandcoffee

https://www.goodreads.com/kcsmithbooks

See all of Katelyn's titles on her amazon page:

https://www.amazon.com/author/kcsmithbooks

* 9 7 9 8 9 8 6 4 5 9 0 8 0 *